DEATH RENTS A BEACH HOUSE

A CAPE MAY MYSTERY

MILES NELSON

 WORKING STIFF PRESS
www.MilesNelsonAuthor.com

ISBN - Print - 978-1-7326405-9-7

ISBN - ebook - 979-8-9887472-0-8

Cover background photo by John Bilous @ Dreamstime

All other artwork and design by Miles Nelson

Thanks to Lee Burton of Ocean's Edge Editing

WORKING STIFF PRESS
www.MilesNelsonAuthor.com

❀ Created with Vellum

This one is dedicated to Dame Agatha Christie and the great Ian Fleming, who first got me excited about this whole writing thing many years ago.

W
ith the first day of spring just a week away, Cape May was already starting to shake off the chill of a long, gray winter. For the first half of March, it had been a graceful transition, with the clear days outnumbering the cloudy by a factor of two to one, and temperatures hovering a few degrees above normal. And as it did every year, the fresh, crisp sea air that made its way gently through the town held a promise of new beginnings and sunny summer days soon to come.

Mallory Vickers was in the middle of one of those long summer days. Well-coated with coconut-scented tanning oil, and drowsy from the heat and the rhythmic crashing of waves, she rose to a sitting position on the brightly striped beach towel to look over towards the nearest lifeguard stand. *There he is! And he sees me!* A well-tanned and muscular young man jumped down to the sand and called out her name as he started to run towards her. She rose from the towel, flashing her brightest smile and opening her arms wide. Just as the young man came close enough for his face to come into focus, he evaporated into the summer heat, along with the sand, the towel, and the waves. Mallory's alarm clock went off, filling the room with the jarring sound of a Wildwood radio station...

Happy Monday morning from WZXL, where we are rocking the Jersey Shore. Hopefully, you remembered to set your clocks ahead yesterday. Coming right up, some Bon Jovi to help you get your day started...

Mildly dejected and already missing the lifeguard, Mallory reached out to hit the snooze button before rubbing her eyes and sitting up. Noting that the clock read 7:02, she realized, with a shake of her head, that the rest of the world thought it was an hour later. Not waiting for the alarm to ring a second time, she switched the thing off and made her way to the kitchen. There wouldn't be time for a workout this morning, but she still had plenty of time to get ready for her dentist appointment at 9:30.

Almost an hour later, and after several texts and calls had gone unanswered, she started to think her friend Boone, who had agreed to drive her to Rio Grande for her appointment, had probably overslept as well. *Well, sheesh, that's just like him*, she thought to herself, *but I guess I'm not one to complain this morning.* She grabbed her coat and purse, checking that her insurance card was handy, and headed out for the two-block walk over to Boone's place on Columbia.

~

Across town, Police Chief Tate Saxby, who had not forgotten to set the clocks ahead, started the toaster and poured the first cup of coffee for the day. Savoring the all-important first sip, he took a moment to look around at the huge kitchen of the house he and his fiancée, Angela, had recently bought together. It had taken him some time, but he had grown comfortable with all the space, and more importantly to him, Angela was crazy about it. *Just four or five more times moving all the pots and pans around from this cabinet to that one ought to do it*, he thought to himself. After he had spread peanut butter on his toast, he settled down on one of the tall stools alongside the long granite island and reached for the newspaper he'd brought in from the porch.

"Well, I guess the honeymoon is over, folks, nobody brings me coffee in the bedroom anymore."

Saxby turned to see that Angela had appeared from the hallway, her hair still damp from the shower and hanging free. She was dressed in one of her favorite outfits of faded jeans, riding boots, and a cable knit sweater. Aside from their long-term romantic relationship, she was indispensable to him as the head of the restaurant division of the local business empire he had inherited from his older cousin a few years ago. She was part of a team of hard-working people who handled the task of running the various businesses so he could focus on his role as Cape May police chief. Most of her typical day-to-day was spent as the on-site manager of the Ugly Mug Tavern, which was a popular destination at the outdoor shopping mall at the center of town.

Saxby laughed. "Sorry, Ang, you were in the shower when I got in from my run, and I really needed to get some toast in me. I'll try to do better tomorrow. Promise."

"Oh, I'll hold you to that." She poured herself some coffee before starting to peel a banana. "I admire you for getting up and running. It'll be really good for you in the long—oops, well, in the long run. Accidental pun, I swear."

"Very funny, but you're right. I'm not running very far yet, and still walking partway, but baby steps, I guess. It feels good anyway, and I know it's good for me. Are you opening the Mug today? Enough people in town, you think?"

"I think so. It'll be quiet, but there are people around, and a lot of other places are closed a few days a week. I totally understand that, but I don't want us to get a reputation as one of the places that does it. I've got a meeting with Velma over at the main office before that. We're going over the plans for the season. What we need to order, what needs a coat of paint, who's coming back this year—you know the drill."

"Actually, I don't know the drill as much as I should, which is why I'm so glad I have you and Velma and the rest of the crew. I'm so lucky Earl made so many good hires over the years. You most of all."

"Well, I don't know about 'most of all.' I'd vote for Velma to have that title, but you're right that it's a good team. Which is a good thing, what with you all caught up in fighting evildoers all the time. By the way, aren't you late?"

"Yeah, a little. My weekly with the mayor got moved to six, so I figured I'd head in a little late. Anyway, you know I'm always on the clock."

At that, Saxby's cell phone buzzed and vibrated a few inches across the counter.

"Speak of the devil," he said, scooping up the phone. "There goes the bat signal. I have to get this."

He tapped the screen to take the call, seeing it was from one of his sergeants, Roy Brody.

"Morning, Roy, what's up?"

"Good morning to you, Chief," Brody said. "Sorry to start your day with this, but we've got a body. It's Boone Roseman, in his apartment over on Columbia. A friend of yours, right?"

"Well, I wouldn't say we were friends, but yes, I know him, just as a guy around town. Seemed like an okay guy. Damn, that's a shame. What does it look like? Accident or what?"

"I doubt it was an accident, Chief," Brody said, "unless you think that a fireplace poker could have somehow fallen onto the back of his head two or three times."

"You have a colorful way of getting right to the point, Roy," Saxby said. He closed his eyes for a few seconds and took a deep breath, letting it out slowly. It was a rare day he didn't reflect back on the fact that he'd had to deal with two separate murder sprees over the past two years. All in a town where things like that just weren't supposed to happen. *Shit. Not again.* "Okay, I assume you've cleared and secured the area and called for Dr. Coyle and the ambulance. Give me a quick summary and the address."

"Right, Chief," Brody said. "So, a friend from a few blocks away found him—lady by the name of Mallory Vickers. She told us he was supposed to drive her up to a doctor's appointment in Rio Grande. He wasn't answering his phone, so she walked to his place and used the spare key to let herself in. Got partway up the stairs and saw him, freaked out a bit but called 911. The body's pretty cold, so I'm guessing whatever happened was yesterday or last night. Anyway, as soon as we got a look at the apartment and the body, I sent Redding and Davis to do a quick check around the block—between the houses and driveways, sheds, you know. It's mostly empty houses around here. And Dr. Coyle's out of town, but his fill-in is on the way."

"Sounds like you have things under control there," Saxby said. "How does the apartment look? All torn up?"

"No, not really," Brody said. "First impression is that it's pretty neat and orderly. One or two things out of place. Could have been a struggle, but if so, not any kind of big fight. There are a few signs of some recent drug use."

After getting the address and a few more details, Saxby ended the call. He saw that Angela had already started to put a to-go coffee together for him.

"Did I hear that right?" she said. "Really? Another murder?"

"I'm afraid you heard it right," Saxby said. "But it sounds like it could have been a break-in. Not that that's much better. Boone Roseman, local. I knew him a little. A friend found him. Do you know Mallory Vickers?"

"Not on a personal level, but I know her," Angela said. "She's a waitress at the Harbor House. She works for you."

"Oh, well, I'll keep that part to myself when I talk to her," Saxby said. He had fastened his gun belt over his jeans, and reached for his coat and hat as Angela set out a bowl of assorted power bars for him to choose from. "I know I don't have to say it, but not a word to anyone about this. I'll call you later."

"No, you don't have to say it, but that's okay, Chief

Saxby," Angela said. "I guess I shouldn't tell you to 'have a good day,' but, well, maybe try anyway?"

Traffic was light enough that he was able to drive swiftly through town without needing to turn on the lights and the siren, and he pulled up across from Boone Roseman's apartment five minutes after leaving home. As he crossed the street, he noticed Sergeant Vicki Barstow getting out of her cruiser a few cars down, just behind an idling ambulance. Their paths converged as they approached the house.

"Morning, Chief," Barstow said. "You know anything yet?"

"Not much, Vic," Saxby said. "Brody got me at home and gave me the rough cut. Boone Roseman. I knew him from some years back. Sounds like some kind of attack, so hopefully you didn't have a big breakfast."

The department's newest addition, Officer Megan Hayward, greeted them at the mouth of the driveway of a three-story Victorian house. She nodded to Saxby and Barstow as they approached. "Good morning, Chief, Sergeant. It's the top apartment at the back of the drive-way. Looks like they converted the garage for rentals. You'll find Sergeant Brody and the others back there. The doctor just went in also. I'm sorry, I didn't get his name."

"No problem, Megan, you're doing fine," Saxby said. "You're the gatekeeper. Just keep doing what you're doing. Stay up here and watch out for any neighbors or other gawkers. No doubt there'll be a few of them. I think we probably have a crime scene here, so don't let anybody else down this driveway without checking with us."

They left her on the sidewalk and continued past two police cruisers and towards the rear of the property. At the end of the driveway was a two-story structure that was done up to look something like a miniature version of the main house. The parallel cement tracks dominating the driveway ended abruptly just in front, as though they had once continued inside through large doors that were no longer there. As they approached, a door on the side opened and Sergeant Brody appeared to greet them.

"Ah, good to see you, Chief. And, Vic," Brody said. "Dr. Lee just got here a few minutes ago and he's upstairs. Davis and Redding are up there too, and they've gotten started with the pictures and the crime scene kit. As you can see, this is the old garage building, but it's been converted into apartments, one on each floor. The lower unit appears to be vacant, and the same for the main house. It was a friend of Mr. Roseman who found him—name of Mallory Vickers. She got concerned when he didn't show to drive her to a doctor in Rio Grande. She said she figured he probably overslept due to the time change yesterday. Apparently, they were good enough friends that she knew where he kept his spare key. She's right there in my car if you want to talk to her."

Saxby looked over at the car to see a woman looking out at them from the passenger seat. He raised his hand in a wave and nodded to her. "You know what, I want to get inside, but give me a half a minute to check in with her." He walked over to the passenger side of Brody's car and opened the door, bending low to speak with the person inside.

"Good morning, Miss Vickers. Mallory, right? I'm Chief Tate Saxby. I know you've had a scare. How are you holding up?"

"Well, I guess I'm okay," Vickers said. Her voice was quiet, but clear. Saxby had the impression she was affected by the shock of finding her friend dead, but was working to remain composed. "It's just, I mean, one of those things that isn't really happening, right? Except that I think it is."

"That's kind of like what it is when these things happen, Miss Vickers," Saxby said. "But yes, I'm afraid that this is real. Listen, we'll try our best not to keep you here any longer than we have to, but first … I understand you were on your way to a doctor's appointment. Are you okay? I mean, are you having a problem that we need to take care of?"

"Oh no, I'm fine," Vickers said. "That's really nice of you to ask. It was just a regular dentist appointment. I'll reschedule it. Thank you."

"Ah, okay, then, that's good to know," Saxby said. "Well, hang in there, and we'll get you out of here soon. Of course, we'll need a statement, but that isn't something we need to deal with out here in the cold, okay? Won't be much longer."

Saxby closed the car door and walked back to Barstow and Brody. "Okay, Roy, let's see what we have here."

Brody held the door open for the other two as they entered a small foyer of about six feet square. A flight of carpeted stairs went up to a door that stood wide open, exposing a partial view of the upstairs apartment. Saxby saw a figure walk across the room as he caught muffled sounds of human activity. A second, closed door, was just off to the left of the stairs.

"I presume this is for the first-floor apartment," Saxby said, as he tried the door, finding it solidly locked. "And we don't think this is rented, right?"

"That's right, Chief," Brody said. "Miss Vickers said someone had been there for a few years but had moved out about two months ago. And nobody's answering. Doreen will be trying to contact the owners of the property, so we'll confirm all that."

"Good. And nothing on the stairs?" Saxby said.

"Nothing as far as we've found," Brody said. "Looks like all the action happened upstairs, and then the assailant pulled both doors shut when he left. The outer door here was locked, but the upper one wasn't."

"So, it sounds like whoever rented here," Saxby said, "would have had two keys, then, right?"

Brody held up a plain metal loop keyring with two keys on it, gesturing through the door to the outside. "Exactly. This is the set Miss Vickers used this morning. It was in one of those fake rocks in the flowerbed alongside the door out there. The square one is for the outer door, the other is for upstairs, though she says that door wasn't locked when she got here."

Saxby nodded and then turned to climb the stairs with the others in tow, entering the spacious apartment. Right away they saw a man's body prone on the floor just to the left of the top step. The man's face was mostly obscured as he lay face down roughly at the center of a pool of blood. A fireplace poker lay on the floor near the man's feet at a right angle. A casually but neatly dressed man, with sleeves rolled up and wearing surgical gloves, knelt over the body.

"Dr. Lee, I presume?" Saxby said.

"Yes, that's me," the man said, looking up from his work. "Filling in for Dr. Coyle in his absence. And you must be Chief Saxby. Good to meet you. Mark warned me that you've been having a lot of murders down here lately, but I assumed he was just having fun with me—pulling my stethoscope, as we used to say back in med school."

"Well, I hope it isn't going to be an ongoing thing," Saxby said, "but I'll admit the last two years have been interesting. So, what's your first impression here? Some kind of fight, obviously, that he lost..."

Doctor Lee stood up and stepped back from the body as he started to peel off his gloves. He was both shorter and younger than Saxby, at a trim five-ten or so, and in his late thirties. A lock of thick, dark hair hung down like a comma to touch the bridge of a pair of black, small-framed eyeglasses. He projected the authority and confidence of an experienced doctor as he spoke, and Saxby realized almost right away that he was inclined to like the man.

"Yeah, that's about right, as far as it goes," Doctor Lee said, gesturing down to the body. "But I'd just add that it looks like the kind of fight where there were two hits. Somebody hit him and he hit the ground. No sign of bruising or cuts on his hands or knuckles. No defensive marks or wounds—no, he was caught off guard. Somebody approached him from behind and whacked him on the head with the poker. Then again ... I think probably two more times, possibly three. Based on body temp, I'd put time of death between nine and eleven last night, give or take a half-hour."

"So, three whacks in all, then," Saxby said. "Do you see anything that tells you if the second two came when he was already on the floor, or do you think it could've been several fast swings as he was standing?"

"I guess I don't know why that would matter," Doctor Lee said, "but you know your side of it more than I do. I'll know more when I get a closer look at him up in the lab, but hmmm, that's interesting. I can't say right now which of the strikes came first, but I can say that they were all vicious. Any one of them should have knocked him to the ground. I suppose that if his attacker was really fast, he could have done a quick one-two-three punch while he was standing. While he was gradually crumpling to the floor is probably more like it though. Could be either. I'll try to answer that for you when I get a closer look."

"Thanks, Doctor," Saxby said. "You're right that it may not make a difference, but details like that can help us reconstruct the whole scene and whatever led up to it. Was this something personal, like a heated argument that got out of hand for example? Or was it some kind of planned killing for who knows why? The little details can add up." He paused a moment to take in the large open-plan space, nodding at the two officers who had moved from taking pictures to dusting key areas of the apartment for finger-prints. He looked down at the body again, and pointed across the room. "You see the way he fell, perpendicular to the stairs. Looks like he was headed from the living room towards the kitchen. Like he was talking with someone over here, a meeting maybe, then he said, 'Hang on, let me go over here and get something' or whatever. Maybe he was going for a glass of water. He starts to walk over that way, but the other guy—or gal—grabs the poker, comes up behind, and *wham*. It doesn't look to me like he was trying to run away down the stairs. Is that what you guys see?"

"I agree with that assessment," Doctor Lee said, looking down at the scene and nodding. "And the way his right arm is stretched out, that could have been an instinctive move to stop himself as he fell."

"That makes sense to me too, Chief," Barstow said. "If the killer had surprised him, like, broken in maybe and gotten up here, then it fits that he might have then tried to run for the door, which means back down the stairs. Seems more likely to me that they knew each other. I don't see any sign of a fight, but I just got here. Roy?"

"It might be nothing, but there's one thing that caught my eye," Brody said. He pointed across the room towards the far wall of the kitchen, where what looked like a small briefcase or satchel lay on the floor against the wall. "That bag over there, like a leather messenger bag with stiff sides. Seems to me that it could have just been leaning against the wall, like, stored there, and gradually slid down, but I think it looks more like it was thrown across the room and landed there. I took a quick look and it seems empty, aside from little scraps of paper and some dust, or crumbs of something or other. It's in the exact position now as when I first saw it, and we have pictures."

"Okay, sure. Worth noting," Saxby said, nodding. He scanned around the room again before looking at Brody. "When you called this morning, you said something about drug use. What was that?"

"Just over here, Chief, about as clear as it gets, really," Brody said, pointing and leading the way back to the living area, where a sofa and matching chairs were on three sides of a glass coffee table. Lying flat on the table was a mirror, about the size of a hardcover book, framed in light-colored wood. There was a small pile of white powder at one end of the mirror, with some more cut into thin linear piles of an inch or so long. A single-edge razorblade lay on the mirror near the main pile.

"Yep, I see what you mean about 'as clear as it gets,'" Saxby said. He knelt down for a closer look. "And hello, there's the little plastic bag and a rolled-up bill too. Looks like someone dumped out, what, at least a half-gram of coke or meth, and cut it up. They snorted some, presumably, and then the party went south. Let's get this all bagged up and printed very carefully. Doctor, you'll be able to tell if Mr. Roseman inhaled any of this shortly before he died, right?"

"Certainly. That won't be any problem after we get him up to the lab," Dr. Lee said. "I can tell you now that when I turned his head to get a look at his face, I noticed traces of what could be that white powder around his nostrils. I'll double-check that."

Saxby started walking the perimeter of the living area as they talked, and he paused at the fireplace that dominated one of the outer walls, framed by a thick oak mantel above and a brick hearth at the bottom. A standard set of fireplace tools, less the poker, stood in a tarnished brass rack to one side. He opened the glass doors to look inside. "Well, there sure wasn't any fire in here last night, and I'm guessing not for a long time. Roseman probably thought of it as decoration. No reason for anyone to be moving around with the poker."

"I think fireplaces are decorative for many people, Chief," Barstow said. "But if I was here in this room, looking around for a weapon of opportunity, the poker would be a good choice. It's long and heavy enough to be a serious weapon. I wouldn't want to be hit with one anywhere."

Saxby was still standing by the fireplace. "Hmmm, that's right, Vic. And if our killer was standing somewhere around here, and Roseman started to walk away, he could've grabbed the poker and come up behind in just a few steps. *Bam.* Or maybe he was holding it already, under some pretense. It could work. Anything else, Roy?"

"Mostly just a normal looking apartment so far," Brody said, "though we'll do another close sweep. There's a few empty beer bottles on the counter beside the sink, and the one there on the coffee table. His pockets were empty, and my thought on that is that he was in for the night. You can see he's wearing slippers, and also, on the dresser in the bedroom is a bowl with his wallet, some cash in a money clip, some change, and a little pocketknife. Normal contents of a man's pockets."

"Did you take notice of how much cash it was?" Saxby said.

"I did, yes," Brody said. He glanced at a small notepad. "It's eighty-six dollars in bills, along with some change. Typical wallet with a few credit cards, ID, insurance card."

"Well, that's not big bucks," Saxby said. "But probably enough to say that robbery wasn't the motive. Cash sitting in plain sight that wasn't grabbed, and this coke left here

—if that's what it is. That's valuable stuff to certain people. Interesting. You find any other drug paraphernalia?"

"No, not yet," Brody said. "And that seems odd, given the mirror there, but I guess someone could have shown up with the coke or whatever, and said 'hey, let's party.' There was beer in the fridge, but no hard liquor. No sign that he was a smoker, and the only ashtray I see is the one on that little table by the stairs. Looks like he dropped his keys in that when he came home. I have a little bowl like that just inside my door at home."

Dr. Lee cut in: "I'm all done here, unless you have any other questions for me right now." He continued after Saxby shook his head: "I'm mostly booked up for today, but I should be able to start on him first thing tomorrow. Give me a day or so after that and I'll be able to get you a fair picture of what happened to him. I'm sure you know full tox results will take a lot longer than that."

"Okay, thank you, Doctor," Saxby said, stepping forward to shake hands. "We can use whatever you can get us as soon as possible. Even best guesses can help point us in the right direction. Call me or my office at any time. Good meeting you, despite the circumstances."

The doctor zipped up his bag, pulled on his coat, and went out. Sergeant Brody used his radio to ask Officer Hayward to send in the ambulance crew.

"Okay, gang, let's focus on doing a close sweep of the whole place before we pack up," Saxby said to all four officers in the apartment. "We don't have a warrant yet, but we can look around at whatever's out in the open. Whoever has the camera, let's be sure to get plenty of pictures of the body, and the area under it and around it as they pick him up and move him."

As the two-person ambulance crew appeared from the stairwell with a folding stretcher and started dealing with the body, Barstow came over to stand beside Saxby. "What're you thinking, Chief? I'm not getting that there's much here that explains away killing a person."

Saxby looked at her, considering that. "I follow you, Vic, and it's important to pay attention to those kinds of feelings. Listening to your gut is part of what makes you a good cop. It's hard for normal people like us to imagine killing another person in cold blood. For money or drugs, or for some old argument. I think it's good that it doesn't make sense to you—to us. As long as you're able to set that 'wrongness' aside and focus on the facts. Sometimes people kill each other for stupid reasons, and drugs and all that crap is probably at the top of the list."

"You're right, Chief," Barstow said with a shrug. "It's probably nothing. I'm sure what happened here last night is probably just what it looks like. Drug deal gone bad most likely. Some kind of old argument bubbled up and boiled over for some reason or other. That's what it is."

"That's what it looks like at the moment, Vic," Saxby said. "If it looks like a duck and quacks like a duck ... not always—but more often than not. But anyway, I meant what I said about paying attention to your intuition. Sometimes your gut steers you right. But for now, we have an apartment to search, and we have a witness outside in the car. I'd like you to drive Miss Vickers home and get her formal statement, in whatever order you think is best. No problem if she needs to come in to the station later today, but talk to her and use your judgement. We need her impression about Roseman's lifestyle. To what extent —if any—he was into drugs, did he have friends in low places, was he hard up for money? You know what to do. She got a little shook up this morning, but she seems like someone who has it together pretty well. I'll stay here and help sweep this place. Let's catch up later back at the station."

It was a few minutes after five that afternoon when Chief Saxby was sitting at his desk, pencil in hand, staring down at a notepad that held a disappointingly small amount of information about Boone Roseman and his recent demise. Pushing the pad to one side, he decided to steel himself for another look at a recent report covering the year-to-date parking violations in town, when he was saved by the buzz of his desk phone. Seeing that the call was coming from the office of Mayor Jack Torrance, he answered right away.

"Afternoon, Jack," Saxby said. "Are we still on for six?"

"Well, that's just it, Tate," Torrance said. "Something's come up and I need to reschedule. No crisis, but something I need to take care of. I didn't have anything for you that can't wait for next week, unless you need to try tomorrow. Sorry about the short notice."

"No problem with next week," Saxby said, "for the regular stuff. But I'm glad you called because I do need you for just a few minutes. Is right now okay?"

"You know, Tate, I'm sorry," Torrance said. "I did get the message that you came up when I was on a call. I'm just frazzled today. It's been hard to find a minute to breathe. What's up?"

"Just a case I wanted you to be aware of," Saxby said. "We found a body this morning. First or second-degree murder is my first impression but we're only getting started. Looks like it could have been an argument that escalated, or might even be drug related. Too soon to tell. In an apartment over on Columbia between Jefferson and French. The deceased was a local guy by the name of Boone Roseman. He was mid-sixties, I think. I knew him only very slightly. We met for some reason or other years ago."

"Oh no, good grief, Tate. Not again," Torrance said. "It's only been what, a little over a year since those last killings? Do you have someone in custody? Or any suspects?"

"No, nothing like that yet," Saxby said. "It was a cold crime scene. A neighbor who had a reason to come over in the morning found him. First glance says that one or more people were with him in his place last night, and at some point, he ended up getting a fireplace poker to the back of his head and went down fast. As far as we know, nobody in the area heard or saw anything, but you know how that is, with so many of those big old houses being empty. We hope to hear more from the ME within a day or so."

"Oh, this is terrible," Torrance said, "but thanks for letting me know. Dammit. What the hell is going on around here? All we need now is for Netflix to show up wanting to do some kind of true crime mini-series on Cape May and scare away all the tourists."

Always the politician, Saxby thought to himself. *And of course, I'm not surprised.* But he also knew that Mayor

Torrance was a good guy at heart, who always had his back and that of the department when it counted.

"Oh, I doubt that'll happen, Jack," Saxby said. "But anyway, that's about what we know at the moment. I'll let you know when we have anything more substantial."

"Okay, yes. Do that please, Tate," Torrance said. "And likewise, let me know if there's any way I can help. You know where to find me. When I get home later, I'll drink to this being a one-off this time."

"Oh yeah, put me down for that idea," Saxby said. "I'll do the same toast myself. Have a good evening, Jack, and I'll speak with you soon."

As Saxby hung up the phone, he realized that Sergeant Barstow had appeared in his office doorway, about to knock on the open door.

"Sounds like you were just filling the mayor in on the Roseman case," Barstow said. "Aren't you meeting with him at six?"

"I was planning to, but he had to cancel on me," Saxby said, waving her in. "Come on in and have a seat. You're right, that was just him on the phone. He was busy as always but I gave him what little we know. Though, right now I'm hoping you know more than I do."

"Not much more than what we talked about at the scene earlier," Barstow said. "A few odds and ends is about it."

"That's okay," Saxby said. "We've got to start somewhere and I'll take what I can get."

Barstow consulted a notepad, using a pencil to sort through her list. "Ah, let's see. First of all, I've already called up to the county offices, and Detective Dooley actually answered the phone. I told him what was what, he checked with his boss, and was able to put himself on the case."

"Oh, that is the first good news of the day," Saxby said. "Tom's always been a good guy to work with."

Though the small-town police departments throughout Cape May County weren't always thrilled about the requirement that they liaise with an assigned county detective in the event of a homicide, Saxby was matter-of-fact about the situation, and had been very glad to work with Detective Dooley on a number of occasions. It had been less than a year since a brutal string of murders had spilled from Cape May into several of the other shore towns, and for that case, he and Dooley, along with Sergeant Barstow, had made an effective team.

"Yeah, I was glad about that too," Barstow said. "So, I've crossed that item off my list. He said he could meet with us here at noon tomorrow. Is that okay for you?"

Saxby looked down at an appointment book that lay open next to his phone before nodding. "Noon's fine with me. So, lay it on me. What do you have that I might not know about yet?"

"Okay, so, you were there for the look around Roseman's apartment after I left, so I'll just go through that quickly. The white powder on the mirror checks out as cocaine. That's per the NarcoCheck test. But there's something else we only learned this afternoon. Remember that leather messenger bag that Brody thought looked out of place? That also had traces of cocaine in it, along with marijuana. Not any significant amounts, but enough for a positive test. I showed Mallory Vickers a picture of it and she didn't recognize it as Roseman's. They were just friends, but to hear her tell it, they were close friends going back some years. They would hang out at his place and watch a movie or do dinner now and then. If she says that bag wasn't his, I'm inclined to believe it."

"Circumstantial, but sure, it's a possibility," Saxby said. "For the moment, let's work with the idea that someone else brought the bag into his apartment. What else do we have?"

"Apart from that and the mirror, nothing else stands out as drug related. I mean, there was a pack of single-edged razorblades on a shelf in the kitchen, but that's a common household item."

"Sure. I have a pack of them somewhere," Saxby said, "and I don't do cocaine. What else?"

"Oh yeah, there was something else that could be a little exciting," Barstow said. "They found two of those paper bill wrappers—you know, like they use at the bank to wrap around a fat pile of bills. Crumpled up on the floor beside a little trashcan under the desk at one end of the bedroom. They were both for five thousand in hundreds. That would be two bundles of fifty hundreds each, or ten thousand dollars. There wasn't any money like that either on him or laying around the apartment."

"Right, except for that torn corner of the hundred we found under the body when they moved him," Saxby said. "Starting to look more like some kind of drug thing, isn't it?"

"I have to admit that it's looking like that," Barstow said. "Though that wasn't my feeling initially. The fact that those wrappers were in the bedroom suggests that maybe Roseman was counting money out or getting it ready for a deal. Getting ready for someone to come over with cocaine and whatever else."

"And so, Mr. X comes over last night," Saxby said, "possibly with that leather bag with drugs in it. They party a little, have a few beers, do a deal, or maybe disagree about the deal, and then it goes south. Roseman ends up dead, and Mr. X takes off with the money and the drugs. That could be pretty close to what happened. What do you think?"

"Well, I guess that's the standard playbook, isn't it?" Barstow said. "But if that's what happens, why does Mr. X leave without the messenger bag that he came with?"

"Fair question. Nothing conclusive, but good one to think about," Saxby said. "One idea is that after he flared up and killed Roseman, he realized what he'd done and went into a panic. Probably wasn't thinking straight. He grabs the money and whatever else he can, shoves it into some other bag, or just inside his jacket maybe, and hightails it out of there."

"Okay, that might be what happened," Barstow said. She nodded slowly, but her eyes held a hint of suspicion. "Only problem is, that scene didn't look like anyone had panicked and hightailed it out. Maybe that's the feeling I had when we were there this morning. Aside from Roseman's body on the floor, the poker, the blood, and the messenger bag, the scene was very neat."

"Neat. Like, you mean 'tidied up?' " Saxby said.

"Just giving you my impression," Barstow said. "And you told me not to ignore my gut feelings."

"You're right, Vic, I get you," Saxby said. "And I'll say that again, but I also said that we've got to follow the facts and the evidence. What else do we have along those lines?"

Barstow took a moment to look over her notes again. "There are a few strange things. It's too early for complete results on the prints, but we did get a reference set from Roseman, and his prints weren't anywhere on the mirror, the plastic bag, or the razorblade, though to be fair we shouldn't expect much from the razorblade. There are some prints on the mirror that we haven't identified yet, just not his. Also, of the five empty beer bottles in the apartment, three of them did have Roseman's prints—and only his prints on them, while the other two had no prints at all on them. And all five bottles seemed fresh, as though they were probably from yesterday—not yet rinsed out."

"Now that is interesting, isn't it," Saxby said. "The three with only his prints doesn't seem weird. It's his place, his beer, and he's the host. But the other two ... Seems like they should at least have his prints, even if he poured it into a glass for a guest."

"I agree, though there were no glasses out or in the sink showing recent use or smelling of beer," Barstow said. "It seems to me that those two bottles were wiped off, which adds to my impression that whoever was there was calm, cool, and collected. Not freaking and running down the stairs forgetting things, such as their nice leather bag."

"I think you might be on to something there, Vic," Saxby said. "We could have a cool customer. I don't see Roseman's prints not being on the mirror as important as the thing with the bottles. Whoever the guest was could have brought the mirror with him—in the leather bag maybe—and set that all up. If Roseman even took part in that, he could have knelt down at the table with no need to handle the mirror. If so, then the only thing he would have had to touch would be the rolled-up bill. And as you know, it's almost impossible to get prints from currency."

"Right, so that's a dead end," Barstow said. "About the only other thing is that I asked Mallory Vickers if she knew anything about Boone Roseman and drugs. Was he a user of anything, what did she know about his past, etc. She said he enjoyed his beers, and the occasional bottle of wine if she brought one over, but that was it as far as she knows. She was aware that he had been caught up in some kind of local pot selling operation way back in the late '70s, but she didn't know details, only that the experience had scared him off illegal drugs. She did say they had smoked pot a few times at parties over the years, but he didn't actually keep a supply himself. And all that fits with our search of his stuff. I mean, apart from the appearance of the mirror and the coke, he seems clean."

"Until maybe some old friend shows up and dredges up his past, and tries to get him back into it," Saxby said. "Whips out a mirror and dumps out a pile of the good stuff. But that doesn't help us with the money, if there even was any money there. Isn't Three back from his trip tomorrow? When he gets back and gets caught up, I'd like him to work with you on this."

"Tomorrow yes, I think he should be in by late morning," Barstow said. "I'll get him caught up as soon as possible."

Sergeant Barstow outranked Deputy Chase Connor III —who was called "Three" by most of his friends and fellow officers—but the two of them had a close and informal relationship, frequently working as partners. Saxby liked to encourage their collaboration whenever the situation allowed.

"Good, thanks," Saxby said. "And hopefully we'll get at least a little preliminary from Dr. Lee, along with some more on all the print work. What else?"

"We did a door-to-door for about a block and a half around, and the bottom line with that is that basically nobody we talked to saw or heard anything last night," Barstow said. "It's only March, and as you know, seven out of ten houses in town are empty, so there's that. I'll start work on Boone Roseman's background tomorrow. For the moment, all we know about him is what we got from his wallet and apartment, along with what Mallory Vickers told me, which wasn't really a treasure trove of information. Okay if I put it all together for our meeting with Detective Dooley tomorrow?"

"Yeah, sure, Vic," Saxby said. "That's probably enough for now. Let's hold the rest for tomorrow's meet with Dooley. If Three gets in before that, all the better and he can join us. This is all just hours old, but I think we're off to a good start. At least we've got the team in place."

Barstow straightened her papers and stood up. "I don't know about you, Chief, but I'm ready for a glass or two of something."

"You're singing my tune, Vic," Saxby said. "I had a power bar for breakfast and another for lunch. I think there's a big sandwich and one of those glasses you mentioned with my name on it somewhere nearby."

"You're too predictable," Barstow said, as she headed for

the door. "My detective instincts are telling me that I think I know where you're headed."

"I need about a half-hour to close up a few things here," Saxby said. "After that, if I bump into you at the Mug, I'm buying."

2

It was about an hour later that Chief Saxby was halfway into a huge BLT sandwich in his favorite booth at the Ugly Mug Tavern. Everyone on the kitchen staff knew that Saxby didn't eat tomatoes, and so, for him, the "T" stood for "turkey." They also knew that both the bacon and the side of fries should be very well-done, and the sandwich should be devoid of any sort of condiments. Though he believed his powers of persuasion to be considerable, and he was engaged to the manager, he had never been able to get any of the staff to either confirm or deny that the kitchen crew referred to his favorite sandwich as the "BL Tate."

Angela had stopped by shortly after he'd arrived and sat with him for a few minutes as he ordered dinner, stealing sips of his beer as they talked.

"So, what are you allowed to tell me?" Angela said, leaning in after a glance around the room. "And what can you tell me that you aren't allowed to tell me?"

"Come on now, Ang," Saxby said. "You know how it

goes. I can't tell you much at all. We don't even know if he had any family yet."

"Of course, right. I understand. That must be just about the first priority. But it is a murder, right? You can tell me that."

"Yeah, I guess I can say that. You were there when I got the phone call this morning anyway. About the only thing we're sure of right now is that one person killed another person in town last night. A break-in maybe, some kind of deal gone bad—we don't know. Too early to tell. Doesn't look like a robbery, but again, too early to tell at this point."

"That is terrible," Angela said, getting up from the booth. "Just so sad. But I know you'll do your best, like you always do. Hey, I need another twenty minutes to take care of a few things, and then I'll come back and let you buy me a drink. Didn't you say Vic was coming to join you?"

"I don't think I said that," Saxby said, "but you may have read my mind. I invited her, and she usually shows when I invite her."

"Lo and behold, there she is," Angela said. She waved across the bar to Sergeant Barstow, who had just come in through the side door. Angela waited for her to come around to the booth. "Good to see you, Vic. You can have some time to talk shop with the boss while I do a few things. Back in a little while."

Barstow slid into the booth across from Saxby as Angela retreated into the kitchen.

"I hope I didn't scare her away," Barstow said.

"No, you're fine, Vic," Saxby said. "She just had to wrap up a few things. She'll be back. I'm surprised you didn't get here earlier. Would you like something to eat?"

"No, thank you though," Barstow said. "I had a big lunch at the station late afternoon and I'm not very hungry yet. Well, I might swipe a few of your fries, if that's okay."

Saxby laughed and pushed his plate to the middle of the table. A waitress came and took Barstow's order for a glass of wine. The jukebox started to play Van Morrison's *Brown Eyed Girl*, drawing claps from a group of fifty-somethings at one of the other booths.

"You know, I think the first time I ever heard this song was here, at the Mug," Saxby said. "I think there's a rule that it has to play at least once a night."

"I know what you mean, Chief," Barstow said. "I'm not the same ripe old age as you are, but the song and the place go together for me too." Barstow's wine arrived and she took a few thoughtful sips before deciding she liked it. "Oh, I wanted to tell you, just after you left the station today, I picked up a message Doreen had left me earlier, about Roseman's next of kin. She said she would do some more checking tomorrow, but it looks like the only relatives he has—*had*—may be a niece and a nephew, who apparently both live and work in the Chicago area. They're the children of Roseman's late brother, Bonner Roseman. Doreen said Bonner Roseman died ten years ago from a heart attack. She plans to try to contact them tomorrow morning."

"Good. Hopefully that'll come together in time for our meeting with Dooley tomorrow," Saxby said. "We need to keep Roseman's name on the QT until we notify the family. If Doreen can even find them, that is."

"Right, got it, Chief," Barstow said. "On the down-low until then. I just had an idea—I wonder if he had a will, because that could have contact information. I'll mention that to Doreen."

Saxby nodded. "That's not a bad idea at all. Also, if he did make a will, we'll need to know what's in it. Hard to imagine he had much money, but he could have had a life insurance policy."

They both looked up as Angela appeared with a glass of wine in hand. "Okay to join you two, or are you in the middle of a top-secret conversation?"

"Please do join us," Barstow said. "Nothing top secret, though the chief says things are on the QT."

"I got it," Angela said. She drew a finger across her lips in a zipping motion. "I won't talk about it until it shows up in the *Star & Wave*."

"So you're aware, Vic," Saxby said, "Angela was with me in the kitchen when I took the call from Brody this morning, so she knows the name and the rough outline of what happened."

"Okay, that makes sense," Barstow said. "But anyway, I don't have anything else that can't wait for tomorrow with Detective Dooley. We can talk about more pleasant things, like, will I have another glass of chardonnay, or should I switch it up for the second round?"

"Detective Dooley? I remember him," Angela said. "He worked with you on that last big murder case. I hope that isn't a sign that you're going to get into a big gunfight again this time. I seem to remember seeing you both in the hospital."

"Ang, that certainly wasn't his fault," Saxby said. "He's a great guy to work with. I'm with you on the gunfight though, and I promise to try to avoid that. What do you think, Vic?"

"Well, I'm thinking there's two important things," Barstow said. "Speaking as the only person out in the rain that night who didn't get shot, I agree with you. Let's try not to go there again."

"You see, Ang, Vic agrees with me, so you don't have to worry," Saxby said. "But you said there were two important things, Vic. What's the other?"

"I think I'll have another glass of chard," Barstow said. "And we can talk about fun, lighthearted stuff. Like horror movies."

3

It was an unusually hot day for late May, with the mid-afternoon temperature hovering around eighty-five degrees and just a few wispy clouds scattered high up across a brilliant blue sky. It was the kind of day that Manny Bowen's older sister Jody would have called a "beach day." With the start of Memorial Day Weekend only a week away, the big arcade on the boardwalk was already open full-time, along with most of the shops and restaurants in town. The local high school students had been surprised and thrilled to learn earlier in the week that school would be closed on Friday, in order for all the teachers to take part in some kind of training. Manny and his friends didn't care about the reason. What was important to them was that it was hot, sunny, and they had the day off from school.

As he waited for his friends Ryan and Frankie to come out of Morrow's Nut House, Manny watched the light traffic go by on Beach Avenue. Directly across the street,

the marquee of the movie theater loudly proclaimed that
Play It Again, Sam was held over for a third week. He
scanned each way up and down the boardwalk, disappointed that it wasn't yet far enough into the season for the
serious girl-watching that was his favorite part of every
Cape May summer. This would be the first summer that he
and most of his friends were going to be sixteen years old,
which meant they would be able to get jobs and make
money. Manny hoped it would be easier to meet girls then
—being able to spend cash on them. He could take a date
over to the Wildwood Boardwalk, where he'd buy tickets
for Dracula's Castle. She would certainly want to take his
hand as they wandered through the spooky darkness, with
all the ghosts and ghouls jumping out from their hiding
places, trying to scare them. At least that's what his older
friend Cliff said had always worked for him. Manny had a
feeling the summer of '72 was going to be the best one yet.

"Here we are, goofball," Ryan yelled to him, as he and
Frankie emerged from Morrow's, small bags of candy in
hand. Manny walked over to meet them in front of the
store.

"What took you so long?" Manny said, reaching into the
bag Frankie held out to him to grab a few Malted Milk
Balls. "I thought I was gonna have to come in after you."

"We had to wait for the lady to go in back and find a
new box of Swedish Fish," Ryan said. "But it was cool
because that gave us time to eat like half the fudge samples
on the tray up front."

They all laughed out loud as Ryan popped one of the
bright red candy fish into his mouth.

"Have you seen any of the other guys?" Frankie said. He checked the Timex watch his uncle had given him for his last birthday. "It's almost two-thirty. They're probably down there already."

"Nope. Haven't seen anyone yet," Manny said. "I bet you're right and they're already down there. Doug told me he thought he could get his brother to buy us some beer. Let's go see."

The three boys, munching candy, walked past Convention Hall and the last few shops to the flight of weathered wooden stairs that took them down to the beach. Being so early in the season, and with the school year not yet over, there weren't many tourists in town, and the beach was sparsely populated. The ocean water was still too cold for all but the hardiest of beach-goers, not yet warmed by weeks of blazing summer sun. Most of the people the boys could see, camped out on towels and folding beach chairs, appeared to be either dozing off their lunch or engrossed in the latest thriller.

At two-thirty, the tide had almost finished going out, and as the sand sloped away towards the ocean, the forest of pilings and the associated framework of huge timbers that supported Convention Hall, the arcade, and all the shops above were exposed. After walking almost to the waterline, and with a final look around to make sure they were unobserved by any passing police or lifeguards, the boys ducked their heads and went in under the boardwalk. They walked farther in, keeping on dry sand but close to the water, where there was plenty of open space between the pilings, and more than enough headroom. They were in a place that was not designed for people to be, and there were no lights, but the bright daylight pouring in from the open ocean side, along with the thousands of slivers slipping through the cracks in the boardwalk above, gave them all the light they needed to see where they were going.

The sounds of teenage boys laughing and horsing around got louder as they approached, until they heard someone yell out, "Hey, Ryan and Frankie are finally here. What a couple a slow-pokes."

"And there's Manny too," another voice said, echoing around the vast and sandy cavern, just as the three new arrivals stepped around a tight grouping of seaweed-covered pilings to enter an open space of dry sand about twenty feet square. The "ceiling" of heavy old boards was several feet above their heads at that point, and Manny figured they must be roughly under the rear of Morrow's Nut House.

The boys began a round of the slapping and arm-punching that was a common greeting for young men of their age. No more than a few minutes after Manny's group had joined the other three friends, Doug Lawson appeared, having made his way under the boardwalk from the opposite direction. He had been lugging a large canvas tote bag, which he set down on the sand with obvious relief.

"Oh man, I think I've carried that thing halfway across town," Doug said, rubbing the spot on his left shoulder where the strap of the tote bag had been riding. "But my brother came through for us."

"Really? What's in the bag?" Frankie said, before stealing a look. "Oh cool! Miller ponies!"

"Yep. Two eight-packs," Doug said. He took a moment to look around at the group, counting silently to himself. "There's seven of us, so we each get two, and we can split the last two."

"Cool man," Ryan said. "The summer's starting off pretty good."

4

Chief Saxby was working at his desk when office manager and primary dispatcher Doreen Watson buzzed him on the intercom.

"Detective Dooley here for your meeting, Chief," Doreen announced, with an electronic tint to her voice. "On his way to your office now."

Saxby thanked her as he got up, making it around the desk in time to meet Dooley at the office door.

"Good to see you, Tom," Saxby said. The two men shook hands warmly and Saxby motioned the county detective to a chair. "Thanks for coming in to meet with us."

"My pleasure, Tate," Dooley said. "You know I'm always happy to work with you guys down here in lovely Victorian Cape May."

"Well, I'm glad you aren't too superstitious," Saxby said. "Angela, my fiancée, reminded me last night that the last time you and I worked together, we both got shot. Geez.

Hard to believe that was less than a year ago. How time flies."

"We were damn lucky that night," Dooley said. "All things considered. It's funny, but on the drive down today, I was thinking that might have been the most interesting case I've ever worked on. That was some crazy stuff. This new one you've got, this Roseman thing, seems a lot more straightforward, at least with what I know so far."

"Let's hope so," Saxby said. "If you've read the summary Vic sent you this morning, you know what I know. I think she got something new from Doctor Lee a few hours ago, but she hasn't shared it with me yet. As a matter of fact, it's about time we headed over to the conference room. We have a few minutes if you need anything. You know where the coffee is if you want some. Doreen's pretty good about maintaining a pot in drinkable condition."

"Drinkable even? That's always a bonus. I can't say that about the coffee up in our office," Dooley said, standing up. "I think I'll take you up on that. See you in there in a few minutes."

Dooley turned towards the kitchen as he went out, leaving Saxby to gather a few items from his desk before heading to the conference room. Sergeant Barstow was already there, seated across the long table from Deputy Connor.

"Welcome back, Three," Saxby said. "Good to see you. Your trip go well?"

"It was good, Chief, thanks," Connor said. "It's nice to get a break and get some good R & R, but it's also good to come home and get back to work after a while."

"Agree with you there on all points," Saxby said. "And you have good timing, because now you can jump right back in with Vic on this Roseman case." Just then Detective Dooley entered with a mug of coffee in one hand and a file folder and legal pad in the other. "Ah, our honored guest. You both know Detective Dooley from county. Tom will be working with us on the Roseman case. And likewise, Tom, you've worked with Sergeant Barstow and Deputy Connor in the past."

Hellos and handshakes were exchanged around the table as everyone settled into their seats and arranged papers, pads, and cups of coffee or water in front of them.

"I've asked Sergeant Barstow to lead the meeting today," Saxby said. "Okay, Vic?"

"Absolutely, Chief," Barstow said. "I'll go ahead and get started then. I already know you've all read the summary I sent out early this morning. It wasn't a very long summary, since we really don't know much yet. There's just a few items we've learned since I wrote that, nothing big, and I'll cover them in a little bit." She paused for a moment to look at her notes before continuing. "I was surprised to see an email from Doctor Lee early this morning with some good information, if not the final report. Apparently, he had some unexpected free time late yesterday and was able to get started on the postmortem. With that in mind, I'll run through the basics of the case as we know it."

Barstow took a long slug of water. "Yesterday morning, Miss Mallory Vickers, of Hughes Street in Cape May, became concerned that her friend, Boone Roseman, who had agreed to drive her to an appointment in Rio Grande, had not shown up at her place and was not answering calls or texts. At about ten after eight, she made the two-block walk over to his apartment on Columbia Avenue. She saw his car on the street, but got no answer when she banged on the door. At that point she used a spare key, from one of those fake rocks in the garden, to let herself in, finding him dead from an obvious violent attack. She told me that she did not look around his apartment at all, but ran outside, calling 911 within a few minutes. That call was recorded at 8:21.

"Sergeant Brody, who had been out on patrol, arrived at the scene within six or seven minutes, with Officers Redding and Davis arriving a minute or two after that. They confirmed that Mr. Roseman was dead and secured the scene. Redding and Davis did a brief canvass of the neighborhood, finding nothing of interest. That canvass was repeated more extensively within the hour, including a door-to-door, again finding nothing of interest.

"Within another thirty minutes or so, by a few minutes after nine, Doctor Lee, the chief, and myself were also at the scene."

"How did Doctor Lee get there so fast?" Dooley asked. "Does he—or she—live in Cape May?"

"North Cape May, actually," Barstow said. "Doctor Robert Lee. I believe he lives somewhere just off Bayshore Road. He told me he was all dressed and about to drive up to the hospital when he got the call. Took him about fifteen minutes to get to Mr. Roseman's apartment. The chief and I pulled up together, and he must have already been there for about ten or fifteen minutes."

"Thanks, Vic, that's a good overall," Saxby said. "How about summing up what we know about Roseman."

"Right, sure, Boone Roseman," Barstow said. "Sixty-six

years old, born in 1956. Local guy, worked a bunch of different jobs, but nothing for more than a few years at a time. Lived off social security and a small inheritance from an aunt who passed away twenty or more years back. No known children or spouses. Or enemies for that matter— per Mallory Vickers anyway. We'll be talking to other people who knew him of course, but for the moment a lot of what we have comes from her. She says they were just friends, like a brother and sister situation. She's forty-eight years old, single with no kids. Married once but divorced years ago. My impression of her is that she's a straight arrow and seems like a good witness.

"So, now back to Boone Roseman. Miss Vickers says she spoke with him for about a minute Sunday afternoon just to firm up the plan for him to drive her to her appointment. She showed me that call on her phone. They did not discuss social plans for the evening. She had something else on with a female friend of hers, and as far as she knew he was going to be home watching TV. At some point later that evening, Roseman had at least one visitor in his apartment. There is evidence that he, along with at least one other person, drank several beers, and there is evidence suggesting that he and some other person may have engaged in snorting some cocaine. In any case, at some time around ten or eleven, somebody, apparently taking him by surprise, hit him repeatedly on the back of the head with a fireplace poker, killing him almost instantly. Whoever that person was left the apartment shortly after that, leaving the upper door unlocked but locking the lower, outer door behind them on their way out."

"What do we have so far on fingerprints?" Dooley asked.

"Looks like somebody was very careful there," Barstow said. "It appears that the doorknobs and door edges were wiped, because the only prints we got from there were ours or Mallory Vickers, along with Doctor Lee's in one spot. As you know, those areas really should be plastered with Roseman's. Also clearly wiped were two of the five empty beer bottles, the kitchen faucet, and around the sink in general."

"So, somebody spent at least a few minutes doing a little clean-up," Connor said. "What about the cocaine setup—the mirror, the baggy—anything there?"

"That is interesting," Barstow said. "Because the mirror does have prints on it, some only partial and some years old. The only one we get a hit on is for a man by the name of Narvel Carter, who passed away two months ago after living in the area for years. He was in the system because he applied for a gaming license back in 1996. Must have been trying for a job in one of the casinos. I haven't got anything on him yet—I mean, apart from him being dead."

"And dead people don't hit other people over the head with fireplace pokers," Dooley said. "I'll be interested to hear what you find out on that."

"Have you asked Mallory Vickers about the mirror?" Saxby said. "Maybe she would recognize it as Roseman's."

"Yes, I did ask her," Barstow said. "I showed her a picture of it on my phone. She didn't recognize it as his, and she's spent a lot of time in his place over the years, including using the bathroom. She thought it didn't belong there but admitted that she couldn't say for sure. I also asked her about the leather bag that was on the kitchen floor, and she seemed pretty sure that was not his either. She didn't recognize it and she didn't think it was the kind of thing he would have had. That bag had traces of cocaine in a few spots on the inside, along with what I think are bits of marijuana."

"Speaking of 'traces of cocaine'," Saxby said. "I remember Doctor Lee telling us he thought there was a little bit of white powder around Roseman's nostrils. Do we know yet if he was able to look into that?"

"Actually, Chief, he was," Barstow said. "And he was puzzled by it. There was a little bit of powder around the opening of each nostril…"

Dooley cut her off with a question. "Wait a minute. A toxicology test can take days at least, and maybe more. What am I missing here?"

"No, you're absolutely right about the tox tests," Barstow said. "From what I understand, Doctor Lee was able to do was just a little bit of specialized poking around. Here, I printed out part of his email. Why don't I read it out loud so you'll get it straight from the doctor's mouth. It's only a paragraph."

She shuffled papers for a moment before holding up a single printed sheet. "Doctor Lee writes:"

You may recall my mentioning that I had observed traces of a white powder around the nostrils. I was able to confirm that when I got a closer look at the deceased in the lab. As you know, full toxicology test results won't be available for as much as two weeks. But, being aware of the evidence in the apartment of recent cocaine use, I was able to focus on that with a simple contact swab test for cocaine (as opposed to a blood test). With that, I can now confirm that the white powder at the opening of the nose of the deceased is, in fact, high-grade cocaine. The interesting thing, though, is that, using the same swab test, I was not able to find any trace of the drug farther up in the nasal cavity, or even as little as two centimeters into the nostril. I pondered this for a while before repeating the test with the same results. With all that in mind, I can't see that the deceased had actually "snorted" anything up his nose, or certainly not with any effort. Could he have pretended to do that for some reason? I suppose he could have made a show of trying to inhale, dabbing a little powder around his nostrils for effect perhaps. I'll leave that for the police to figure out. There is a specific test for cocaine in the blood that gives results within hours. I have done that test on Mr. Roseman and will pass the results on to you as soon as I get them. I will be very surprised if it turns out that his bloodstream has any trace of the drug at all.

"Well now, that is interesting, isn't it?" Saxby said. "Why would he be faking it—you know, putting on a show? If the visitor had arrived to do a drug deal, with some amount of cocaine in that leather bag, intending to sell to Roseman, why wouldn't Roseman want to try the goods? Vic, yesterday you mentioned that Mallory Vickers was under the impression that he had been involved with selling pot a long time back. What do we have on that?"

"Right, Chief," Barstow said. "I was just about to go into that. Mallory Vickers thought that had been in Wildwood, back in 1978. She told me she knew the year—just one of those funny things—because when he told her about it, she had realized that she must have been four years old at the time. Anyway, so, I called over to Wildwood, and one of their people dug it up for me pretty quickly. It was just a thin paper file, but the gist of it is that Roseman was one of several young guys who got busted selling a bag of pot to an undercover cop. Looks like it was a small-time thing. They scrape up the money to buy a half pound or a pound of Mexican up in Atlantic City or Philly, split it up and sell small bags up on the boardwalk in the summer. Charges were dropped after Roseman and the others got scared and told whatever they knew about the people they bought from. I figure he was twenty-two at the time."

"And no doubt that kind of thing happened all the time," Saxby said. "Especially in the summer. And that experience put him off having much to do with any kind of drugs, isn't that also what Vickers told you?"

"Right, that's what she believed," Barstow said. "She had seen him smoke a little weed a few times, if it was being passed around a party, but that's it as far as she knew."

"So, if we believe her," Dooley said, "or, I should say, if we believe that's what she believes, then how does that jibe with the idea that he pretended to snort the coke? In the summary you sent me, Sergeant, there was something about a few of those paper bill wrappers in the trash, along with a torn-off piece of a hundred-dollar bill under the body. Was there any other evidence related to money?"

"Not that we found, no," Barstow said. "And that's another thing I asked Mallory Vickers about. According to her, Roseman was comfortable but not wealthy in any way. He paid his bills on time and had a decent car, but wasn't the sort of person who could go to the bank and take out ten grand in cash. He had social security and some savings, and he also had income from a trust that his aunt had left to him about ten years ago."

"I'm thinking about that torn bill under the body," Connor said. "To me, that implies that there was some kind of struggle. Like, 'I've changed my mind and I don't want to do this. Take your coke and get out of here.' But the visitor doesn't want to leave without the money."

"That could be. Yeah, I was leaning that way myself," Dooley said. "So, whatta ya think we have here, folks? Seems pretty cut and dried, doesn't it? Would you like to go first, Deputy Connor?"

"Sure, Detective," Connor said. "I'll give it a shot. There isn't a lot of evidence, but what there is sure does point to a drug deal gone wrong for some reason. There must have been a part of Roseman's life that Mallory Vickers didn't know about. Either he's been doing a little dealing on the side for a long time, or else he recently bumped into someone from his past and they decided to do a deal. They make plans, he comes up with the cash somehow, and the guy comes over to his place the other night. They have a few beers and sample the product, except that he doesn't really. On that, to me, that might just mean that he's up for selling, but not for putting any up his own nose. He just wants some extra money, but he's not into the lifestyle. Anyway, after a while they disagree. Over the terms maybe, or maybe Roseman gets cold feet. The visitor doesn't like that, picks up the poker and wham. He looks around, takes a minute to wipe down for prints, then grabs the money and the coke and leaves."

"Good summary," Dooley said. "I agree that what little we have right now is pointing towards some version of that. What are you thinking, Tate?"

"Hmmm. I agree that Three's scenario is what we have

to work with at the moment," Saxby said. "As you say, 'some version of that.' It has holes in it, and we need to work on filling in those holes or explaining why they aren't holes. Was Roseman actually able to come up with that money? Or, while we're on that, was the money even there? If the killer was calm enough to wipe the place down for prints, why wasn't he calm enough to take the leather bag, or the mirror?"

"We need to find some more people who knew Roseman apart from Mallory Vickers," Dooley said, "and get their take on him. About drugs mostly, but also about state of mind, possible enemies, anyone who had threatened him—the usual stuff."

"I can get to work on that right after this meeting," Connor said.

"Good, thanks, Three," Saxby said. "Talk to Brody about who you can borrow to help with that, if you think you need it. Where are we on a warrant?"

"I've got that," Dooley said. "I put the paperwork in this morning. I'll see where it stands when I get back to the office. Shouldn't be any problem, and that'll allow us to look into his finances."

"That will be interesting," Saxby said. "It'll also be interesting to see if there's any secret stash of money or drugs in his apartment. What's next for you, Vic?"

"Well, if we can get a signed warrant today," Barstow said, "I'll grab who I can and take a close look at Roseman's apartment. Aside from that, my priority is to get what I can on this Narvel Carter person whose prints are on the mirror, and we'll see where that goes. If I have time in between, I'll help Three with talking to some other people who knew Roseman."

"Okay, good, then," Saxby said. "Sounds like we have a plan for the day. Anything else, Tom?"

"I think we've covered things for now," Dooley said, standing up. "I've got some things to work on up the road, but I'll check on that warrant and let the sergeant know as soon as I can."

"Okay, then," Saxby said. "Good work so far, everyone. I'll be at my desk for most of the rest of the day, but please interrupt if I can help in any way. Vic and Three, check in with me for a quick end-of-day chat to go over any updates."

Everyone gathered their papers as the meeting broke up, and Saxby walked Dooley out to the reception area, where they chatted for a few minutes before the detective left.

By four-thirty, Saxby couldn't help smiling to himself as he tallied up the progress he'd made on reducing the ever-present stack of paperwork on his desk. Throughout the day, the pile in the "Out" box had grown slowly taller than the one in the "In" box. He was jotting down some notes for the next day when a knock on his office door announced the arrival of Barstow and Connor.

"Is this a good time, Chief?" Barstow said. "You asked us to get with you around the end of the day on the Roseman case."

"Yeah, yeah, come in and have a seat," Saxby said. "I was just finishing up and making my 'to-do' list for the morning. I'm all ears. What's the latest?"

"You wanna start with the people?" Barstow said, looking at Connor as they both took their seats.

"Sure, I can do that," Connor said. He took a few seconds to consult a large notepad. "I spent most of the day after our meeting finding and talking to people who had known Roseman. There were six people, and Vic helped me with a couple of them. We talked to a guy he worked with at his most recent job, where he was assistant manager of a seafood warehouse up in North Wildwood, a woman he'd apparently been friendly with at the job before that, and two friends here in town. I got those names from Mallory Vickers. And Vic spoke with the homeowner—his landlord—a Mrs. Warner. She gave us the name of the man who had rented the apartment on the first floor for several years—a guy by the name of Steve Sullivan. She said she remembered Roseman being on friendly terms with him."

"That's right," Barstow said. "And he sure was an interesting character. Nice guy, but I finally had to cut him off. Kept going on and on about his ham radio habit."

"Hmmm, I didn't even know that was still a thing," Saxby said. "So, what's your feeling after talking to all these people?"

"Vic and I compared notes after," Connor said, "and we agreed that they pretty much backed up the version of Roseman that Mallory Vickers gave us. Decent person, got along with people, worked well with others, not rich or flashy with money but did okay and paid the rent on time. Not especially ambitious. One of his friends here in town, a guy named Vern Deetz, admitted that he'd seen Roseman take a few hits of pot at a party once or twice, but apart from that nobody was aware of him having any involvement with illegal drugs. Everyone we talked to was surprised at the suggestion that he might have had."

"And as far as we can tell," Barstow added, "Mallory Vickers is the only one who had heard anything at all about the pot bust back in the late seventies."

"Interesting. The plot thickens, doesn't it?" Saxby said. "Now we have seven people, with at least several of them knowing him socially, who seem surprised that he would have anything to do with drugs. Now, we need to bear in mind that lots of people are surprised when they hear about someone they know being involved in this or that. So, not all that unusual, but worth thinking about. Good work on that. What else?"

"I got another message from Doctor Lee," Barstow said. "He got the results from that specific blood test, and it was negative for cocaine. Looks like his theory was correct and Roseman didn't really snort any cocaine. I guess he must have faked it for reasons unknown."

"Sure seems that way," Saxby said. "Though I can't figure why he would have some around his nose. That will just have to be a puzzle for now. What else? Have you gotten anywhere on the man whose prints were on the mirror? Can't remember the name, but it was something strange."

"Yes it was, Chief," Barstow said. "Narvel Carter was his name. Rhymes with 'marvel,' near as I can tell. He had a fatal heart attack about two months ago and died at seventy-eight. The obit mentioned a younger sister who was nice enough to answer her phone, and from her I got that he had been volunteering at the Liberty Thrift store on Bayshore Road in Town Bank before he died. When I walked around the store I saw a display of twenty or more small mirrors, and it hit me that could be the reason his prints were on Roseman's mirror. Because he worked at the store where it was sold."

"Sure, that could be it," Saxby said. "Whether our mystery visitor bought it, or Roseman himself. Whoever you spoke with at the thrift store—I don't suppose you were able to show them a picture of the mirror?"

"I was, and I did," Barstow said. "I had a picture of the mirror on my phone and I showed it to the lady I talked to there. She had worked on the mirror display herself about three weeks ago and thought she recognized it as one she had unpacked and hung up. She was pretty sure but wouldn't go a hundred percent. We looked around and didn't find anything that looked like the one she was thinking of, so I figure it could have been Roseman's, and had been sold recently, complete with Narvel Carter's prints. It's a busy place with tons of small cash transactions, so I don't think we're going to do better than that."

"I'm just wondering," Connor said. "What are the odds that Roseman went up to the thrift store in Town Bank and bought that mirror? You know what—I'll ask Mallory Vickers if she knew of him ever going there."

Saxby was just nodding at that idea when a distinctive pinging sound came from Barstow's cargo pocket. She fished out her phone to check it. "Ah, Detective Dooley just sent over the search warrant for me to print out." She looked at her watch. "It's a few minutes to five. Who's up for a search party?"

It was almost three hours later that Saxby, Barstow, and Connor, having completed the search of Boone Roseman's apartment, were starting to dig into their dinners at the Dragon House Chinese Restaurant in Wildwood. Only a few other tables were occupied, but the brass bells hanging from the door rang every few minutes as a steady stream of takeout customers came and went.

"I'm so surprised at how clean that place was," Barstow said, in between bites of sesame chicken.

"You mean because it's a man's apartment?" Connor said. "Like, a man would be more of a slob?"

"No, sorry, that's not it," Barstow said. "The cleanest apartments I've seen have been mens', actually. No, what I meant was, no evidence at all to support the idea of him having anything to do with what he was apparently up to the other night. No drug paraphernalia at all, no large amounts of cash…"

"And you saw the bank statements," Saxby added, scooping some fried rice onto his plate. "No oddly large amounts of money or unusual transactions."

"It is strange," Connor said. "It looked to me like all we saw was the remnants of an ordinary life. Decent, and even boring maybe."

"I agree, Three," Saxby said. "But if it was a boring life, it worked for him until somebody killed him."

"Hey, isn't that the Wildwood police chief, picking up takeout?" Barstow said. She pointed with her eyes across to the cashier's counter. "I think that's Chief McGarry."

Saxby twisted around for a look just as Chief Jean McGarry turned away from the counter with a bulging bag of Chinese food. Her glance happened to take in their table and Saxby motioned her over.

"Well, hello there," Chief McGarry said. "Nice to see

that Cape May's finest appreciates the Dragon House too. Hello, Chief Saxby, and I think I remember Deputy Connor, is that right?"

"Yes, that's right," Saxby said. "And this is Sergeant Barstow, who you may also have met some time or other. And, guys, this is Chief Jean McGarry. Good to see you, Jean. I suspect you need to get all that hot food home to your family, so we won't hold you up, but I just wanted to say hello. I hope you and yours are doing well."

"We're good. Thanks, Tate," McGarry said. "The family's fine, and things have been very quiet in Wildwood, which I think is just fine too. I hear you have an exciting new mystery over in Cape May though. How's that going?"

"We were just talking about it," Saxby said. "As a matter of fact, we came straight here from searching the victim's apartment and were talking it all out. Interesting case and a bit of a puzzle. One of your team already helped us out with it, right, Vic?"

"Yes, that's right," Barstow said, looking at McGarry. "Just yesterday. Your Officer Wright was very helpful with digging up some background for me."

"Good, that's what I like to hear," McGarry said. "Thanks for letting me know. I'll be sure to mention it to him. Let us know if there's anything else we can help with. Look, I'll let you folks get back to your dinner and your mystery, and I'd better get this home to the starving masses. Call me tomorrow if you have time, Tate. I'd like to hear about your case."

After goodbyes were said, she turned to walk away, but stopped, turning back to the table with a finger in the air. "Sorry, I just remembered something, speaking of puzzles.

I assume you're aware of the case they've got up in Ocean City, right?"

"No, I don't think so," Saxby said. He looked at Barstow and Connor, who both shook their heads. "I don't remember seeing anything serious on the police blotter. What do they have going on up there? Not another murder I hope."

"Yep, afraid so," McGarry said. "And a strange one, as far as what I've heard. A man killed in his condo—last Thursday I think it was. Surprised you hadn't heard about it, but you know, everyone's busy with their own turf. Sorry, this isn't a pleasant dinner topic, but you know cops. Give the locals a call. Maybe it would help to compare notes."

Chief McGarry turned again, leaving the restaurant as the others returned to their dinners.

After a while, Barstow said, "I know there's no reason at all to think there would be any connection, but I can't help but remember that the last time there were murders in Cape May and the other shore towns within a few days, it turned out that they were connected."

"I hear you, Vic," Saxby said, "and I'm tempted by the idea too, but we don't know the first thing about that case yet, whatever it is. Let's not get ahead of ourselves. I'll find out what I can tomorrow. Meanwhile, we've got our own to deal with, and that's enough."

5

The next morning dawned gray and cold, with temperatures in the low twenties. All the weather people on TV and the radio were engaged in a conspiracy, it seemed to Saxby, to bring a late-winter blast of icy cold down upon the Jersey Shore. Saxby was fixing himself a mug of coffee in the small station kitchen when Sergeant Barstow came in.

"It's been so nice lately," Barstow said. "I wasn't ready for that wind chill out there. Yikes."

"Me either," Saxby said. "But with luck, the powerful spell of the 'Cape May Bubble' will hold, and if any snow tries to come here it'll divert off into the bay. I'm about ready for spring, myself."

"I second that motion," Barstow said. "Hey, I was thinking about what Chief McGarry mentioned last night, about that case up in Ocean City. Were you going to call up there today to find out what's what?"

"Yes, that was near the top of my list for this morning," Saxby said. "How about joining me in my office in about ten minutes so we can go over next steps on the Roseman case. Grab Three too, if you see him."

It was closer to fifteen minutes later when Barstow came into Saxby's office and sat down in one of the chairs across from his desk.

"I tried to get Three to join us," Barstow said, "but he's out on a call right now. Doreen told me that he went over to one of those big houses on Harbor. Apparently, there was a break-in last night. Somebody rooted around and stole some tools or something. Anyway, I'll fill him in on whatever we find when he gets back in."

"Okay, sounds good," Saxby said, starting to punch buttons on his desk phone. "Before we start, I just wanted to give Dooley a call to see about the Ocean City thing."

Detective Dooley answered on the third ring. "How are my friends from Cape May doing this fine winter morning?"

"All good here, Tom," Saxby said. "And hoping we've seen the last of the snow for the year. Hey, Sergeant Barstow is with me, and you're on speaker."

"Good morning, Sergeant," Dooley said. "I got your note about the search of Roseman's place. So, nothing really of interest, then—is that the consensus down there?"

"We didn't think so, Detective," Barstow said. "A normal apartment filled with normal stuff for a man his age and with his background. Nothing related to drugs, or money, or any sort of illegal activity."

"That is interesting," Dooley said. "But not finding anything does fit in with what we've learned so far about him. This is a strange one, isn't it? No stash, no cash, no triple-beam scale, nothing. Could it be that his first foray into the underworld since the seventies is what got him killed?"

"Seems like it's shaping up that way, doesn't it?" Saxby said. "But we've still got a few angles to work. Something may turn up."

"That's the spirit," Dooley said. "Keep plugging away. I'll be going over everything we have so far myself this afternoon, and I'll let you know if I think of anything."

"Thanks, Tom," Saxby said. "And there's another thing I wanted to ask you about. We happened to run into Jean McGarry over at the Dragon House in Wildwood last night. Only spoke with her for a minute, but she mentioned a homicide last week up in Ocean City. I can't figure out why that wasn't on the county report. Are you aware of it?"

"I'm aware of it, yes. And I've been aware of it for about forty-five minutes," Dooley said. "And I bet I also know why you haven't heard about it too, and that's because it wasn't in Cape May County at all. The crime wasn't Ocean City, but across the bridge in Somers Point, which as you know is Atlantic County. Apparently, there was a mix-up with the original communication that had to do with the fact that the call first came in from an Ocean City number, and also some OC units responded to the scene. I just tracked that down this morning after I heard one of the other guys mention it. Anyway, that's why it didn't make our reports."

"Ah, okay. Well, that explains a few things," Saxby said. "Sounds like an understandable mix-up. I'll drop McGarry a line to let her know. So that was last Thursday night. Do you know enough details to give us a two-minute version?"

"I know just about enough to give you a two-minute version, sure," Dooley said. "Male victim, single, mid-sixties, name of Francis Deutsch. Around midnight, a neighbor made a couple of late trips to take the trash out, and noticed that his door had been open for a while. He went up to check on him and saw him lying on the floor with a knife in his back, and called 911. Somers Point Police arrived, and also two units from Ocean City, who happened to be in the area having just gotten off the Parkway."

"And that helped to cause the confusion about Ocean City—got it," Saxby said. "Go ahead, Tom, what else do you have?"

"Cause of death was stabbing," Dooley said. "Several times, and left with the knife still in him. Apparently, the knife was some kind of fancy Asian antique, like a ceremonial thing maybe."

"Oh, yikes, that hurts just to think about it," Barstow said. "Horrible. Did it look like there had been a big fight? Signs of a struggle?"

"Not that I'm aware of," Dooley said. "Or robbery for that matter. As far as I know, somebody broke in, or was invited in, and stabbed him to death. Nobody heard or saw anything out of the ordinary. The detective I talked with here who knew something about the case said that there was some evidence that it may have been a revenge killing of some sort. Something to do with this guy's involvement with a big industrial accident somewhere in Asia a long time ago. Look, now, I'm firmly in 'whisper down the lane' territory, so I'd better stop. Anyway, it's got nothing to do with you guys, but if you're interested, I'll get you a copy of the latest report. Doesn't hurt to know what's going on around the state."

"That would be great, Tom," Saxby said. "And thanks for that info. You're right that it's good to know what's going on with our neighbors in other counties. I'll watch for your email on that, and also, we'll keep you updated on the Roseman case."

It was just as Saxby was ending the call that Deputy Connor came in. "Hey, Chief, Vic, Doreen says you were looking for me. Did I miss much?"

"No, Three," Saxby said. "Your timing is good, have a seat. We just got off a call with Detective Dooley, asking him about that Ocean City case Chief McGarry mentioned last night. Somers Point actually, as it turns out."

Saxby and Barstow took a few minutes relating to Connor what they had learned about the case from Dooley.

"So, now we know why we hadn't heard about it," Saxby said. "I'll pass the report on to both of you when I get it. What was the call you went out on, Three? Anything I should know about?"

"Just something that needed to be checked out," Connor said. "No big deal. There was a minor break-in last night at one of those big houses over on Harbor Cove. You know, just down from the Fisherman's Memorial. Someone broke a glass door and rooted around. The contractor says they stole a miter saw."

"I think I know the house you mean," Saxby said. "That's the Tanner company working on that, isn't it?"

"That's right," Connor said. "As a matter of fact, it was Paul Tanner who called it in, and that's who I met with.

The owners are out of town until June and they're working on a bunch of improvements."

"Improvements, huh?" Saxby said. "Seems to me that house can't be more than ten or fifteen years old."

"Thirteen, as a matter of fact," Connor said. "According to Tanner. But you know how some of these people are, with these houses that they don't even live in. You get tired of the wallpaper so you hire someone to replace the wall. Good revenue for local business I guess, is how we should look at it."

"Yeah, you're right," Saxby said, with a laugh. "Okay, so you're on that. Anything else going on?"

"Well, two things," Connor said, "though I don't know if either is worth mentioning. Sally Moss, over on Howard Street, called again to complain about her neighbor's dogs barking all night. I had to explain to her again that her neighbors didn't have any dogs, which is true. She seemed to accept that. I get the feeling that we're going to have to explain that to her every few months. The only other thing is that someone swiped a takeout sandwich from Starla's Café without paying. Starla thinks she has footage of the perp. She's going to send it in and Doreen will put it up on our webpage."

"Whew, you've had a busy morning so far," Barstow said. "I think Sally Moss may have a crush on you. I'm thinking she might call in about the dogs hoping you'll come over for coffee."

"You know, Vic," Connor said, "I hate to admit it, but I think you may be right. She's a nice lady, and she does make a good cup of coffee. One of those old stovetop percolator things."

"Ah, the small sacrifices we make in the name of keeping the peace," Saxby said. "So, what new do we have on the Roseman case, and what's on tap for today?"

"We still have a few people to talk to—friends or former co-workers," Barstow said. "People who were busy or out of town when we first tried to contact them. I was hoping Three would help with that." She looked over at Connor, who nodded his assent. "I finally heard back from the niece and nephew out in Chicago, and it sounds like they've had basically zero relationship with him for twenty years or more, so nothing to add there. Also, we're going to be looking at footage from a camera at the base of the bridge. Only problem there is, there are hundreds of cars coming in and out of town Sunday and Sunday night, so I don't have high hopes for that."

"Right. That's probably a needle in a haystack kind of situation," Saxby said. "But let's give it a try anyway. I suggest you focus on any cars leaving Cape May in the hour or two after our estimated time of death. Get whatever help you need from the other guys for that and don't worry about overtime. Anything else?"

The three of them spoke for a few minutes more about general department business before the meeting broke up. Barstow and Connor went out, leaving Saxby to redirect his attention to the contents of his in-box, which had grown substantially since the day before.

6

Years later, as Bobby Hallman recalled the events of that afternoon under the boardwalk, it was Ryan who had pulled out the bag of pot. It was the kind of small, rolled-up bag he'd seen a few times before at parties. He had the impression back then that everybody but him seemed to know the way to roll up the bag nice and tight and lick the flap before folding it over as a seal. Ryan had a small pipe that didn't look anything like the pipes Bobby's grandfather liked to puff on when he was sitting out on the porch at night. He said he had bought it at a shop up on the Wildwood Boardwalk.

"We can only do a little," Ryan said. "Like two hits each." He gestured towards the cracks between the boards above them, his arms imitating swirls of smoke rising up and through. Several of the others nodded in understanding.

Twenty minutes later, with the pipe put away and most of the boys finishing up their second beer, Manny and Ryan started up a game of clamshell pitching, having dug two holes in the sand about twenty feet apart. Manny's mother had taught him to play the horseshoes-like game years before, including the art of picking shells that could be accurately tossed toward the holes. Ryan soon learned that he was overmatched, and was replaced in the game by Doug Lawson, who quickly proved to be able to hold his own against Manny's skill level. As they started their second round of the game, two of the others started facing off against each other in a mock battle, each pretending to be a favorite superhero. Another of the guys joined in and they all took turns running at each other while throwing fake punches in lumbering slow motion.

The third round of the clamshell game ended with Manny as the clear winner. He and Doug did their best to give a few of their shells an honorary toss out into the sunlit surf. Brushing sand from his hands, Doug walked back past the raging superhero battle to where Bobby was leaning against a piling by himself.

"So, are you and Peggy Barnes going steady now?" Doug asked. "I saw you kissing her when I was walking over to the gym the other day."

"Oh, I don't know," Bobby said, holding up a hand to try to hide the red that was suddenly rushing across his face. "What do you think? I think she's pretty cool but I don't know."

"Hey, I think she's cool too, and you're lucky," Doug said. "Only thing is, you know, it's about to be summer, and this town is going to be crawling with girls. And I mean out-of-towners. They're the best, 'cause they go home as soon as September hits. For me, I'm planning to—"

Doug stopped talking abruptly and they both turned in

the direction of the sharp yell that had come from some-where around the superhero fight.

They ran over to join the others, the boys all coming together, no more than an arm's length apart. Six of them stood looking at the seventh, transfixed by what they saw...

7

Tate Saxby had never been one of those people who could fall asleep with ease and get in a solid seven or eight hours of rest. Though the nightmares and other strange dreams that had been a big part of much of his nocturnal life had subsided in recent years, it was still common for him to lie awake for long stretches. While the quiet rhythm of his fiancée's breathing, along with the ambient sounds of the house were peaceful and reliable company, he frequently tried to follow the common advice to "get up and do something" when he couldn't sleep, rather than just lying there in the dark.

Downstairs, in the room they had set up as their "TV room," he was halfway through an old movie about radioactive ants the size of school buses terrorizing people in the New Mexico desert when his phone rang. The display told him that it was exactly midnight. He hit the mute button on the remote and answered the call.

"Saxby here, what's up?"

"Hey, Chief, Dunnigan here. We've got a body over here

at a house on Harbor, just in from Texas Avenue. It's kind of a construction site really. Looks like they're doing some heavy-duty remodeling or something. A man fell from high up and landed headfirst on a stone patio. I hope I'm correct in thinking that I'm supposed to call you, even for an accident."

"Your memory is correct, Jim," Saxby said. "I'd like to know right away whenever anyone dies in town. I'm awake anyway, so don't worry about that. Couldn't sleep and I've been flipping channels. Tell me who's there with you and what you're seeing."

"Bill Lathrop is here with me," Dunnigan said, "and Sergeant Barstow should be here any minute. She was off-duty, but heard it on the scanner and wanted to come over. The ambulance is here too. They checked out the body and now they're waiting on us. The deceased is Jeffrey Tanner, according to the guy who found him, who appears to be his son, Paul Tanner. He's still here. It's their company doing the work here—Tanner Construction."

"Okay, I know the house. I'll get it together and get there as fast as I can," Saxby said. "Take as many pictures as you can and don't let anyone else near the scene or the body. I'll be there in ten or fifteen minutes."

As Saxby got out of his car fifteen minutes later, Sergeant Barstow came over to meet him, handing him a warm cup of coffee. "Pretty damn cold. I figured you might need this."

"You figured right, Vic. Thanks," Saxby said, taking a sip as he looked around at the scene. They were in one of the newest neighborhoods in town, with none of the homes being more than twenty years old. Saxby knew that even the "plainest" houses in the area would go on the market for at least two million dollars. There was no sign of any vehicles on the street apart from police and the ambulance, and the houses to either side were dark. The house they stood in front of had been built in what seemed to Saxby to be an awkward cross between classic Victorian and European Chateau. The defining feature of the house was a round turret that rose a full story above the highest point of the second floor. Looking up at it through the fog, he wondered how tall it was.

The broad driveway in front of the three-car garage had been set up as a staging area for the construction crew, with piles of lumber, shingles, bags of cement, and other materials lined up on either side. Half of the remaining space in the driveway was taken up by a black Mercedes sedan. One of the officers had pulled his cruiser up beside the Mercedes, as close as possible to the house, and the car's searchlight was positioned to illuminate a wide stone patio that extended out from the side of the house into the lawn.

Saxby and Barstow took the matching pathway that came up to where Officers Dunnigan and Lathrop were standing near the prone figure of a man, mostly covered by a foil emergency blanket. A pair of legs, bent at unnatural angles, protruded from one end of the blanket. Saxby nodded to the other officers. "I don't see Paul Tanner. Wasn't he here?"

"He left just before you got here," Barstow said. "He was very concerned about his mother, and I told him to go home and take care of her. From what he told me, his father had texted her around 9:30, saying he would be home soon. She got tired and fell asleep. When she woke up around eleven, she got concerned that he hadn't come home yet. He wasn't answering his phone so she called their son, who drove over and found him. He was pretty shaken up."

"Okay, that sounds fine. No need for them to be here right now," Saxby said. Bending over, he pulled the foil blanket aside to have a look at the body. A small pool of blood under and around the man's head appeared to be partly frozen over, and most of the face was visible. His right arm was extended up near his head, with the hand resting in the blood puddle. "Yeah, that's Jeff Tanner all right. Looks like he probably died on impact. Fractured his skull most likely, based on all the blood." He gestured over towards the idling ambulance across the street. "What did they have to say?"

"Same thing you just said, Chief," Dunnigan said. He pointed up to the tower that rose above that part of the house, painting it with the beam from a powerful flashlight. "There's a kind of wraparound walkway up at the top there. Before the son left, he told us that one of the things his company was doing was replacing part of the railing. He thought maybe his father had stopped in to check on the work, and fell somehow."

With Dunnigan still shining the flashlight up at the tower, Saxby walked to the far edge of the patio to look up at it. "That's a widow's walk up there. An unfortunate term in this case, it appears. They were built high up on seaside houses so worried ladies could watch the coast, hoping for their husbands to come back from the sea." Nodding to himself after a moment, he let his eyes follow an imaginary path from the top of the tower down to where the body lay. "I'd have to agree with Mr. Tanner on his theory. It makes sense. Why his father felt the need to go up there late last night in this weather may make less sense, but it's his company and his project, so who knows. Working on these houses is a big money business."

"Is this something?" Officer Lathrop asked. Coming over to Saxby from the other side of the patio, he held out his hand to display a tiny white object. "I see a few of these around here. At first, I thought it was a little mint, like an Altoids or something, but I think it might be some kind of pill."

Barstow came over to look. "You know what that is—I bet you anything that's nitroglycerin. My father used to have those pills. It's an emergency thing for people with a heart condition. They take it when they feel pain coming on, like to stop a heart attack."

"There must be ten or more of them around," Dunnigan said, coming over to drop a few of the little pills into Saxby's hand.

"And bingo, take a look at this," Lathrop said. Saxby and the others came close as he pointed his flashlight into a formed cement flowerpot.

Saxby produced a tissue and used it to pick up a small, shiny bottle in brown glass, holding it up for a close look.

"That's the prescription bottle, isn't it?" Barstow said.

"Yep. Fifty pills," Saxby said. "Point-four milligram. Jeffrey Tanner." He handed the little bottle to Barstow and again stood back to look up at the tower, and then down at the body. "He probably felt the need to take a pill when he was up there, but fumbled with the bottle in the wind and dropped it. That's why the cap was off and the pills went all over the place. He had an attack or maybe the pain just got to be too much, and he tumbled over the railing."

"So, he may have had a heart attack," Barstow said, "but it had to be the fall that actually killed him."

"Well, look, it's freezing out here," Saxby said. "You guys get lots of pictures?"

"Over a hundred, Chief," Dunnigan said. "All over the place. Plus, I took a film of a walk around the property and looking up at the tower."

"Good work," Saxby said. "Let's give the ambulance guys their go-ahead to take him. Be sure to get more pictures of that, along with the area under the body when they move him. You know what to do. And pick up as many pills as you can see around the area, but no need to go to any heroics to find every last one. Oh, has anyone found a phone? I understand he texted his wife earlier."

"No phone that we've seen yet, Chief," Lathrop said. "Could be in the house or his car."

"You're right. I'm sure it'll turn up," Saxby said.

A few minutes later, as the EMTs were strapping the body onto their gurney, headlights flashed across the house as a vehicle came down the street and stopped at the end of the driveway. Saxby saw that it was a late model Ford pickup with the logo of Tanner Construction emblazoned across the door. Saxby walked up to meet Paul Tanner as he got out.

"I'm surprised to see you, Mr. Tanner," Saxby said. "I'm Chief Tate Saxby. Is your mother doing okay?"

"Okay, yes, not great," Tanner said. "I was able to get a neighbor of ours to sit with her." He was looking past Saxby at the men starting to load the gurney into the back of the ambulance.

"I'm sure you'll be able to see your father tomorrow, up at the hospital," Saxby said. "Your mother too, if she likes. We're all sorry for your loss, but you really didn't have to come back out tonight."

Tanner looked away from the ambulance and back at Saxby. He pulled a folded handkerchief from a coat pocket to dab at his eyes. "Thank you. And yeah, I know. Our neighbor was doing a better job at comforting my mother than I was, and I thought I might be able to help you here somehow. I knew he had been working in his office till late yesterday. His health had been getting worse and worse over the past few years, but man, when he had a burst of energy, he would go with it."

"We found a handful of what we think are nitroglycerin pills spread out around the area where your father fell," Saxby said. "Along with the prescription bottle. Am I correct in thinking that your father had some sort of heart condition?"

"He sure did," Tanner said. "He's had two serious heart attacks already, going back maybe four or five years. His doctor thought the next one might likely be his last, if you know what I mean, so he's had those pills for about a year now. He was supposed to take one, or a few I guess, if he felt something coming on. You put them under your tongue, you know, so they dissolve quickly. It's supposed to be a very fast-acting thing."

They both watched the ambulance drive away. Saxby

motioned to Barstow. "Excuse me just a minute, Mr. Tanner, then I'd like to take a look around the inside, if you don't mind." He went over to speak with the other officers, thanking and dismissing Lathrop and Dunnigan, and asking Barstow to join him with Tanner.

"I know you met Sergeant Barstow earlier, Mr. Tanner," Saxby said. "We won't keep you much longer, but why don't we get inside where it's warm. I'd like to hear whatever you know about what happened tonight, and I'd like to get a look at the top of that tower."

Tanner unlocked the front door and led them inside, flicking up several nearby light switches. They had come into a large open foyer, capped by a pair of skylights in the ceiling high above. A living room and a dining room flanked the entryway on either side, all in a scale double that of most people's homes. The furniture had been moved to sit along the outer walls, creating a large central space that was obviously being used as a staging and work area. Saxby did a quick scan, taking in sawhorses, all manner of power tools, a jumbo Shop-Vac, coiled extension cords, and other signs of carpenters and craftspeople at work.

Tanner sniffed the air in several spots as he moved around. His face had a puzzled expression. "I keep smelling cigarettes. Do you smell that? It's not me—I don't smoke."

"Neither of us is a smoker," Saxby said. "I don't smell anything, but my nose could be half-frozen from the wind out there."

"Well, no matter," Tanner said. "I'll just remember to talk to the work crew and make sure nobody's smoking here in the house. Anyway, not your problem."

"Deputy Conner told me about the break-in you had the other night," Saxby said. "Was that right here?"

"You know, all this with my father..." Tanner said. He shut his eyes and paused a moment before continuing. "I almost forgot about that. Yes, somebody rooted around in here, looking for whatever was valuable, I guess. Stole a brand-new miter saw, a pretty nice one—DeWalt. That and a few Makita battery packs. They came in through the kitchen door to the patio. We've already replaced the glass."

"That's good. Unfortunately, thefts like that are fairly common at construction sites," Saxby said. "I'm surprised at how cold it is in here. You must have the heat on for your workers, right?"

"Certainly," Tanner said, "but you're right that it's pretty cold. When I got here earlier, looking for my father, I noticed that the door was ajar by a few inches. That must have been letting cold air in since he got here."

"Was that like your father?" Saxby said. "To leave a door open like that, at a job site?"

"No. Not at all," Tanner said. "I thought about that when I came in, but after a minute I figured he'd pushed it closed but it didn't quite latch, and the wind did the rest. Anyway, that's why so much cold got in." He walked over to look at a digital thermostat on the wall off to one side. The thing let out a few beeps as he pushed buttons. "I turned it up a few degrees, though I guess we won't be here long enough to feel it."

"So, as you can see, we've been doing a lot of work in here," Tanner continued, gesturing to all the tools and materials sitting around the foyer. "I don't think the owners—the Doyles—spend more than two months out of the year here, but they gave us a long list of things they wanted done before summer. My father was keeping close tabs on the work here while I handled some other things. This job was kind of his project. Look, there's his stuff right over there." He pointed to a long buffet in dark hardwood that stood against the dining room wall near where it opened to the foyer.

Saxby walked over to where a leather portfolio sat on the black marble counter, along with several file folders and a large notepad. A number of loose papers were spread out nearby. "Looks like your father was working here for a while. May I?"

"Sure, go ahead. Whatever you want to do," Tanner said. He stood near where Saxby was looking through the papers. "So, you had asked what I remember about earlier. I only spoke with him for a minute or two yesterday, and that was about another job we have going over in Wildwood Crest. He did mention that he would be working late in his office, which is just across town on Park Boulevard. My mother told me that he had sent her a text at around 9:30, saying he was almost done at the office but wanted to check something at the Doyle house —that's here—and would be home soon after that. She fell asleep after a while, and then woke up about eleven. She got worried when she realized he hadn't come home, and wasn't answering his phone. She called me and asked me to check on him. I went to his office first and then came right here. That was about eleven-forty or forty-five. Somewhere in there. His car was in the driveway but I didn't see him in the house. It wasn't until I went out on the widow's walk and looked down that I saw him and realized what must have happened. You know the rest."

"Okay, thanks for that," Saxby said. "I see your father was a list maker." He held up the legal pad. "Almost everything on the to-do list for today is crossed off, except for the bottom. He's got a little section for 'Doyle House,' with a few items. The last one is 'check tower railing.' That sounds to me like the widow's walk up there."

"Right. I'm sure that was it," Tanner said. "The railing's less than ten years old, but that kind of thing takes such a beating with all this salt air right here by the harbor. Our people were removing the teak and replacing it with a carbon fiber setup. We had never used it before and my dad was very interested in how it would turn out. I knew that if he said he was going to look at the work here, he would definitely want a look at those railings. That's why I went up there almost as soon as I'd come into the house. Shall we go up and have a look?"

With Tanner in the lead, they went up a wide flight of white marble stairs that curved gracefully up from the foyer. At the end of a hallway on the second floor, a set of wooden circular stairs took them up into the tower, where they emerged at the top into a small round room of about eight feet in diameter. A circular bench seat, built of shining mahogany and topped with thick cushions, ran along all of the wall apart from a break large enough to accommodate a sturdy wooden door to the outside. Tall windows ringed the room above the benches. Saxby thought to himself that the overall effect was like being at the top of a small lighthouse.

Tanner paused with a hand on the door to the outside

walkway. "It's the railing and supports out here that my father was interested in, and the stretch just outside isn't fully fastened yet. This is definitely a work area, so I'm sure I don't have to tell you to watch your step, if you even want to come out." He opened the door and stepped out, holding it open behind him. "It's thirty-five feet straight down to the patio from this side."

Saxby stepped out onto the walkway, carefully testing the grip of his shoes on the decking, which shone here and there with small patches of ice. A whistling wind blew in from the harbor and seemed to whip rings around the tower. He pulled the zipper of his coat up the last two inches to the top. Moving to the railing, and taking a firm grip on the nearest vertical support, he tested the horizontal rod that was attached to it. "I see what you mean. This is very loose. Why is that?"

"That's because they have to fit the sections together precisely, like, tweak it," Tanner said, "before they install the permanent fasteners. They do two sections at a time before moving on. That's why they keep the yellow safety tape all around the area." He took a moment to look around, seeing no evidence of yellow safety tape. "Though clearly that all seems to have blown away. I'll get that taken care of."

"I can't help but think that if somebody had a sudden need to reach out and steady themselves by grabbing that railing," Barstow said, from her position halfway through the door, "it could be quite a scare to find it so loose."

"You're right, Vic," Saxby said. "That would be startling, and at precisely the wrong moment. That could terrify someone."

"I'm sorry, guys," Tanner said, "I need to head back downstairs. This has all happened so fast. I mean, I spoke to him only hours ago. I just can't be up here right now. Stay as long as you want. I'll do my best to answer any questions you have when you come down."

"Right, that's fine, Mr. Tanner," Saxby said, as Barstow stepped aside to let Tanner back in. "I think we've seen enough out here, and you've been through enough already. We can go downstairs now."

Tanner started down the stairs as Saxby took a last look around at the widow's walk. Just before he stepped back inside, the glint of something shiny caught his eye near where the decking met the vertical wall off to the side. Thinking that it didn't look like one of the patches of ice, he knelt down for a closer look, realizing that what had caught his eye was the reflective black screen of a cell phone. As he reached to pick up the phone, he noticed another, smaller object about two feet further along the wall, and he moved to pick that up as well. He brought both inside where Barstow was waiting for him at the top of the stairs. He pulled the door to the outside shut, making sure it was closed tightly and locked. He held up the phone to show Barstow.

"Well, here's the missing phone," Saxby said. "He must have dropped it out there before he fell. Let's see if Tanner knows the code. And look at this ... I'll bet this is the cap to his prescription bottle."

Barstow fished the little bottle out of her pocket and tested the cap for fit. "Yep, I would say so. The cap even has the same logo as the bottle. Must be the manufacturer."

They started down, finding Tanner sitting on a stool in the foyer.

Saxby held out the phone for Tanner to see. "I found this outside on the deck just as I was coming in. Does this look like your father's phone?"

"Looks like it could be," Tanner said. "Most of the family got new ones around the same time last year. That looks like one of them."

"Do I have your permission to look through it?" Saxby said.

"Sure, that's fine. Whatever you need to do. Try 'KENO' for the code. That was a favorite dog he had years ago."

"Thank you," Saxby said. "That appears to be the right code. We'll get it back to you as soon as possible." He handed the phone to Barstow, who looked briefly at it before dropping it into a pocket. "Well, I think that's enough for tonight. We can cover whatever we need to cover tomorrow morning at the station. Our condolences again to you and your family, and also, thanks for coming back out tonight to help with this. One more thing I have to ask you, Mr. Tanner. We need you to shut down the work on this house and keep it locked up, probably just for tomorrow. I hope that won't be any problem."

"No, of course not," Tanner said. "That won't be any problem at all. In fact, it's the right thing to do anyway. When I get home, I'll make some calls and give everyone in the company the day off tomorrow. Out of respect for my father."

"That sounds like a good idea," Saxby said. "And where can we get a key, in case we need to take any more pictures, check measurements—that sort of thing? Routine stuff."

"I think we can handle that right now, Chief Saxby," Tanner said. He handed over a small keychain. "You can hang on to this one. We have others. I'll see you at your station tomorrow at ten."

It was just before two in the morning when Saxby was back in his kitchen, fixing a hot cup of herbal tea, complete with a generous slug of aged rum. Angela appeared in the doorway, bundled up in a thick robe.

"Sorry if I woke you," Saxby said. "I'm trying to be quiet but I guess I don't know where everything is in the kitchen yet."

"Don't worry about it," Angela said. "I've almost got it figured out, so I can stop moving everything around soon. I'm not jealous of the way you get called to rush out and go look at bodies."

"Part of the job, I'm afraid," Saxby said. "And to keep it in perspective, that's really only a very small part of the job. It's just that they don't wake me up when someone steals a bike from the boardwalk."

"I know, I know," Angela said. "So how did it go anyway? Somebody fell off the roof? In the middle of the night?"

"Well, now it's the middle of the night," Saxby said. "But it must have happened around ten or so. A contractor working late and stopping by to check up on a job site. Damn shame really."

"Did you cut your hand?" Angela said, having seen

something on his right hand as he lifted the mug to drink his tea. She came over for a close inspection.

"Not that I know of," Saxby said. Noticing for the first time that he appeared to have traces of blood on his hand. "You know what … there was blood at the scene. I must have brushed against some without knowing it. I'll go take a shower. Sorry about that."

"Okay, and if you come to bed soon," Angela said, "I'll rub your back to help you fall asleep. Maybe you can get a few hours before the next body turns up."

8

In addition to their regular staff meetings, something Saxby tried to do every day was a casual check-in with all the officers on duty. He liked to take a few informal minutes with each of them to chat about how their week was going, what special projects they might be working on, and what problems or difficulties they might be experiencing. He had learned that a few minutes like that, on a regular basis, was time well spent, and seemed to him to pay dividends in terms of maintaining a real team, as opposed to simply a group of people who had to work together.

By half-past nine the next morning, having completed his tour around the station, he settled down at his desk with Sergeant Barstow in one of the chairs across from him.

"You know, Vic, I noticed something when I got home that I thought was strange. Actually, it took me a while to realize it was strange. I was having a cup of tea before I went to bed, and Angela noticed blood on my hand. We looked all over for a cut but didn't find one. I figured I must have gotten some of Mr. Tanner's blood on me somehow, right? Thing is, the more I thought about it—you know, what I touched, where I knelt down—I really don't think I got blood on my hand that way. Did you see blood anywhere around the place other than right by the body?"

"Funny you should say that, Chief," Barstow said, "because I also noticed a little bit of blood on my hand when I got home, and I did what you did—looked around for a cut. What I finally figured out is this." She held up a plastic baggie containing a late-model cell phone. "Neither of us noticed it last night, but the phone you found had some blood on it. I guess it was probably frozen, but then when we came inside where it was warm and handled it… So, that's why I bagged it up. Before you got in this morning, I got one of the guys to check it for prints and blood type, which was A-positive. He's going to try to get back to me later today with the print results. The way phones go in and out of pockets all the time, particularly for men, I'm not expecting much. My prediction is that it's probably you, me, and the late Mr. Tanner, but we shall see."

"Very interesting," Saxby said. "And good work on your part. In hindsight, I shouldn't have picked up that phone with my bare hands, but all I was thinking was 'tragic accident.' That mistake is on me, but let's both keep it in mind. It's part of our job to be diplomatically suspicious, if only initially, at any death scene. So, moving on, then, why was there blood on his phone? If he dropped the phone before he fell, or as he fell, was there some reason for blood to be present? Call up to the ME's office and see if you can find out if he had a cut on one of his hands, nasty paper cut, whatever. Another thought is … if he was feeling heart pains coming on, could that cause bleeding in any way? For example, would a nosebleed be part of an attack like that? I know that's a reach but it's worth asking. There's got to be a reason for that blood to be there."

"I'll get on that after this meeting," Barstow said. "Other than that, regarding the phone, I do see the phone call with his son, which Paul Tanner mentioned last night. That call was at 4:18 and lasted for three minutes. That was the last call of the day. I don't know how active of a texter he was—some older people aren't much into that—but anyway, whatever text threads there were have been deleted. We know he texted his wife at 9:30, but his phone doesn't show anything. I'll confirm that with Mrs. Tanner, but late night at the construction site seems like an odd time to be cleaning up your phone."

"It does, doesn't it," Saxby said. "Not impossible, but odd. Seems to me that's more the kind of thing you do while you're in the waiting room at the dentist, but that's me."

Just then Officer Watson stuck her head in the door. "Chief, Vic, Mister Tanner is here to see you. I put him in interview room one. He says you were expecting him and that he's anxious to show you something."

"Okay, thanks, Doreen," Saxby said. "Please tell Mr. Tanner we'll be right in."

"How are we playing this?" Barstow said. "We still think it was an accident, right? I mean, aside from the blood on the phone."

"Yeah, I think that's where we are right now," Saxby said. "The blood on the phone deserves an explanation, but apart from that, I haven't yet seen anything that points to something other than an accident. So, what I said a minute ago is the play. Diplomatically suspicious. Diplomatically and respectfully."

When Saxby and Barstow came into the interview room, they found Paul Tanner looking at something on a laptop. He hit a few buttons and stood up to shake hands.

"Good morning, and thank you for coming in, Mr. Tanner," Saxby said. "How is your mother doing this morning?"

"Hanging in there I guess is the right way to put it," Tanner said. "She took something to help her sleep, so that helped. She'll have some friends over today for company, and she's a tough lady. For a couple of years, with all my father's heart problems, she's lived with the idea of something suddenly happening, but still, this was a surprise. Anyway, thanks for asking. Will you need to have her come in also?"

"We will need to speak with her, yes," Saxby said. "Just to check all the boxes, but I don't think there's a need for her to come in. We'll give her a call and schedule a visit for when she's up for it."

"Right, okay, well, whatever you need from the family of course," Tanner said. "Look, I guess you've got boxes for me to check too, but I've got some ideas and something to show you. I've been thinking about what happened, and the open door, and my head is kind of…"

"Okay, let's take it slow, Mr. Tanner," Saxby said, motioning for him to sit. "Have a seat and we'll go over everything. What is it you wanted to show us?"

Tanner settled back down into his chair and took a few

deep breaths. "I'm sorry. It's just that I've been up all night rerunning the whole thing in my head. Okay, right, so, there was that break-in at the Doyle's house the other night. Tuesday night—that's right, because your Officer Conner came out yesterday morning. Anyway, it must have been him who suggested we install a camera, like, to keep an eye on the yard and the driveway, just in case the guy ever came back."

"I don't remember Deputy Connor mentioning that to me," Saxby said, "but sure, that sounds like a good idea. So did you put one in?"

"Yes, but with everything that happened last night," Tanner said, "I just didn't think of it until I got home. One of our guys found a spare camera, and they put it up under a corner of the second-floor roof, so it was there last night. I wish they had put it somewhere with a better view, but whatever. Anyway, I drove over early this morning and downloaded the images. Can I show you?"

Saxby and Barstow came around the table to stand behind Tanner as he opened a window on his laptop. The image on the screen was of a length of residential road, with part of a wide driveway. Tanner pointed. "So, this is the road in front of the house—Harbor Cove—and this dark area here is the beginning of the driveway. That white shape there is the bottom corner of a garage door across the street."

"I see, and I remember that pile of two-by-fours there," Saxby said, pointing to part of the screen. "What time is this?"

Tanner pointed to a small display at the top of the screen. "Here's the timestamp, so this particular shot is

20:03, so 8:03 yesterday evening. As far as I know, it starts at 7:00 and takes pictures every five seconds until six the next morning."

Barstow was using the calculator on her phone. "That's 720 shots an hour. Can you scroll through them, like a fast-forward?"

"Yes. Let me show you," Tanner said. He moved the mouse and the images on the screen changed slowly, and then more quickly as he made adjustments. He stopped at an image that appeared to be the same as the first one he'd shown, but with slightly different lighting. "This is the same view at 8:36. I've been all through this very slowly, and there isn't much going on at all. A few cars drive by, someone walking a dog, a couple bike riders. But then here, at 9:22, my father's car appears, like it's about to turn in. A few seconds later, it's in the driveway and you can just see the rear end. See—in the next few pictures you can see the interior light through the back window."

"So, that syncs up with the text your mother got," Saxby said. "Half-past nine I think that was. Within about ten minutes after he pulls up at the house. Seems right. Is there anything else?"

"Yes, there is," Tanner said, "and that's really what I wanted to show you. Give me a sec to get to it. There it is, six minutes later—9:28."

This time, the view was the same, except that the figure of a man appeared in the upper corner, and in a jerky, stop-motion action that spread across five or six shots, moved diagonally across the driveway towards the house, disappearing just after coming alongside the parked Mercedes. He wore dark clothes and dark shoes, with a hooded sweatshirt obscuring his face. Tanner backed up so they could watch it again, repeating several times.

"At first I thought he was all dressed in black," Barstow said, "but in those last two shots you can see that his hoodie is actually red. It looks black in the dimmer light."

"Right. It looks like black shoes, black or dark blue pants, and the red hoodie," Saxby said. "We could probably enhance it some, but we're not seeing his face at all. It's certainly a man, moving very slowly. Not much reference to say how tall he is, except maybe that pile of two-by-fours. Over six feet is my guess. We're going to need a copy of this film, Mr. Tanner."

"I kept thinking about that door being open last night," Tanner said. "And the more I thought about it, the more it doesn't seem like my father would've done that. And then I see this. I've watched this over and over, and the thing is, I think I know who it is."

"Really? Okay, then, I'm all ears," Saxby said. "There isn't a lot to go on in this video. What about him looks familiar to you?"

Tanner sat back in his chair and ran the fingers of both hands through his hair. He shrugged and gave his head a quick shake before he spoke again. "I don't know. Maybe it's crazy. His size and shape. He's slim, about the same height as me. And something about the way he's moving. Stealthy, like serpentine almost. Watching this, I keep coming back to a man who used to work for us up until about six or eight months ago, when my father fired him. His name is Barry Vaughn. I didn't have a problem with him, but my father got tired of him always pushing for us to take on different types of jobs. They finally had it out one day, in front of some of the crew, and that was it. I wasn't there, but I heard he really blew up at my father. Yeah, I really think that's the guy in the video. He lives right here in Cape May."

"Now, Mr. Tanner," Saxby said. "Remember what I said a little while ago about not jumping to any conclusions. Inside this room, I'm taking your comments seriously, and we will look into it, but I have to caution you not to go around making accusations or sharing these ideas with people outside the police department. Can I count on you for that?"

"Right. I mean yes, Chief Saxby," Tanner said. "I'm not going to go around talking about this. I haven't even told my mother about it. I'm really just trying to give you information and to help however I can. Last night, I thought my father had a terrible accident. This morning ... I'm not so sure. Here, I already made you a copy of the video." He handed Saxby a thumb drive.

"Great, thank you," Saxby said. He dropped the drive into a shirt pocket and sat back down across from Tanner. "It seems like the matter of your father's death may be taking a substantial turn. Let me ask you, Mr. Tanner, can you think of anyone who might have wanted to harm your father? Or had any reason to do so?"

Tanner hesitated before speaking, and seemed to Saxby to be considering the question carefully. "It's so strange to even think of something like that. I mean, that question wouldn't have occurred to me a few days ago. So strange. But, since last night, I have asked myself that. My father was in business for years, and I'm sure he stepped on some toes along the way, like any successful contractor does, but to be mad at him enough to kill him? That's a whole crazy thing, isn't it? That thing I told you about, with him and Barry Vaughn, that's the biggest blow-up I can think of."

"Yes, as you were just saying," Saxby said. "We'll be checking with Mr. Vaughn. Can you tell us again what that was about? Flesh it out a little?"

"I can sure try," Tanner said. "I don't know it all, but I can give you the rough idea. You probably know that big construction projects get kicked around all the time, for years even, before they ever break ground. Someone has a property and an idea for a hotel, but the financing never comes through. Or maybe it's all in place, including the financing, but then someone finds out they can't get all the right permits. Or someone stumbles on an old cemetery on the property—that'll slam the brakes on things. There's been one project idea kicked around the county for two or three years now by a company called the Barness Group. They wanted to build three big condo complexes all at the same time, in three different towns. One was going to be in Wildwood Crest, and I forget where the other two were going. It never did take off, or not yet anyway. I don't know where it stands now, but for a while, they—the Barness people—were after my father to take on the job. They liked our reputation in the area for quality, is what they said. Thing is, we would have had to double the size of the company to take it on, and my father didn't want to get involved with that. I thought we should do it, but he shut me down the few times I brought it up. Barry Vaughn was gung-ho for the idea, and tried to talk to my father about it too. My father got sick of hearing about it and finally canned him. Not long after that, Barness backed off and stopped coming around. That's about what happened. That must have been last September or October. Sorry if that turned into a long story."

"No, that's fine," Saxby said. "I'd rather have more detail than less. But I think that's enough about it for now. Changing tack, Vic, you were going to ask about the phone…"

"Yes, right, Chief," Barstow said. She took the bagged phone out and set it on the table. "Just a strange thing, Mr. Tanner, that we wanted to run by you. In the Doyle house last night, just before we came downstairs, the Chief picked up this phone from out on the walkway. After handling it later, we realized that there was blood on it. We don't yet know if it was your father's blood, but that does seem most likely. Would you happen to know your father's blood type?"

"Yeah, same as mine," Tanner said. "A-positive. Is that what was on the phone?"

"We've got a forensic test in the works," Barstow said. "Hopefully by the end of the day we'll know if the blood on the phone was your father's. When you found your father, it's totally understandable that you were very upset, and possibly in shock to some extent. With that in mind, Mr. Tanner, is it possible that his phone was with him, or very near him, and you somehow—unconsciously maybe—picked it up and took it up to the tower?"

"What? No. I was on the patio last," Tanner said. "I only saw he was there when I looked down from the tower. What are you saying?"

"Nobody is accusing you of anything, Mr. Tanner,"

Saxby said. "We're just asking for your help to make sense of why there was blood on the phone. Vic?"

Barstow continued: "That's right. We're trying to fit the pieces together. We'll also be checking to see if maybe your father had cut his hand on something before he went up in the tower, or even before he arrived at the house. Alright, then, while we're on the topic of the phone, tell me, did your father do much texting at all? With you or with others?"

"Well, I know he did sometimes," Tanner said, "but certainly not as much as many people today. He texted me every once in a while, and of course he texted my mother just last night. May I ask why you're wondering about that?"

"It's just an odd thing I noticed," Barstow said. "All the text threads on his phone have been deleted. Last night, I gather, and after he texted your mother, because that isn't there. It's probably nothing. We do see the call to you yesterday afternoon."

Tanner reached into a coat pocket to pull out his own phone. "Here, let me see if I can find the last time he texted with me. Here it is—that was Tuesday morning. Something about the work schedule at a job in Wildwood. Before that was Sunday. Would you like to look?" He offered his phone to Barstow, who looked at it for a moment before handing it back.

"Thank you. That is interesting," Barstow said. "Maybe your father had a habit of regularly deleting texts. It's a possibility."

"Mr. Tanner, I think that should do it for now," Saxby said, standing up. "Thank you for coming in and for the copy of that video, which we will be looking at closely. I'd appreciate it if you could keep these things we've discussed here to yourself for now."

"No problem with that," Tanner said. "I've got a lot to do and lots of calls to make, but if someone brings it up, it was just a freak accident. Nobody's going to ask more than that."

"Thank you. On your way out," Saxby said, "Doreen Watson, out at the front desk, can help you with where to go up in Cape May Courthouse to see your father and take care of that paperwork. She can help you with who to see and what to expect. Oh, and when you talk to Doreen, would you please give her the name of a contact we can talk to at your company for a list of employees. If we need that."

After they had shaken hands and Tanner had left, Saxby and Barstow sat back down at the table.

"I wasn't expecting that when I came in today," Saxby said. "What was your impression of Mr. Tanner?"

"You mean, aside from going a little heavy on the cologne? Sheesh," Barstow said. "I know, I know—that's not nice. He's just one of those men. Aside from that, well, I think he's upset but collected. I think he did the right thing to come in and show us that video, so he seems eager to help."

Saxby laughed and wagged a finger at her. "Now, now, Vic. I appreciate that you have a superhuman sense of smell, but let's cut the man some slack. I'm not ready to say his father's fall wasn't an accident, but that video deserves a close look. Also, I don't want to dismiss Tanner's concerns, even if it does seem like he went pretty quickly to pointing at this Barry Vaughn character. One of the next things we need to do is to find Vaughn and have a chat with him. We'll frame it like we're having routine interviews with a handful of current and former employees."

Saxby stood up again and gathered his notes. "For now, Vic, unless you have anything urgent with the Roseman case, I'd like you to contact Mrs. Tanner and set up a meet with her as soon as possible. Maybe you just want to knock on her door—you decide. Get a sense of her overall state of mind and go with your gut. We need to know if she has any inkling at all that her husband's death was something other than an accident. Oh, and I know you'll check her phone to verify that she really did get that text last night. Who will be running the company and how is her relationship with Paul Tanner? Also, Paul has a sister, Susan. See if you can get a feel for how she figures in. I think with the timing what it is, this kind of conversation would be better coming from you than from me. Are you okay with all that?"

"All fine, Chief," Barstow said. "I'll see how she is and go with it as best as I can."

Just then Deputy Conner appeared in the doorway. "Morning, Chief, Vic. How did your interview with Tanner go?"

"It was interesting to say the least, Three," Saxby said. "He came in with some video footage that shows an unidentified man appearing to approach the house right after Tanner Senior went in last night. Good work on your part suggesting that he put up a camera."

"Oh, thanks," Connor said, "but I think it was him that brought that up first. Anyway, what good timing."

"Yes, good timing is right," Saxby said. "I've got Vic doing a few things related to this case for the next few hours or so. What do you have going on?"

"Well, on the Roseman case," Connor said. "Two friends of his who I've been trying to catch up with finally got back to me, and I was just about to head out to have a chat with them. One lives here in town and the other is off Rt. 9 north of Rio Grande. After that, I was going to go out on patrol unless you can use me for the Tanner case."

"Yes, I can use your help with Tanner," Saxby said. He gestured in turn to Connor and Barstow and handed her the thumb drive Tanner had given him. "You two coordinate getting together later, and I want you to go over to the Doyle house and take a look around, inside and out. Take a laptop so you can look at the video for reference. Try to get a feel for where that man may have been lurking around. Knock on some doors and see if the neighbors heard or saw anything. You know what to do. I'm going to call Detective Dooley and run all this by him. We've got a day, maybe two, to decide what sort of investigation this is, and I want his take on it."

"Got it, Chief," Connor said. "After I meet with Roseman's friends, I'll see where Vic is and we'll meet up. By the way, just this morning I read that report from Somers Point, about that man who was stabbed to death. Did either of you read that yet?"

"I completely forgot about it," Barstow said, shaking her head.

"Haven't read it yet myself either," Saxby said. "Seems like we've got enough of our own stuff going on down here. Anything interesting or important to us?"

"I don't think there was anything important to us," Connor said. "But I thought it was interesting to read that the man who was killed was from Cape May. Grew up here and all. Moved away thirty or more years ago. Frankie Deutsche was his name. That's all."

"That's a shame," Saxby said. "Can't say the name is familiar to me, but I don't know everyone. Did the report say how old he was?"

"Pretty sure it said he was sixty-six," Connor said. "Had an interesting life. Ex-corporate bigwig or something. Anyway, that's something that caught my eye. It's not our case. I'll get on those calls now. Vic, I'll catch up with you as soon as I can."

Saxby spent the next several hours working at his desk, and was glad for the interruption when Barstow knocked on his open office door. "Got time for an update, Chief?"

"As a matter of fact," Saxby said, "yes, this is a great time. I just got all caught up on the latest notes on the Roseman case, and I've opened a file on Tanner, though there isn't much at all in that one yet. I could use a stretch and a little fresh air. What's going on with the weather?"

"It's chilly, but not terrible," Barstow said. "Mid-forties, I think. The sky is gray but no rain."

"Sounds like March," Saxby said. "Join me for a walk down to Starla's. I could use the cool air and a hot coffee." He checked in with Doreen at the front desk to let her know they would be stepping out while Barstow went to get her jacket.

"So, you first," Saxby said, as they started the two-block trip to Starla's Café and Coffee Shop, which was on a side street adjacent to the popular outdoor shopping mall that was the main focus of the center of Cape May.

Barstow began by relating the details of her meeting with Mrs. Tanner, which had been a civil and mostly pleasant encounter. "Very stoic was my impression, but obviously shocked and deeply affected. She told me right out that she's been bracing herself for losing him ever since the second heart attack, but hadn't expected it to be because he goes and falls off a building."

"Did you get any sense that she might be thinking that her husband's death was something other than an accident?"

"No, I can't say I did, and I was watching for it. If she was thinking anything like that, she was keeping it to herself. Other than that, she told me that she expects her son to run the company now, and she planned to mostly stay out of it. Her daughter is a couple years younger than Paul Tanner, and apparently doesn't have much to do with the company. Susan Bingham is her name. I don't think I could tell you exactly why, but I got a feeling that she loved her two kids but it wasn't a warm and cuddly family. According to Mrs. Tanner, both of her children will be going with her up to the ME's office this afternoon to see the body and take care of all that. I did mention that I might want to check in with her again and she seemed genuinely fine with that."

"Good, so you've established a rapport," Saxby said. "Were you able to confirm that she got the text from her husband?"

"Yes, she did get it," Barstow said. "I brought it up in the context that I wanted to note the exact time it came in, and she was happy to show me her phone."

Saxby nodded as he opened the door of Starla's Café for Barstow. The owner, Starla Sloan, greeted them from the other side of the counter.

"How nice to see my favorite Cape May police chief," Starla said, "and one of my two favorite sergeants escorting him!"

"What, so the chief is a favorite and I'm not?" Barstow said, feigning indignation.

"Oh, of course you are, but I like Sergeant Brody too," Starla said. "I just didn't want to show favoritism. Chief Saxby is the only police chief, so I don't have to worry about that with him. What can I get you today? Whatever it is, I'll need you to try my latest cookie experiment to go with it. It's a new chocolate chip oatmeal, but with a hint of toasted coconut. I need to know if they're fantastic or just almost fantastic."

The three of them chatted for a few minutes while Starla's barista put their coffees together. Saxby and Barstow tried the new cookies, carefully considering taste, texture, and appearance, before agreeing that they leaned more towards a rating of "fantastic." When they noticed one of the few small tables in a quiet corner had opened up, they excused themselves to take their coffees and a second cookie over to sit down.

"Now, tell me how things went after that at the Doyle house," Saxby said.

"Okay. Well, Three and I were over there for about two hours," Barstow said. "We spent some time looking around inside. Not a close search, but a pretty thorough look around. We didn't see anything that jumped out at us. As far as family stuff, there isn't much there at all. It has the look and feel of a vacation house that's been cleared out for the next renter."

"That makes sense," Saxby said. "The owners probably did some tidying up before they turned the whole place over to workmen who were going to be in their house for a month."

"When I showed Three the loose railing up there outside the tower," Barstow said, "he had the same reaction that you did. I mean, if someone had reached out to steady themselves suddenly, and grabbed that wobbly thing, that could be very disorienting.

"Nothing new outside or around the patio that I could tell. We brought out a few buckets of hot water and washed away most of the blood puddle. Just seemed like the right thing to do, instead of having some neighbor's dog licking it up."

"That was a good idea," Saxby said. "I'm glad you thought of it. So, it sounds like nothing that might be related to the man in the video, then."

"Well, actually, we did find something," Barstow said. "And maybe it's nothing, but it's damn sure interesting. Can you picture Tanner's video, where the man came from somewhere off to the left of the driveway, like if you had your back to the house?"

"Yeah, I can picture that," Saxby said. "He came from the direction of Pittsburgh Avenue as opposed to the harbor."

"Right, you've got it," Barstow said. "We walked all around the area, just looking for anything odd or out of place. The second house down has a garage building that comes out almost to the road. I first looked at it from across the street and it kind of jumped out at me as a good place for someone to hang out if they were watching the Doyle house. You know, like staking it out. There's a little gravel area at one corner, with lattice around it, probably for where they put their trash cans on trash day. Anyway, I found three cigarette butts on the ground there, all the same brand."

"Potentially interesting," Saxby said. "Whenever I see a bunch of cigarette butts in one place on the ground like that, my first thought is usually that somebody was waiting there for something. But it sounds like a good spot also for someone working in the area to go over and have a smoke. I remember when we first went into the house last night Tanner was sniffing around, wondering who had been smoking."

"I remember that too," Barstow said. "So, it could have been one of the people working in the house. Took a little break and maybe walked away to that spot so they could make a private phone call. But there's something else. Remember late yesterday there were a few snow flurries that went through town?"

"I remember," Saxby said. "That must have been between about six to eight, or near there. But there wasn't really any accumulation."

"Right, Chief," Barstow said. "Except in some sheltered spots, like next to a wall or fence. Places where the snow might have been protected from the wind. The area around the corner of this garage is a spot like that. There's a thin layer of snow there, or at least there was overnight."

"Okay, so somebody smoked a few cigarettes and dropped the butts onto a patch of snow," Saxby said. "That what you're getting at? If they were really on top of the snow, then it makes sense that they were dropped there after seven or eight last night."

"Bingo, Chief," Barstow said. "There's only a little bit of snow, but they were on top of it. But hang on, because there's a cherry on top."

"Oh, a cherry even," Saxby said. "I can't wait."

"We bagged them up and brought them in to the station," Barstow said. "Where we could take a really close look at them in good light and with a magnifying glass. They're cowboy killers. Marlboros."

"Okay, probably the world's most popular brand," Saxby said. "What else did you see?"

"All three of them had a little bit of sand stuck to them," Barstow said.

"Well, they don't call this the seashore for nothing," Saxby said. "There's sand all over the place."

"Not on that driveway there isn't," Barstow said. "I even drove back over there and took another close look, and there's no sand around there. It's gotten warmer today so what little snow was there was all melted when I went back, but I remember seeing a few specks when I first picked up the butts."

"So, we've got a few cigarettes that appear to have shown up shortly before Tanner comes by to check on the house," Saxby said. "Plus, a little bit of sand that shouldn't be there at all. You might be onto something, Vic, but what? Let me pay for this and we should start walking back."

Saxby settled the bill, adding a box of Starla's new cookies for the crew at the station, and they started on the walk back.

"I'm trying to keep an open mind about why there would be sand on cigarette butts," Saxby said, "when there isn't any sand in the area. Sure, it's possible that the pack of smokes was in the same jacket pocket where someone had carried around a few pretty seashells that they picked up on their last beach walk. Possible, but not likely. No, there's some other reason for that sand. Have you heard back from the ME's office on the blood that was on Tanner's phone?"

"Yes, about an hour ago," Barstow said. "It was his own blood, but there weren't any cuts on his fingers or hands that could explain it normally, like a papercut in the office."

"So, the blood on the phone that we found up on the widow's walk was a bit of the blood from his injuries sustained by the fall to the patio. That's worth a good ponder." They paused on the sidewalk outside the City Hall building. "This is the second death in Cape May in less than a week—one obviously a murder and the other an apparent accident—where there's a number of things that just don't add up."

"Are you still thinking Mr. Tanner's death was an accident, then?" Barstow said.

"If it was an accident," Saxby said, "at a minimum, it's been interfered with. You follow me? This thing with the blood on the phone with no good explanation, all the texts deleted, someone breaking into the house the day before, and now this with the cigarette butts. No, I'm having a hard time still calling it an accident."

"Have you talked to Detective Dooley about Tanner yet?" Barstow said.

"Not yet," Saxby said. "I left him a message earlier, so he should get back to me. I just thought of something. If someone wanted to wait around near the Doyle house, and they had a car, they wouldn't park right near there, because that's a very quiet and very ritzy residential street. If I was a crook and I wanted to watch that house for some reason without being noticed, I think the edge of the Wawa parking lot might be a good place to park. It's a busy place, with cars in and out, but also some of the people working there would park along the edges for hours at a time. And from there, it's just a two or three block walk or run over into the Doyle's neighborhood."

"That's not a bad idea," Barstow said. "That would be a good place to park and not be noticed. I'll stop in and see if they have surveillance footage from last night."

Saxby nodded. "That's a good next move for us. Ask for the manager—Don Zipper—he's a good guy. He should be able to burn you out a copy of whatever they have. I'll probably be chained to my desk for the rest of the day, but let me know if you need anything, and feel free to interrupt."

It was just after four-thirty when Detective Dooley returned Saxby's call, finding him at his desk.

"Sorry it took me so long to get back to you, Tate," Dooley said. "This week seems to be another of those times when a crimewave has suddenly erupted in the county. I'm busier than a one-legged man in an ass-kicking contest. I think I'm up to date on Barstow's notes on the Roseman case. Anything new on that?"

"Nothing that I'm aware of offhand, Tom," Saxby said. "Deputy Connor was planning to talk to a few more of Roseman's friends today, but I haven't heard from him on that yet. I'll let you know. There's something else I wanted to run by you though. We had an accidental death here in town yesterday evening—a local contractor fell off a house and hit a stone patio, basically. But there are some aspects to it that are really odd, and I'm thinking more and more that it may not have been an accident at all. Let me tell you what I know and you can give me your take on it."

Saxby spent the next fifteen minutes relating everything he knew about the death of Jeffrey Tanner, including the details of Barstow's return visit to the Doyle house.

"That thing with the sand on the cigarettes is interesting," Dooley said. "I know we're just spit-balling here, but I've been around the block a few times with crime scenes and evidence, and that kinda smells like something that was planted. Just a gut reaction. Don't hold me to it."

"Right. Sure, that's fine," Saxby said. "And just to go with that idea for a minute, if those butts were picked up from the beach or some other sandy place, and dropped there, why? What's the point in that, other than to maybe create the impression that somebody was loitering around that area."

The two men spent another ten minutes discussing the circumstances of Jeffrey Tanner's death before breaking off the call. Detective Dooley said he would start a file on the matter, and would run it by his supervisor. He and Saxby agreed that, pending further investigation and the medical examiner's report, they would call the Tanner death accidental, but with a big question mark.

After the call with Dooley, Saxby was making a few "end-of-day notes" and working on his to-do list for the next day when Sergeant Barstow and Deputy Connor appeared in his office doorway.

"Are we too late to update you on a few things, Chief?" Barstow said.

"No way," Saxby said, motioning them in. "I want to hear what you've both been up to. Let's take it in order and start with Roseman. What's new on that?"

"That's me, then, Chief," Connor said, "so I'll start. Since we talked this morning, I was able to meet with two of Roseman's friends here in town that I've been trying to get time with. Actually, it was three people, because one of them suggested someone else I should talk to and I went with the suggestion. I'll put it all in my case notes, but to sum it up for you, each of them was surprised to hear about his death, but more surprised at the idea that he might have been involved with drugs—dealing or even using. All three of them insisted that just wasn't like him. Other than on that point, the story was pretty much the same. He was friendly but quiet, got together on occasion with a small circle of friends, and worked well with people but wasn't much of a joiner. Which is pretty much the same version of the guy that I've gotten from all the people I've spoken with about him."

"Okay, so not much help there," Saxby said. "Where are we with looking at any video footage from cameras in the area?"

"Mostly where we are on that," Connor said, "is that finding cameras in that area is a tall order. There just aren't many at all along Columbia or Washington. The owner of the C-View Inn gave me several DVDs that are my next priority. That could show some percentage of the people coming in and out of town. The cameras in the marina area aren't much help, with hundreds of cars zipping by in a blur on Sunday. Without help from the NSA, I don't see us getting much value out of that."

"Yeah, and I don't see help from the NSA as being forthcoming," Saxby said. "Anyway, good work on that so far, Three. Hopefully, you'll see something on the C-View footage. Switching to Tanner now, is there any update on that? Vic?"

"A little bit, Chief," Barstow said. "I talked to your friend Don Zipper at Wawa, and he made me a copy of the parking lot video from six to twelve last night. I haven't looked at it yet, but I plan to start on it tonight. Speaking of the Wawa, Three met me over there and helped with a test. We made a few trips, on foot, from the Wawa parking lot over to the Doyle house. It's less than a thousand feet away, with a few turns. You can do it in about three or four hundred paces, or five or six minutes. Faster, obviously, if you run or walk fast."

"We didn't try it running," Connor said. "We thought about it but decided not to risk freaking people out. People see uniformed police running past their house, they might get all worked up."

"Good thinking," Saxby said. "No need to scare people. So then, if someone was walking at close to normal speed, because running might attract attention, let's just say five minutes there and five minutes back. If they made that trip no more than a few minutes before Jeffrey Tanner arrived, let's just say another five minutes. Then what? Maybe eight or ten minutes to get inside the house, kill Tanner, and then get out. Seems like they would need to park at Wawa for at least twenty-five minutes. And that's with everything all planned out and going off perfectly."

"Right. And that timeframe certainly doesn't allow for someone to stop and smoke three cigarettes," Barstow said.

"I agree," Saxby said. "The scenario of rushing over from Wawa doesn't fit with the idea of standing there by that garage and having a smoke. Okay, then, anything else?"

"I don't have anything else to report for now, Chief," Barstow said. "Later on, I plan to open a bottle of wine, put on an old sweatshirt, and have an exciting time looking at hours of footage of the Wawa parking lot."

"I'm not sure if that sounds exciting or not," Saxby said, "but please don't stay up all night with it. Give me a call if you find anything."

At half-past nine, the Thursday night crowd at the Ugly Mug was starting to thin out as Saxby ordered a second round of bourbon on the rocks. Angela was finishing up her work day just as he arrived, and had joined him with a glass of wine. Saxby had told her what he could about the Roseman and the Tanner cases.

"You sure have had a whirlwind couple of days," Angela said. "I hope you can get some sleep tonight."

"You and me both, Ang," Saxby said. "I think the odds of my getting rousted out of bed tonight are pretty low."

"Oh, I hope you're right about that," Angela said. "But they do say bad things come in threes."

"You know, someday I'm going to find out just who 'they' are," Saxby said. "And why they say all that crazy stuff."

"I want another glass of wine," Angela said, "so you can help me try one of the new bottles the wine rep dropped off today." She caught the attention of the bartender and made a series of gestures that made no sense to Saxby, but apparently had the effect of asking for a certain bottle of wine and a pair of glasses to be brought over. Two minutes later, the bartender delivered the wine and poured out a generous sample for each of them.

"Thanks, Cody," Angela said. "Try a glass yourself if you want. I'd like to get your take on it too."

"Thanks, boss, I'd like that," Cody said. "Leave me a little and I'll have it when I'm cleaning up." He retreated back behind the bar, leaving them to sip the wine.

"It's a Washington State Chardonnay," Angela said. She took another sip of the wine and considered it carefully. "Slightly oaked, but not overdone. I like it now, but it could also be nice for a hot summer day outside. What do you think?"

"It's very pleasant," Saxby said. "I would say it's delicious, even if my tastebuds are a bit numb from the whiskey. I agree it could be a good wine for a hot summer day." He picked up the bottle to read the label. "Hmmm, Chateau 66. I wonder what that means. It can't be the year."

"Certainly not," Angela said. "This bottle is probably

two or three years old, but it's good, and has a good price. I think I'll get a few cases."

"Sixty-six," Saxby said. "That's funny. Just a couple of songs back was that Route 66 song—the Rolling Stones version. It's about driving west or something like that. Jeffrey Tanner was sixty-six and so was Boone Roseman. I hadn't put that together before. Hang on a minute, Ang, I need to make a quick call."

Saxby excused himself to walk over to a quiet spot near the door, and used his cell phone to call Deputy Connor, who answered on the second ring.

"Hey, Chief," Connor said. "What's going on? Is everything okay?"

"As far as I know, Three," Saxby said. "A quiet night in town is what I'm hoping for. I'm sorry to bother you, but I'm kind of brainstorming and thought of something you would know. This morning at the station, you mentioned that you'd been reading the case report on that fatal assault up in Somers Point last week."

"Right, yeah, you and Vic said you hadn't read it yet," Connor said. "Frankie Deutsch was the guy's name. It caught my eye that he had grown up in Cape May."

"Yes, I remember that you mentioned that," Saxby said. "But there was something else. I think you told me how old he was, didn't you?"

"I may have," Connor said. "It was in the report. He was sixty-six."

"That's what I thought I heard," Saxby said. "But I wasn't sure. Thanks for confirming. It's just something I was kicking around. I'll explain when I see you tomorrow. Have a good rest of your night."

Saxby ended the call and started back to rejoin Angela, his mind full of numbers that were all made up of two sixes. *What does it mean? Does it even mean anything? It doesn't make sense.* He stopped when his phone buzzed. Seeing that it was Sergeant Barstow calling, he tapped the screen to answer.

"Evening, Vic," Saxby said. "I hope you haven't been spending your entire night watching the parking lot video."

"Almost, Chief," Barstow said, "but I'm about done, and I found something that I think you're really gonna like."

Saxby had worked with her long enough to know that she was obviously very excited about something. "Lay it on me, then, Vic, what are you seeing?"

"Well, right around the window of time that we thought would fit in with someone hurrying over to the Doyle house, like a little after nine last night, a car pulls in and parks. Some of it's blurry, but we get a flash of the license plate."

"Oh, that's fantastic," Saxby said. "That could be a really good break. We need to run that plate as soon as we can."

"Already did, Chief," Barstow said. "The car's registered to the guy that Paul Tanner thought was the man on his video—you know, the man in the red hoodie. Barry Vaughn."

"Whoo-weee, that's a big one," Saxby said. "This might be coming together fast. I think I'm going to move talking with Mr. Vaughn to the top of my list tomorrow. How about meeting me at George's for an early breakfast? I have a feeling tomorrow's going to be a busy day."

9

The Friday morning regulars at George's Restaurant were just beginning to trickle in when Saxby and Barstow sat down to order breakfast at seven-thirty.

"The usual for me, Lexi," Saxby said. "Burn the bacon and keep the coffee coming please."

"Of course, Chief," Lexi said. Having waited on him many times over the years, she had mostly given up trying to get him to try one of their excellent daily specials. "Vinnie probably started cooking it when he saw you pull up outside."

"I, on the other hand," Barstow said, "am adventurous, and will try your Friday special—the veggie omelet. Hold the shrooms if you can. Thanks, Lexi."

Their food was delivered in less than ten minutes, and Lexi topped up their cups with the strong, dark coffee that the restaurant was known for.

"So, I know you ordered me to get some sleep last

night," Barstow said, between bites of her omelet. "And I did, a few hours anyway, but after I talked to you, I realized I should get a copy of the footage from inside the Wawa around the same time. I drove over there again and was able to catch your friend Don Zipper before he left, and he burned a disk for me. The footage we have of the parking lot shows Vaughn's car driving in and parking, but then just as he starts to get out, a big Herr's potato chip truck pulls in and blocks the view, until almost forty minutes later when we see the car pull out from behind the truck and leave. I'm hoping the inside footage will show if he ever actually went into the store."

"I'm looking forward to seeing this video," Saxby said, "but are you saying that the Herr's truck blocks us from seeing whether or not Vaughn walks from his car to the store, or somewhere else?"

"Unfortunately, yes," Barstow said. "We can see that he pulls in, and gets out of the car, and we can see something red, but it's hard to tell if he's wearing it or carrying it. But then he turns back to the car, like maybe he forgot his keys or something, and right there is where the Herr's truck appears and blocks everything."

"Damn. A lucky break followed by a lousy break," Saxby said. "I want you to show me all this when we get to the station."

"We know that Vaughn worked for the Tanner company for a few years," Saxby continued, "until Tanner Senior fired him last fall. Paul Tanner said he lived here in town. Do we know anything else about him?"

"Not much yet, apart from the basics," Barstow said. "White male, fifty-two years old, address on Lafayette

Street—that's all per his driver's license. There's a 2019 Acura TL registered in his name, and no criminal record that popped up. I haven't gotten any further than that yet."

"You can dig a little more when you get time later," Saxby said. "I'm going to get in touch with Dooley as soon as I can and get hold of Vaughn for an interview."

"I talked to Three for a minute this morning," Barstow said. "He mentioned that you had called him last night. Is there something going on with that case up in Somers Point?"

"Oh, I don't know, Vic," Saxby said. "It's probably nothing. I was sitting with Angela at the Mug last night, talking about this and that, and something made me realize that our two unrelated deaths this week, Roseman and Tanner, were both sixty-six years old."

"A lot of people are sixty-six years old, Chief," Barstow said. "Remember, the Cape May population skews older. Interesting though."

"I know, I know," Saxby said, taking a last bite of bacon. "I can't imagine how it would mean anything, but I thought I remembered Three mentioning that the guy up in Somers Point had also been sixty-six. It just seemed odd, all of them from Cape May and all dead inside less than a week. Anyway, I think I'll call up there and see if I can get read in on that case, just out of interest if nothing else."

Back at the police station, after taking time to check messages and make a few calls, the two of them convened in the conference room to view the video footage, going through each recording several times.

"Seems like what we're looking at," Saxby said, "from the time the Herr's truck pulls in and blocks the view of his car, up to when we see him enter the Wawa, is a gap of about twenty-two or twenty-three minutes. That would give him just enough time to hustle over to the Doyle house, find Tanner, help him over the railing, and get back in time to go in and get a hoagie or whatever it is he buys."

"Yeah, it does look that way," Barstow said. "And hustle is the right word. Tough, but possible."

"Really good work putting this together, Vic," Saxby said. "At least now we have a person of interest, who conceivably could have made it over to the Doyle house and back."

Just then, Deputy Doreen Watson opened the door and stuck her head in. "Excuse me, Chief, but I was able to contact that gentlemen, Barry Vaughn, for you. He said he would be happy to come in to the station to talk any time this morning. Shall I call back and give him a time?"

After a glance at his watch, Saxby said: "That's great, Doreen. Please do that and ask him to be here at eleven. Vic, does that give you enough time to hook things up in here so we can watch on the big screen? We'll want all three videos, starting with the one Tanner gave us, then the one with the Herr's truck, then the one inside the store."

"Sure, Chief, no problem with that," Barstow said. "I'll have it all queued up."

"Wonderful, and I'm going to call Dooley and see if he can be here for this," Saxby said.

Barry Vaughn arrived at the station five minutes early, and Doreen showed him to the conference room to join Saxby, Barstow, and Detective Dooley.

"Thank you for coming to meet with us this morning, Mr. Vaughn," Saxby said, as he stood to meet Vaughn and gestured to a chair. He set a water bottle down on the table.

Barry Vaughn was a tall man, at six-one or six-two, with a trim physique that had apparently not yet started to gather the extra pounds around the middle that commonly appeared on men around his age. His light-brown hair was starting to thin on top, and had been stylishly cut three to four weeks before. He was clean shaven and well put together in pressed khakis, a slate-blue sweater, and a dark gray overcoat. "Well, I'm always happy to assist Cape May's finest when I can," he said, as he folded the coat over an adjacent chair and sat down. "Though I am looking forward to hearing what this is about."

"Certainly," Saxby said. "But first, joining us today is Detective Tom Dooley from the County Detectives Office, and Sergeant Vicki Barstow. I think you already know that I am Chief Tate Saxby. We are investigating the circumstances of the death this last Wednesday evening of Jeffrey Tanner, owner of Tanner Construction."

"Aha, then I guessed correctly that I was here in relation to that," Vaughn said. "Didn't he fall off a walkway up on that big house they're working on over by the harbor?"

"That's correct, Mr. Vaughn," Saxby said. "At least at first appearances, it was an accident. But there are some aspects to the events of that night, and the scene, that we are trying to reconcile. Your name came up early on as someone who might be of some help."

"I hope I can be of some help, Chief Saxby," Vaughn said. "But please, don't be so shy in getting to the point. If Jeff Tanner fell to his death, I'm guessing you have reason to suspect that somebody may have helped him fall. And my name came up because he publicly fired me last fall after a dozen people saw us having a big argument. That must be why I'm here, which is understandable. To be clear, I don't mind that he's dead, but I didn't have anything to do with it. So, ask me anything you like."

"All right, then, Mr. Vaughn," Saxby said. "Your directness is noted, and frankly, appreciated. We can all save time that way. You are correct that we are looking into the possibility of foul play in the Tanner case, and yes, your name came up as someone who was known to have had a heated public argument with him in the recent past. Would you please give us a compact version of that argument, and what led up to it?"

Vaughn did so, taking less than five minutes to relate a version that was close to the one they had gotten from Paul Tanner.

"So, yes, as the most senior crew boss," Vaughn said, "I strongly advocated for Tanner to take on those projects. He would have had to do some fast expansion, but the company would have had great exposure and would have made a ton of money."

"Do you have any guess as to what kind of money you're talking about?" Dooley asked.

"It's hard to say, Detective," Vaughn said. "But I think a

reasonable estimate would be that the company could have cleared between fifteen and twenty million dollars. Most of that would have gone to the Tanner family of course, but there would have been very nice bonuses spread over the crew. If you're wondering what I might have gotten out of it myself, that is also hard to say, but it could have been between fifty and a hundred thousand or so. It's completely reasonable to say that a number of people were upset about Tanner turning it down."

"What about Paul Tanner?" Barstow said. "How did he feel about it?"

"Paul wanted them to take it on too," Vaughn said. "He lobbied his father for it, but not as vocally as me. I guess I was the big mouth and I was the one who took the fall."

"Thanks for that background," Saxby said. He motioned to Barstow and to the flat screen monitor mounted at the end of the room. "At this point, I'd like to show you something. This is a few minutes of video footage that was taken Wednesday night. Sergeant, will you narrate please."

Barstow hit some keys on her laptop and a still picture of the Doyle house driveway appeared on the big screen.

"This is actually a series of still pictures that were taken by a time-lapse camera mounted on the house on Harbor Cove, where it appears that Mr. Tanner fell to his death. What we're interested in first is this sequence of shots that starts at 9:22." She clicked through the series of pictures, narrating as they went by. "Just to recap, we see Mr. Tanner's Mercedes appear on the street, and then for the rest of the shots it's in the driveway, with the first two showing that the car's interior light was on. We can only see the rear end of it, obviously. Now I'll skip forward to 9:27."

Images flew by on the screen at high speed, until Barstow slowed them to a stop before again clicking through them one by one. They watched as the figure of a man crossed the driveway and passed the car on a trajectory towards the front door of the house.

"As you can see in those middle shots," Barstow said, "he appears to be wearing dark pants and dark shoes, with a red hoodie sweatshirt."

"Mr. Vaughn," Saxby said. "We have a witness who has known you for at least several years who has stated their belief that the man in these pictures is you. That, along with your history with Jeffrey Tanner, is why we've asked you to come in today."

"I understand," Vaughn said. "I mean, it makes sense that you would have wanted to talk to me, but nevertheless, that isn't me. It couldn't possibly be me."

"Would you please enlighten us, then," Dooley said. "As to why it couldn't possibly be you?"

"It's very simple, Detective," Vaughn said. "As the sergeant has just pointed out, the man in these pictures is clearly wearing a red hoodie."

"That's right," Barstow said. "Which is a very common item of clothing. There must be ten stores right here in town where you could buy something like that. Why couldn't it be you?"

"It's obviously not me," Vaughn said, with a shrug. "I would never wear red. Or any sort of hoodie for that matter. Good God no."

"Oh, cut it out, Vaughn," Dooley said. "You may think

this is funny, but a man is dead. I strongly advise you to take this seriously."

"I assure you, Detective," Vaughn said, "that I am taking this very seriously. I can see that there's a man in those pictures, and you've already considered the possibility that he killed Jeff Tanner, and then someone—presumably someone with the company—has told you that they think that man is me. So, sure, I take it seriously. But either way, it isn't me. I would never wear red."

"Are you telling me, then," Saxby said, "that if we were to get a warrant and search your car and apartment, we wouldn't find a red sweatshirt, or a red jacket?"

"You wouldn't need a search warrant," Vaughn said. "I'll invite you in. You'll see that my closet is a symphony of blues and grays. I mean, there could be a little accent stripe here or there on a collar or pocket, but that's all. Actually, I don't wear yellow or green either."

"Okay, then," Saxby said, gesturing to Barstow. "Sergeant, if you would please roll the parking lot footage."

Barstow hit some keys on her laptop and the view of the Wawa parking lot appeared on the screen. "This is footage from the Wawa at the intersection of Washington Street and Texas Avenue on Wednesday night. This is roughly a thirty-five-minute span beginning at 9:23, which is one minute after the camera on the Doyle house shows Mr. Tanner pulling into the driveway."

She narrated as the video started, pausing the playback at several points.

"There is your car, Mr. Vaughn, pulling in and turning to the right to park nose-up to the building. It's a black

Acura TL, and we can clearly see your license plate in several frames."

"Do you acknowledge that's you?" Saxby said.

"Yes, I'm sure that's me," Vaughn said. "I don't think I would have remembered the exact time, but I did go to Wawa on Wednesday night. I was craving a meatball sandwich."

Barstow advanced the video, a few frames at a time. "About a minute after parking, there, your door opens, and just as the Herr's delivery truck pulls in, we can see you step out, and look right there—it's dark, but in that flash of the truck's headlights you can see the red around your arm and chest."

"Well, that is interesting, isn't it?" Dooley said. "Do you still want to insist that you wouldn't wear a red sweatshirt, Mr. Vaughn?"

"Unequivocally, Detective," Vaughn said. "It would go against all my better instincts, and would clash with my personal color palette. Chief Saxby, I don't want to waste anyone's time, and I think I can explain this. My car is across the street, right outside. Would you have an officer who you could task to retrieve the two items they will find sitting on the passenger seat?" He pushed a set of car keys across the table in Saxby's direction."

Trying unsuccessfully to stifle a frown, Saxby picked up the keys and stepped out of the room, returning a minute later.

"That'll take a few minutes," Saxby said, looking at Barstow. "In the meantime, please continue."

Barstow entered commands to make the video advance quickly. "After the Herr's truck pulls in, Mr. Vaughn's car is completely obscured until we see it back out and drive away at 9:56." They watched the screen as Vaughn's Acura appeared from behind the truck and drove off. "Rounding by a minute or so, the car sat there for thirty-three minutes. Now, switching over to a camera inside the store, here we see Mr. Vaughn appear inside for the first time at 9:49. About six minutes later we see him paying and leaving the store."

"Would you agree that's you in the store now, Mr. Vaughn?" Saxby said.

"Yes, that's certainly me," Vaughn said. "I got a meatball sandwich and some chips. Oh—and a bottle of Coke. I remember thinking, 'What the hell, I'm already having a meatball sandwich and chips, why not go for the Coke too? Nobody lives forever.' "

"I'm so glad you're having fun with this, Mr. Vaughn, but you must see the problem," Dooley said. "From our point of view, you pull into the parking lot and we see you start to get out of your car, but then it's what … twenty-four minutes later before you enter the store? I suppose you're going to say that you just decided to sit in your car for that whole time?"

Vaughn was about to answer when they were interrupted by Officer Hayward knocking on the door. "Excuse me, Chief. These two shopping bags were the only thing in the car, and they were sitting on the passenger seat just as you said." She handed the two bright red Wawa shopping totes to Saxby, along with Vaughn's keys.

"Ah, thank you, Officer," Vaughn said, as Hayward excused herself and left the room. "So, there you have the 'red thing' I was holding when I first got out of the car.

Wasn't it last year that New Jersey outlawed single-use plastic shopping bags? Since then, Wawa markets have done a brisk business in these red bags. I wish they weren't red, but they are a decent little tote bag for under a buck. If you rewind that footage at your leisure, and with these bags in mind, I think you'll see that's what I'm carrying. You can also see it on the counter inside the store when I'm paying for my items. I don't see it when I'm walking out, which I suppose is due to the camera angle."

"Can we get back to my question please, Mr. Vaughn," Dooley said. "What about the more than twenty minutes before you finally entered the store?"

"Oh yes, certainly, Detective," Vaughn said. "When I first got out of the car—that's when you saw the red—I stopped for a few seconds to make sure I had cash with me, and that's when the Herr's truck pulled in and someone yelled out my name. It took me a minute to recognize him, but the truck driver was an old friend from high school. Chip Tillerman. We both went to Wildwood Catholic."

"You're saying Chip Tillerman was driving that truck," Saxby said, "and you recognized each other?"

"That's right," Vaughn said. "It was very amusing to realize that my old friend Chip is now driving a potato chip truck."

"So, you chatted with him for a while then," Dooley said. "That right?"

"That's right," Vaughn said. "He had the radio playing in his truck. They were doing some kind of salute to 'long songs.' It was WCFA, the station right here in town. While Chip and I were catching up, they played two old Doors' songs."

"And no doubt you're going to tell us what those songs were," Dooley said.

"They were old favorites of mine, so that isn't much of a challenge," Vaughn said. "*The End* was just starting as Chip pulled up, and that went right into *When The Music's Over*. The station's CD skipped at the very end of the first song. I didn't realize that a CD can skip but I guess it can. Anyway, after that, Chip went about his snack stocking work and I went into the store. I'm sure Chip would vouch for me."

Nobody around the table said anything for half a minute, instead shuffling papers or sipping their coffee or water.

"Can you account for your whereabouts for the next few hours after you left the Wawa?" Saxby said.

Vaughn thought for a moment before answering. "Well, right when I got home, I bumped into my upstairs neighbor on the stairs and we chatted for a minute. That must have been right about ten. I invited her to share my sandwich and watch some TV, but she declined. I watched about an hour of *Vertigo*, which had just started, but I was alone so I guess I can't prove that."

"I have two more questions, Mr. Vaughn," Barstow said. "Do you happen to know your blood type?"

"Yes, it's O-negative," Vaughn said. "The Red Cross is always after me to donate because apparently that's the universal donor."

"Thank you. And do you smoke cigarettes?" Barstow said.

"No. I fooled around with that a little when I was a teenager," Vaughn said, "but I never could see the appeal of it."

Saxby looked at both Dooley and Barstow in turn before speaking. "I think that's about it for now, Mr. Vaughn. I'd appreciate it if you could just write down your neighbor's name, and number if you have that, in case we need to check with her. Otherwise, I thank you for your time and cooperation."

"So, aren't you going to tell me not to leave town or something like that?" Vaughn said.

"No, that's something from the movies," Saxby said. "I can't really tell you that. I will ask you, though, to please— voluntarily—let us know if you plan to travel in the near future, just in case we have further questions. Other than that, again, thank you for your cooperation."

After Vaughn had left the room, the three of them sat in silence for a minute.

Saxby was the first to speak. "So, what do you think, Vic?"

"I think he's a character all right," Barstow said. "But I gotta say, Chief, I'm inclined to believe him. Of course, I'll contact the Herr's distributor and check with this Chip Tillerman, and I'll have a chat with Vaughn's neighbor."

"Also, give Mark Allen at the radio station a call," Saxby said. "He'll be able to look up what songs they played Wednesday night and the exact times. What are you think- ing, Tom?"

"Hmm, what am I thinking?" Dooley said. "I'm thinking that there's a part of me that wanted this guy to be guilty, but I've got to admit that it looks like he's probably got nothing to do with it. He's guilty of being irritating, but we can't arrest him for that. Shit."

"So now we're back to the bloody phone, with the

erased text threads, and cigarette butts that shouldn't have been there," Saxby said. "But there's something else that's been haunting me."

"Oh, I know what you're going to say, Chief," Barstow said.

"You know me too well, Vic," Saxby said. "Sixty-six."

10

After the meeting with Barry Vaughn, Sergeant Barstow excused herself to catch up on some desk time, leaving Saxby and Dooley alone.

"How's your schedule this afternoon?" Saxby said. "Got a few hours to spare?"

"Oddly enough, I'm pretty flexible for the rest of the day," Dooley said. "What did you have in mind?"

"I've had a few things bouncing around my head for a while now," Saxby said. "And I'd like to try to shake 'em loose and see where they fall. Do you know Chief Valentine up in Somers Point?"

"Yeah, I know Leo. Haven't seen him for a while, but he's a good man," Dooley said. "I guess you want to head up there to talk about that attack last week, right? Frankie Deutsch was his name, I think."

"That's right, Tom," Saxby said. "I've read the report, but I'd really like to sit down face to face and go over it with him—you know, get his take on the whole thing. Might be something. Might be nothing—but I think it's a good next step."

"Are you thinking there could be some connection to this Tanner case?" Dooley said.

"Actually, I was thinking more about Boone Roseman," Saxby said. "But sure, as long as we're throwing spaghetti at the wall to see what sticks, we can include Tanner too. I'm trying to keep an open mind about these three men from Cape May, all sixty-six years old, and all dead from non-natural causes inside a week. I think that's something worth looking at."

"Alright then. I agree it's worth a closer look, so count me in," Dooley said. "And after, I know a great place for lunch right there on the bay. I'll call Leo and set it up."

"No need for that," Saxby said, glancing at his watch. "He's expecting us in about forty-five minutes. If you want to drop your car at your office, I'll drive us the rest of the way up."

Somers Point Police Chief Leo Valentine greeted them warmly, offering coffee and showing them into a small meeting room. "It's good to see you again, Tom, and to finally meet you, Chief Saxby. Naturally, I've read about those last two big cases you had down there in Cape May. And to think, all this time I thought you had a quiet little town down there. Anyway, good work."

"Oh, I think it's still mostly a quiet town, all in all," Saxby said. "Even if it does seem like we've hit our twenty-year quota of crazy in two short years. I don't get all the credit though. I have a good team, and Tom here was a big help too."

"A good team is the best thing any police chief can ask for," Valentine said. At that moment, another man came to stand beside him, holding a file folder and a large notepad. "And speaking of that, allow me to introduce Detective Dikko Wilkes." Everyone shook hands as Valentine introduced the detective to the two visitors. "Sorry, but as it happens, something's come up and I have to run over to the county office for a meeting. You gentlemen are in luck though, because Dikko here has been working the Deutsch case from the beginning, and he can tell you everything you want to know." They chatted for a few minutes more before Valentine had to leave.

"Well then, it's good to meet you gentlemen," Wilkes said, taking a seat at the table. "Are we okay with first names? Mine's Dikko—pronounced 'dee-koh,' and if you guessed Japanese, you're right. My father was a California kid who joined the Air Force and went to Japan, and my mother was a local girl in Osaka. Hence my membership in the Funny Name Club, but I like it."

"First names are just fine," Dooley said. "And by the way, thank you for your time. I'm sure you've got other things you could be working on, so we appreciate it."

"Don't mention it," Wilkes said. "I'm really glad to be meeting with you two. It's funny, Tate, because you beat me to it. I was thinking of giving you a call to talk about one of your cases. That Roseman thing from the other night, Sunday I think it was. Is that right?"

"Yes, that's right," Saxby said. "This past Sunday night. Guy named Boone Roseman was attacked and killed in his apartment. It was a fairly clean scene, but a few pieces of evidence suggest that it may have been some kind of drug deal gone bad. I'll be happy to talk about that and we can compare notes."

"I find it interesting that you say 'a few pieces of evidence suggest...'" Wilkes said, with a quick laugh. "Yes, let's compare notes. To start off, if you don't mind, how about if I take you through the outline of the Deutsch case. You can always read the report if you want to know the address or other background, but let me distill it down to the main points for you. After that, you can both tell me what your impression is. Okay?"

"Sounds good to me, Dikko," Saxby said. "Give us the main facts and we'll do our best detective impressions." Dooley laughed and nodded in agreement.

"Okay, great. So, our dead man is Francis Deutsch," Wilkes said. "Everyone seems to have called him 'Frankie,' but I'll just call him 'Deutsch.' Sixty-six years old, divorced years ago and living alone in a second-floor condo not far from the bridge into Ocean City. Retired from a long career with Barker Chemical, where he made a big pile as the CFO. Spent a few years at their international head-quarters in Indonesia, and was there when that big chemical spill happened in 2003 at one of their plants outside Jakarta. Something like seven hundred people were killed. The company paid some huge fines and covered the clean-up costs, but nobody was ever prosecuted. So, Deutsch was one of several execs who retired with a big payout and quietly went away. In his case, he came home to the Jersey Shore, where he's been running a pair of small hotels and apparently living a quiet life. No police record at all, and the neighbors seem to have liked him. Older brother out in Arizona tells us they talked on the phone once or twice a year, but weren't close. No other family that we know of.

"So, that brings us up to last Thursday night. It's just before midnight when a neighbor remembers that the next day is trash day. He goes outside, and he's rolling the cans down to the end of the driveway when he looks up and notices that Deutsch's door is ajar. Ten minutes later, when he goes out to put something else in the trash can, he sees that the door is still open. He decides to be a good neighbor and goes up to knock and let Deutsch know his door is open. Only thing is, there's no answer. The guy pushes the door open a little farther, sees him laid out on the floor with a big knife in his back, and calls 911." Wilkes paused to take a long drink from a water bottle.

"Okay, now we're getting to it," Wilkes continued. "The scene. Deutsch had been stabbed in the back three times, with the knife left sticking out of him the third time. The ME thinks he was whacked on the back of the head first, probably with a small marble statue that was lying on the floor. That knocked him out or at least stunned him, and the stab wounds followed immediately after. He never got up after that, and bled out within fifteen or twenty minutes. The weapon was an antique kris dagger—you know the knife with the blade that curves back and forth. It's a traditional Indonesian knife, mostly ceremonial, but could certainly be a deadly weapon. This one had an eight-inch blade and a carved ivory hilt."

"Sure sounds like revenge for that chemical spill," Dooley said.

"It does, doesn't it?" Wilkes said. "But indulge me a little longer and let me finish the story. I think it'll be worth the wait."

"It didn't appear to be a robbery," Wilkes said. "Because there were a number of potentially valuable items around the place that could have been grabbed but weren't. There was about two hundred bucks in his wallet, and a Breitling watch on his wrist. That alone was probably worth over two grand. No, it wasn't a robbery. There were no signs of a struggle, the place wasn't torn apart, and nobody in the area heard or saw anything. Time of death was around ten, give or take a half hour."

"So, the neighbor found him only about two hours after he was killed," Saxby said.

"Right, but, as I said, nobody saw or heard anything," Wilkes said. "The only thing out of place in the apartment was a newspaper clipping about the chemical spill. The headline was cut off, but someone had written 'Jakarta Globe, March 15, 2003' at the top, along with 'You've gotten away with it for long enough.' The clipping was laid out on the kitchen table as if it was meant to be seen as a message."

"Aside from that, and the murder itself," Wilkes continued, "there was no indication that anyone else had been in his place. Now we go outside. Deutsch had an end unit on the second floor, and the stairs down to the side parking lot are just outside his door. There's a long flowerbed along the back of the parking lot, and then about fifty feet of lawn, and then a few acres of woods. You know this crazy weather we've been having recently, with all those warm, sunny days, the plants are getting confused. Some daffodils or something were starting to come up in that flower bed, but someone has trampled over them. I think that the killer came down the stairs and went across the flowerbed and into the woods. About twenty feet in, there's something of a path that takes you to another apartment building on the next street. I think he took that route back to his car somewhere around there and took off.

"Let me tell you what we found in the woods and then I'll be done with the first part of my story. I'm certainly no kind of tracker, but a couple of the guys here have gone hunting up in Pennsylvania for years, and they know a little bit about tracking game in the woods. We think we found where somebody went into the woods near where I thought was likely, and made their way that twenty feet or so to that pathway in the middle. It looks like they got caught up in some thick, thorny bushes in there—brambles they tell me, blackberry bushes—and tore off the pocket of a jacket they were wearing, spilling a bunch of stuff from a pocket. We found part of the ripped pocket stuck on a branch. It was something like one of those old 'Members Only' jackets, in black.

"On the ground right around there, we found a torn piece of a note saying something about the 'Port of San Pedro' and 'pier 16.' Near that was a torn page from a national Amtrak schedule. A few feet away was a gum wrapper, a few Indonesian coins, and one banknote, which was for 500 Rupiah, which is their official currency.

"And that, my friends, is the first part of the story of the murder of Frankie Deutsch. Let's pause for discussion before I give you the second part. What do you think?"

Saxby looked over at Dooley, who shrugged and pointed a finger back at him.

"Obviously you have something in mind with this, Dikko," Saxby said, "but I'm game. I'll take a shot at it. It's clear to me that the evidence points to Deutsch having been killed in revenge for that chemical spill. Someone—an Indonesian, presumably—traveled across the Pacific on a ship that came into the Port of San Pedro, which is Los Angeles, and one of the world's busiest ports. If you wanted to enter the country on a ship and slip somebody some money to not be noticed, that place would be a good candidate. From there, he took an Amtrak train across the country to … Philadelphia maybe, or New York. Made his way down here, found Deutsch, probably watched and followed him for a while, and eventually killed him. He used the kris dagger that he'd brought with him, and left the newspaper clipping as a final message. When he was making his way through the woods, he got hung up and tore his coat, dropping some stuff on the ground. He either didn't realize what he'd dropped, or just didn't want to take the time to try to find it and pick it up in the dark. After that, he could have gone anywhere. If I heard you right, it's been almost exactly twenty years since the chemical spill, so it could be that the twentieth anniversary triggered him to finally act. Like … it's been twenty years since my daughter was killed, I'm finally going to get some revenge —something like that. How am I doing?"

"You're doing good, Tate," Wilkes said. "That all sounds reasonable and fits the evidence. What do you think, Tom?"

"Well, like Tate said, I figure you're up to something with this," Dooley said, "but yeah, I think he summed it up accurately. That's obviously how the story presents itself."

"Good, so we all agree on that," Wilkes said. "Now, if you'll let me tell you the second part, I'll try to be as brief as I can. First, the murder weapon—a beautiful but deadly Indonesian kris dagger. As it turns out, the antique ivory hilt is not ivory at all, but is actually an epoxy-based ivory substitute made by a company in Vermont. There were faint markings on the base of the blade indicating that it was made within the last ten or so years by a knife company in Denver that specializes in replica knives of all sorts, and only sells their products in this country. Next, the newspaper clipping from the *Jakarta Globe*. One of our people spent some time reading up on anything she could find about the chemical spill, and one thing she looked at was coverage of the accident in some of the major U.S. papers. While looking at a digitized copy of a *New York Times* article, something caught her eye, and she ended up doing a side-by-side comparison of the Deutsch clipping and the *Times* article. Turns out, that wasn't from the *Jakarta Globe* at all, but was actually a printout from the *New York Times*."

"Wonderful," Dooley said. "So, they took a copy of the *Times* article and wrote '*Jakarta Globe*' on it. Simple, but effective. Someone's been having some fun with this."

"Right, Tom, that's what I've been thinking too," Wilkes said. "Stick with me—almost done. Next, let's go outside to the items we found in the woods, where, apparently, our killer tore open the pocket of his jacket on a thorny bush. There was a scrap of paper with a handwritten reference to 'pier 16' at the Port of San Pedro. An old friend from my time at UCLA is an LA County Detective, and I gave him a call about that. It took him less than a half-hour to find out that there is, in fact, a pier 16 at San Pedro, but it's been undergoing repair work for the past six months, with zero shipping traffic. The other thing we found in the woods worth mentioning is the Indonesian banknote, which is for 500 Rupiah. Ten minutes of online research tells us that the smallest note in circulation today is the 1000 Rupiah. I wouldn't have known this, but apparently due to decades of inflation and currency devaluation, even the 1000 Rupiah note is only worth about sixty-five cents. The point is that it doesn't make sense that an international traveler would be carrying an old 500 Rupiah note."

"But it could probably be picked up on eBay," Saxby said, "or at any of those coin and currency collector type booths at flea markets all over the country."

"Exactly," Wilkes said. "Which brings me to my last item, which is Deutsch himself. He was the chief financial officer for Barker Chemical when he was over there in Jakarta. In his role, he wouldn't have had anything to do with the running of a physical plant. If you were a local person wanting to pin the blame on somebody, there are a bunch of more likely targets. Plant managers, the executive in charge of safety or security, any number of workers— even the CEO himself. But, as far as we can tell, none of those other people have been threatened, much less attacked."

"Sure does seem like that whole chemical spill connection is a distraction," Dooley said. "A false trail."

"I think you're right, Tom," Saxby said. "Or, as Agatha Christie would have said, a red herring."

"Somebody killed him," Wilkes said. "That's for sure. But that's about the only part of the whole thing that doesn't look staged to me. And whoever killed him was probably someone he knew, or at least someone with a reasonable expectation of gaining entry to his place without a fuss, because there were no broken windows or locks or anything like that."

"I can't help but see the parallels to the Boone Roseman case," Saxby said. "Just like with Frankie Deutsch, the only thing that isn't strange is the fact that he was killed. Also, he was whacked on the back of the head, if that means anything."

"When I read up on that case the other day," Wilkes said, "I kept thinking about that woman who killed her husband up in Mays Landing last July. Do you remember that? He'd been abusing her for years and she finally had enough one day, and put five bullets into him. She walked away on self-defense, and the guy probably deserved it, but the reason I thought of it is that he had been found with methamphetamine around and up in his nose, but he had none in his sinuses or his blood. She eventually admitted to putting the crap in his nose after she killed him, thinking to make it look like he was more dangerous and out of control than he really was. Reminded me of the cocaine you found on Roseman."

"And then we have the little mirror that didn't belong in his place and didn't have his prints on it," Dooley said. "And that leather bag that shouldn't have been there, and the bill wrappers for money that wasn't there and he didn't have."

"The big one for me," Saxby said, "is that nobody who knew him—without exception—thought that he was, or could be involved with cocaine or other drugs. Nobody thought that was something he would do."

"So, what do you think, guys?" Wilkes said. "Do we agree that both of these killings appear to be staged? Or at least, the crime scenes have been 'arranged' to some extent?"

"At this point, I don't see how we can avoid thinking that," Dooley said. "But then that leads us to the next question, which is—are they connected?"

"It was you who pointed out to me that Roseman and Deutsch were both sixty-six years old," Wilkes said, looking squarely at Saxby. "And both grew up in Cape May."

"Right, I've been chewing on that for a while," Saxby said. "And since we're there now, we need to toss in Jeffrey Tanner, also from Cape May and also sixty-six years old."

"I remember something you said earlier, Tate," Dooley said, "about 'throwing spaghetti at the wall.' Let's go with it, then. Roseman and Deutsch are obvious murders, yet the Tanner situation is different. If that was a murder too, why was it made up to look like an accident? If only at first glance?"

"Opportunity? Maybe something about the situation led the killer to go with the accident idea rather than revenge or drugs, like Deutsch and Roseman," Saxby said. He stood up as he was speaking and started to walk around the table. "Just a guess. But let's talk about Tanner for a minute while we're on it. If it wasn't for the blood on the phone, the man on the video, and those three cigarette butts, I'm not sure we'd still be talking about it. He had a history of heart problems that could have contributed to his fall, which actually was the cause of death. The circumstances of the fall were a little odd, but I can't say it couldn't have happened. It already looked like an accident. I mean, why bother adding the mystery?"

"Check me on this, Tate," Wilkes said. "I want to make sure I'm getting you. I think what you're saying is, if Tanner's death was a murder, set up to look like an accident—successfully perhaps—why then muck it up with other stuff which only makes it look like it wasn't an accident?"

"That's a damn good question, isn't it?" Dooley said. He was also standing now, leaning against the wall. "If we're now operating under the idea that Tanner's death wasn't an accident, then now we have three murders that all were staged to some extent. If that's really what we have, then what do you think the chances are that they aren't connected?"

After considering for a moment, Wilkes appeared to resign himself to an idea and did a slow shake of his head. "Somewhere between none and zero is what my gut is telling me."

"Yeah. I have to agree," Saxby said. "Except I was going to say slim to none."

"Okay, so we all agree on that," Dooley said. "And I suggest that should be our next focus. Just what is it that connects these cases? I mean, these men."

"Well, we know three things right off the bat," Saxby said. "They were all originally from Cape May, they were all sixty-six years old, and last but not least, somebody wanted them all dead."

11

After the meeting with the two detectives in Somers Point, Saxby drove Dooley back to his office. They talked about the three cases for the first half of the ride, before settling into silence for the second half. Inside Saxby's head, he went over and over the known facts of the cases, while also taking some mental stabs at the unknown facts. He guessed that Dooley was probably doing the same thing. It was after four by the time he got back to his office, and he set about sorting through calls and emails to see what might need attention.

It was a quiet afternoon in the station, and he had been making good progress when, an hour later, Sergeant Barstow knocked on his open door.

"Good timing, Vic, come on in," Saxby said. "I'm mostly caught up and my brain could use a shift of gears. What do you have going on?"

Barstow sat down and took a moment to look at some notes she'd brought with her. "It seemed like a day of being put on hold or driving around trying to find people, but I did somehow manage to cross a few things off my list. I was able to get hold of the Herr's delivery driver that Barry Vaughn said was a friend of his—Chip Tillerman is his name. He confirms Vaughn's story and the timing. He drives around with a logbook where he records all his stops, and he showed me that. He also remembered the same two Doors' songs that Vaughn said were on the radio."

"That's right," Saxby said. "I remember him saying they were doing some kind of show on long songs."

"Yes, and, on that note…" Barstow said, making a face at the unintended pun, "I talked with Mark Allen at the radio station. He looked up what they played Wednesday night and it matches up with what Vaughn and Tillerman said. So, I guess that puts Vaughn in the clear at least as far as the timeframe we've been looking at. I'm afraid that's about it for me, Chief. How about you? Didn't you head up the road with Detective Dooley?"

"I sure did. We went up to see what we could learn about that case up in Somers Point," Saxby said. "We had a very interesting meeting with the detective who's been leading that investigation, a guy by the name of Dikko Wilkes. I think we're going to shake up the way we've been looking at things. Let me tell you all about it…"

The parking lot of the Cape May Winery was almost full when Saxby pulled in just before eight that evening. "Oh man, there's a lot of people here. What do you say we head back home, open a bottle of something, and watch a movie?"

"Oh stop that," Angela said. "Anybody who's anybody will be here and it's for a good cause. Remember, you're not only the police chief, but one of the largest business owners in the county. People are expecting you to show up."

"Okay, okay, but let's try not to stay too long," Saxby said. He had picked out a parking spot and started to back Angela's Mustang into it. "My schmoozing powers are very low right now."

"I hate to be the one to break it to you, sweets, but your schmooze-powers are never all that high," Angela said. "But it's okay. You're good at a lot of other stuff. Let's get a few glasses of wine into you and you'll be fine."

"That does sound good," Saxby said. "But you know what, I'm going to figure out where to drop off these checks first, so I don't forget about that. What is this benefit for again?"

"It's for the fund to fix up that big old Victorian house that the family left to the city last year," Angela said. "You know the place. It's about a block behind the Chalfonte. We always called it the 'Old Quigley Mansion.' Everybody thought it was haunted back when we were kids. We used to dare each other to go up on the porch and look in the window."

"Yeah, I remember now," Saxby said. "That could use a lot of work that isn't in the city's budget. You go ahead and mingle around and I'll catch up with you."

The winery was closed for the benefit event, and Saxby's first guess that a table for donations would be set up in the main lobby proved correct. He went straight off in that direction as Angela went the other way in search of wine and with hopes of pleasant mingling.

"Well, if it isn't my favorite police chief," said the elegant, silver-haired woman who appeared to be set up to receive and log donations. Saxby was almost immediately relieved that he recognized her as Pat Younglove, a long-time employee of Harbor House Fisheries, the largest of the local companies his cousin had left to him. He knew that she had a history of working with the various benefits that the Harbor House had been involved with over the years, so was not surprised to see her at the table.

"And hello to you, Pat," Saxby said. "It's been a while since I've seen you. Thing's going well for you?"

"Everything's just fine, Tate," Younglove said. "And it's good to see you as well. Is Angela with you tonight?"

"She sure is, somewhere off in there with a glass of wine by now, is my guess," Saxby said. "I have a check from the Harbor House, and also one from the Ugly Mug. Are you the person I should give them to?"

"I would be happy to take those off your hands," Younglove said. She took the checks from him and made the corresponding entries in an open logbook. Saxby refused the offer of a receipt and made his way back towards the tasting rooms. He was halfway across the lobby when he heard a familiar voice call out his name.

"Hey, Tate," Jack Torrance said. Saxby stopped and waited while the mayor made excuses to a small group of people he'd been talking with and came over to him. "I'm glad you could make it. I know this isn't really your thing, but I hope you're having a good time."

"We just got here, but it looks like a good bunch of people," Saxby said. "I was just about to head in to the tasting room to find Angela and a glass of cabernet."

"I won't hold you up very long, then," Torrance said. "I know you've been busy with the Roseman thing and now this with Jeff Tanner. Such a shame." Torrance checked to make sure nobody was within earshot. "Have you made a determination yet about whether or not that was foul play?"

"I think so, Jack," Saxby said, nodding. "Actually, I'm almost sure of it. Detective Dooley and I spent a good chunk of the afternoon up in Somers Point today, learning about a case they have up there, from last week. There are some really strange parallels with Roseman, and probably Tanner. Can we find time to meet tomorrow, and I'll bring you up to speed?"

"Wow. So, you're thinking they could all be connected," Torrance said. He seemed to grit his teeth as he shook his head slowly. "Good God. But hey, yes, let's not talk about all this now and ruin the evening. As the mayor of Cape May, I order you to have a good time, and let's try to find time to catch up tomorrow. I think I see Jeanne and Joe Farnsworth over there—I'd better grab them to say hello. I'll catch you later, Tate. If I miss Angela, say hi for me."

Ten minutes and several brief conversations later, Saxby was making his way towards the outside firepit with a glass of Cape May Cabernet when he almost bumped into his friend Mark Allen, a local radio host and well-known man-about-town. Allen was coming from the other direction while looking down at his phone and hadn't noticed Saxby. They recovered quickly, with Saxby managing to avoid splashing wine onto his blazer.

"Hello, Chief Saxby," Allen said. He broke into a wide smile and held out his hand. "I'm so sorry, why did they have to give us all these damn phones anyway? Did I make you get any wine on you?"

Saxby made an exaggerated show of checking himself for signs of wine splashes. "I think I'm in the clear, Mark, but I may have to ticket you for a pedestrian traffic violation."

"I hope you'll consider letting me off with just a warning," Allen said. "Especially since I was such a big help to Sergeant Barstow today."

"That's right, with the long song list," Saxby said. "Or whatever that show was. Yes, thanks for your help with that. It may sound silly, but it did help us with the case."

"Any time, Tate, you know that," Allen said. "No trouble at all. You've had a hell of a week, haven't you? I only knew Boone Roseman a little bit, like, you know, to say hi in the Acme, but he seemed like a decent person. Older than me by a few years, I think. But then when I heard about Jeff Tanner's accident, *sheesh*. Let's hope there's nothing to all that jazz about bad things coming in threes."

"Well, it's funny you should say that," Saxby said. "Because it looks like—"

Saxby was cut off when a thirty-something executive-looking woman who he didn't recognize appeared by Allen's side and whispered something in his ear. After a moment she appeared to realize she had interrupted the two men and stood back, looking at Saxby.

"Oh, I'm so sorry for cutting in like that, Mr. Saxby—I

mean Chief Saxby—but I'm afraid I need to grab Mark for his presentation."

"No, it's my fault. I'm sorry, Tate," Allen said. "Tate, may I introduce Ellen Yates. Ellen organized this thing, and drafted me to narrate a little slideshow about the restoration fund. Guess I lost track of time and now the hour is upon me. I'll try to catch you later. I had a few thoughts about what we were talking about. You know, some ideas about those guys. Okay, gotta go."

"Don't worry about it. Do what you gotta do and we'll talk soon," Saxby said. "Good meeting you, Ellen. Break a leg, Mark."

Allen gave Saxby a thumbs-up before turning to follow Ellen Yates back indoors. Seeing Angela standing and talking with a group of people near the firepit, he moved off in that direction to join her.

Back in his house, ninety minutes and several glasses of wine later, Saxby realized that he had missed a call from Mark Allen during the drive home. Allen answered the return call on the second ring. "I'm glad you called back tonight, Tate, and I'm sorry we didn't get to talk more at the winery. After that slideshow I was surrounded and got all embroiled in discussions about the restoration. I don't know why. I hardly know anything about it, but I guess people saw me as the expert. Expert on what? Your guess is as good as mine. But I faked my way through it— admirably, I think."

"I'm sure you did just fine, Mark," Saxby said. "You have

'the gift of gab,' as you once told me. Right after we were interrupted though, by ah ... Yates, right? Ellen Yates it was. Before she pulled you away, you mentioned something about an idea you had about Roseman and Tanner, right? Can we meet at Starla's for coffee tomorrow? Either that or the police station or the radio station. I'll take whatever I can get right now, and if you've got any ideas, I'd like to hear them."

"How about we don't wait for tomorrow," Allen said. "It's barely after ten now, and I've got a bottle of something you're going to like."

Saxby thought for a moment before answering. If Mark —or anyone else—had some constructive information on the cases he was working on, he was in a mood to hear it sooner rather than later. Angela had already announced that she wasn't feeling well and was headed straight to bed. *And what is this mysterious bottle he's gotten his hands on?* "Sure, Mark, if you don't want it to wait for morning, I can come over. You're about four blocks away, so I think I'll just take the walk. See you in a few."

It was less than a ten-minute walk to Allen's house, and Saxby found the door open. As he came in and shut it behind him, he heard Allen yell a greeting from the kitchen.

"Glad you were up for coming over tonight, Tate," Allen said, appearing in the hallway. He motioned for Saxby to join him in the kitchen. "I thought of something but didn't want to just shout it at you in front of everyone else at the winery."

Saxby looked around the kitchen, where a set of high stools were spaced out on either side of the marble-topped island. Allen had set out a pair of heavy rocks glasses, a small ice bucket, and a squat, roundish bottle of amber liquid.

"Blanton's, huh? Pretty fancy, Mark," Saxby said. "You must have friends in high places."

"Or at least a friend who owns a liquor store," Allen said. "And I knew you'd appreciate it. Help yourself to ice if you do that."

Saxby dropped a trio of ice cubes into one of the glasses. "Is Gretchen around somewhere, or are you a bachelor tonight?"

"She's doing a girls' weekend away with a few friends, before the season kicks off around here," Allen said. "One of her friends has a family house in Montauk, so I guess they're up there drinking wine and eating lobster."

"Ah, wine and rubbery butter—good for them, then," Saxby said. He took a careful sip of the bourbon Allen had poured, savoring it thoughtfully, before taking a second, larger pull. "Mmm, that's good, thanks. Don't let me have too much though, I have a lot to do in the morning."

"Roger that, Tate," Allen said, "and don't worry about a late party or anything like that—I've got an early meeting myself at the radio station."

They had settled down on stools across the island from one another. Allen produced a thin folder from one of the shelves under the counter. "So, like many of us in town, I've been thinking about Boone Roseman a lot this week. And then there was the news about Jeff Tanner. I knew them both only slightly, but still, it was a sad news week. The thing is, I thought about the one, and I thought about the other, but I didn't think of them together in any way.

As if, for example, they were family members, or business partners. They were just two completely separate incidents. Am I making any sense?"

"I think I know what you mean," Saxby said. "There was no reason for you to think of them as anything other than two strange things that happened in town."

"That's right, you got it," Allen said. "But then, when I saw you at the winery, something must have knocked the dust out of my head, because I started to remember a few things. And then Ellen came up and interrupted us. You probably already know they went to high school together, right?"

"Actually, I hadn't gotten that far yet," Saxby said. "But we did know they were within a few months of the same age, so that makes perfect sense. Lower Regional you mean, right? Or Wildwood Catholic?"

"Regional. Same as you and me," Allen said. "Though they were older than me, and even more older than you. They were both LCMR class of 1974."

"Okay, which stands to reason if they were both born in 1956," Saxby said. "But that doesn't necessarily mean they knew each other. Or are you saying that you know they did?"

"I can say for sure that they knew each other back in high school," Allen said. "But I don't know much about after that. They shared something, which is what I remembered tonight at the winery. Something that happened back in 1972. Here, let me show you."

Allen took an old newspaper clipping out of the file folder, unfolding it and smoothing it out before pushing it across to Saxby.

The print at the top of the clipping indicated that the article was from *The Cape May Star & Wave*, and the head-line read *Local Boy Dies in Freak Accident*. Saxby took a few minutes to read the short article, before skimming over a few sections a second time. "How the hell did I not know about this? So, a kid named Ryan Dunne was killed when a group of friends were horsing around under the board-walk is how I read it. But the article doesn't name the other boys. Are you telling me that Boone Roseman and Jeff Tanner were there?"

"That's what I'm telling you, Tate," Allen said. "Their names weren't in the paper because they were minors. They were all sixteen. But, look at this…" He took a large photograph from the folder and passed it over to Saxby. The faded black and white photo appeared to be of a dozen or more people milling about at some sunny outdoor function, and the focus was on a group of six teenage boys standing together and looking uncomfort-able. The boys were all wearing button-down shirts and had their hair combed neatly. A few of them wore clip-on ties and one was wearing an ill-fitting suit jacket. "This was taken about a month later, at a memorial service for Ryan. I was only twelve, but my uncle worked for the *Star & Wave*, and I was tagging along, helping him with his cameras and whatever else he needed. I actually took this picture myself. I was up on a small deck, and was looking down at the people on the lawn, when the crowd sorta opened up and there they all were, standing together. Far as I know, none of the pics from that day ever made it into the paper."

"So, this accident was May of '72. I'm going to have to

dig up the police report," Saxby said. "Were these boys charged with anything?"

"I don't think so," Allen said, "but you'll have to check me on that. My memory of it is foggy, but I think it was eventually ruled an accident. A few of them were messing around, wrestling or whatever, and Ryan got pushed against a piling that had some kind of big spike sticking out of it. They must have just about pissed their pants."

Saxby was looking closely at the photo. He pointed to the leftmost boy in the group. "This must be Jeff Tanner. He sure didn't change much over the years. Yeah, that's him. Which one's Boone Roseman? Do you know?"

Allen consulted another sheet of paper from his folder, before pointing at another of the boys. "Third from the left there, that's Boone Roseman. And the others are…"

Saxby cut him off before he could go any further. "Hang on, Mark. Hang on. Wait a minute. I hope you're not going to tell me … is Frankie Deutsch one of these boys?"

"Frankie Deutsch," Allen said, looking back at the paper. "Yes, that's him on the far right. That's Frankie Deutsch. How'd you know he was one of them?"

Saxby stood up and started to walk the perimeter of the kitchen. "Oh man. This is just too crazy. All three of them are right there. The world has gone nuts."

Allen was watching him with a look of amused suspicion. "Are you okay, Tate? What do you mean by 'all three of them?' " He picked up the bottle of bourbon and refilled Saxby's glass. "I think you need this."

"Sorry, Mark," Saxby said. "Yes, I'll be okay. Right before your friend Ellen interrupted us earlier, I was about to tell you something, and I guess I never did get it out.

Earlier today, I spent some time with a detective from Somers Point learning all about a case they had up there a little over a week ago. It was definitely a murder, but the circumstances were strange, like, evidence that pointed in different directions. No leads at the moment, as far as I know. Anyway, I only mention that because the murdered man…" He looked down at the photo, and Allen watched carefully as he lowered his index finger to point at the boy on the far right. "Frankie Deutsch."

Allen made a sharp intake of breath as he looked around the room as though he had suddenly heard a loud knocking in the middle of a séance. He reached a hand around to feel the back of his neck. "It's true what they say about your hair standing on end. The world gone nuts is right, Tate. Three of the guys in this picture have been killed in the past week? Or, well, Tanner—that was an accident, wasn't it?"

"This is all confidential, Mark," Saxby said. "Are we on the same page about that?"

"Sure, yes. Absolutely, Tate. No problem," Allen said. "Doesn't leave this room."

"It's been a long day," Saxby said. "And before I went over to the winery and bumped into you, I came to realize that there appeared to be a connection between the three deaths. Now, with all this…" He gestured to the photo and other papers on the counter. "…I think we know what the connection is."

Allen nodded his head slowly, and several times before speaking. "Someone is killing those boys. The boys who were there when Ryan Dunne died. Somebody is getting revenge."

"You can say that," Saxby said. "But as the police chief, I can't say that yet. I mean, yeah, I can see what's in front of me, and I admit that's a tempting idea, but wow, that's a lot. I need to learn whatever I can about that accident and the aftermath. For starters, who are the other three boys in the picture?"

Allen pointed them out as he said their names in turn, referring to his page of notes. "That's Manny Bowen between Tanner and Roseman there. Then Bob Hallman, Doug Lawson, and then Frankie Deutsch on the end. I see Doug Lawson around now and then, but I don't think I know the other two."

"Same for me. I know Doug just to say hello," Saxby said. "But I can't recall ever meeting the other two. Can I borrow this photo and your notes there? I'll make a copy and get the originals back to you."

Allen put the papers back into the folder and handed the whole thing to Saxby. "Sure thing, Chief, no hurry. You know, I've been trying to think of anyone I know who might be familiar with the Ryan Dunne case and how it turned out. I wish I could tell you more about it, but I was too young, and have never had a reason to dig into it. There's someone who I bet knows all about it. Remember you met Ellen Yates earlier, at the winery?"

"Sure, I remember her," Saxby said. "But she can't be more than thirty-five or so, right?"

"You're right," Allen said. "That's about how old she is, but I'm not thinking of Ellen. I'm thinking of her grand-mother, Trilby Yates. Trilby not only worked in the high school office in the seventies, but she also worked at the *Star & Wave* for years. If there's anyone in town who could tell you all about what happened with Ryan Dunne and what the police did about it, or if anyone was sued, Trilby would be the one. She must be close to eighty, but you wouldn't know it the way her mind works. She lives in Cape May Point. I'll write down her number for you."

"Thanks, Mark, I'll look her up tomorrow," Saxby said. "And thanks for the drink too. Man, this thing took a hell of a turn today. I need you to keep it under your hat for now, right?"

"No problem, Tate," Allen said. "Let me know if there's any way I can help, even if you just need to have a drink and bounce ideas off someone. I'm good for that."

Saxby downed the last swallow of his whiskey and started on the short walk home, his mind swirling with variations of a story about tragedy, revenge, and murder. The story seemed almost cinematic to him, and too fantastic to be true. Yet, with real bodies turning up in his quiet town, it was also too deadly to be ignored.

12

Saxby gave himself an early start the next day, and by the time Doreen got in at eight he had already spent most of an hour searching through boxes of old files in the basement of City Hall. Coming back upstairs to the police station, he followed the smell of fresh-brewed coffee into the small kitchen, where he found Doreen fixing herself a cup.

She reached to his shoulder to brush a cobweb from his shirt. "What on earth are you doing down there in the basement so early? And on a Saturday morning no less. Is there some emergency going on that I need to know about?"

"Well, I hope not," Saxby said. He picked one of the paper cups off the top of the stack and poured himself some coffee. "But the Roseman and the Tanner cases have taken an interesting turn, to put it mildly. A turn for the worse. I need to see anything we have about an accidental death that happened back in May of 1972, and I can't find anything at all down there. Why do you think that might be?"

"First of all," Doreen said, "are you sure there is—or was —a file? I mean, was there a police investigation? What happened?"

"It was an accident that killed a local teenager," Saxby said. "From what I understand, a group of local boys—all sixteen—were messing around under the boardwalk. They were running around, or wrestling, or whatever, and one of them—Ryan Dunne—slipped, or got pushed up against a piling and hit his head on some kind of spike. Killed him right away is what I was told. I only heard all this late yesterday, so that's all I know about it right now, and I'm not even sure I've got that much straight."

"And you're thinking the deaths of Boone Roseman and Jeff Tanner could be related to that?" Doreen said.

"Well, I've seen enough in the past few days," Saxby said, "that I think it's worth a good, hard look. Both of those men, along with Deutsch up in Somers Point, were under the boardwalk that day. We have to consider the possibility of some kind of long-simmering revenge as a motive, crazy as that may sound."

"Oh my God, Tate," Doreen said, "that's just incredible. Let me help by looking for that file for you. I'm probably more familiar with what's down there than anyone else."

"Thanks, Doreen," Saxby said. "That would be a big help. Whatever we have, if anything, I need to see it. Before you go down there, could you do two things for me please? First, check if Vic and Three are on the schedule for today, and second, see if you can contact a lady named Trilby Yates and set up a time for me to come over to meet with her as soon as possible. I'm told she lives in Cape May Point, and here's her number."

Doreen took the scrap of paper that Mark Allen had written out. "Trilby Yates sounds familiar. I think I've met her once or twice. Nice lady as I recall. Is this morning okay, if she's available?"

"That would be fine," Saxby said. "Meeting with her is a priority right now."

Doreen went out towards her desk, leaving Saxby to top off his coffee and take it to his office. It was only ten minutes later that she buzzed him with the intercom feature of his desk phone.

"First item, Chief," Doreen said, with the usual metallic 'trebly' sound that the device gave to everyone's voice. "Both Vic and Three are scheduled for six-hour shifts starting at noon. Do you want me to try to find them and bring them in earlier?"

"No, I don't think there's any need for that," Saxby said. "I'll catch up with them when they get in. Any luck with Trilby Yates?"

"Better luck with her, yes," Doreen said. "You're seeing her at her house at ten. If that's all for now, I'll take my coffee down to the basement and see if I can find anything for you on Ryan Dunne."

It was ninety minutes later when Saxby turned off Sunset Boulevard into the quiet beach community of Cape May Point, making his way to the address he'd looked up for Trilby Yates. The house he pulled up to was built in a classic Cape Cod style, with a central door flanked on both sides by a pair of wide double-windows. A neat row of three dormer windows jutted out from the gray-shingled roof, with a red brick chimney rising up from the left end of the house. The house was clad in cedar shake shingles, weathered by the sun, wind, and time to a soft gray. As Saxby walked to the door, he thought to himself that the house perfectly matched the New England, old-money-sounding name of Trilby Yates. The door knocker was a model of a boat anchor in old but well-polished brass, and the door was opened right away by a tall, slim woman. She wore pressed, navy-blue slacks, topped with a pink cashmere sweater with a green whale embroidered on the left breast. *Yes, if ever I've seen someone who should be named Trilby Yates, this is her,* Saxby thought to himself. Her silver-gray hair was long and straight, and was pulled back into a loose ponytail and bound with a ribbon that matched not only her eyes, but the color of the whale on her sweater.

"Well now, you must be Chief Tate Saxby," the lady said. She had a warm and natural smile. "It's nice to meet you. I'm Trilby Yates."

"It's good to meet you as well, Mrs. … sorry, or … Miss Yates," Saxby said.

"Miss is just fine," Yates said. "My husband's been gone for so many years. It might be silly, but 'Miss' makes me feel just a little bit young again. Please come in. When Doreen, your dispatcher, called earlier, I remembered that I knew her, though I haven't bumped into her for some time. She told me that you wanted to talk to me about something that happened in town fifty years ago, but it was clear that she didn't know much about it." Yates led Saxby into a small sitting room at the rear of the house and gestured to a grouping of chairs around a low table. They took seats opposite one another.

"Yes, that's right. And thank you for seeing me on such short notice, Miss Yates," Saxby said. "I do appreciate it. As part of a case, or possibly several cases, we're working on, I need to learn everything I can about something that happened back in May of 1972, and Mark Allen told me that you were the person I should speak with."

"You want to know about that boy," Yates said. "Ryan Dunne was his name, and he was only sixteen. I remember it well. Such a terrible, terrible thing. I knew his family, though only casually. Why on earth would that come up again all of a sudden?"

"First, Miss Yates," Saxby said, "I have to ask that you keep whatever we discuss to yourself for the time being. If you agree to that, I'll explain what I can. Can I count on you for that?"

"Certainly, I can keep the lid on, if you like," Yates said. "I'm happy to help however I can."

"Thanks for that," Saxby said. He paused for a moment, gathering his thoughts. "In a conversation yesterday evening, Mark Allen was able to tell me a little bit about the accident. A group of kids were hanging out, or horsing around, under the boardwalk, and Ryan Dunne hit his head on something and was killed. As of a half-hour ago, we aren't finding any kind of file on it at the police station, so that's about all I know. I'd like to know more about what exactly happened and what any follow-up was. Was anyone blamed, what were people saying, all of that. Whatever you can tell me could be helpful."

"It was a terrible tragedy," Yates said. "Very sad. I remember it well. I saw him there, you know. Stuck on that piling, with the tide coming in. On my deathbed I'm sure I'll remember that sight."

"You say you saw him," Saxby said, "how is that? Were you one of the people on the beach that afternoon?"

"Oh no, didn't Mark tell you?" Yates said. "I was there with the rescue squad. Mark must have forgotten that. I must have been twenty-five or six. Yes, that sounds right. I'd been taking classes for nursing school back then, and I thought that volunteering for the rescue squad would give me some good experience. I was on call that afternoon. There were four of us who got there right about the same time, along with the police. He was an average-sized boy—Ryan. He must have been shoved, or just slipped maybe, I'm not sure. But he hit one of those giant wood pilings that support Convention Hall and the rest of the boardwalk. There was a sharp, jagged piece of metal sticking out, like a rusty bolt, almost like a giant nail or something like that. That just went right into the back of the poor boy's skull, and he was stuck there, dead as can be but standing up. It was horrible. They said it killed him instantly, which I suppose was a small mercy. My partner at the time, Clayton Pelt, was one of the men who lifted him off that spike, and I remember him telling me that it was about four inches long, and had gone all the way in." When Miss Yates stopped talking, she dabbed at her eyes with a lace handkerchief.

"I'm sorry to have to ask you to relive this," Saxby said. "It certainly was a terrible tragedy, but you are helping me by filling me in on all of it. Mark told me that there had been six other boys there, hanging out or playing with Ryan that day. Were they still there when you and the police arrived? Did they run to get help?"

"No, none of them were there that I recall seeing," Yates said. "At that time, I was also working at the *Star & Wave* newspaper, and a friend of mine at the paper was the reporter who researched the story, so a lot of what I know about the case comes from him. He passed on years ago, so I'm afraid you'll have to settle for my secondhand version."

"That's just fine, Miss Yates," Saxby said. "It's clear to me that your memory is razor-sharp, and I'm glad to be hearing your account. Do you know who called the police?"

"Well, my friend Wally—my reporter friend from the *Star & Wave*," Yates said, "he told me the other boys ran away right after it happened. That's hard to imagine, but I don't know, teenage boys aren't generally the finest examples of responsibility. In any case, as I understand it, they realized right away that Ryan was dead and became terrified that they would be blamed, and ran away home, or to somewhere else to hide for a while. Wally told me that it was almost an hour before one of them went to his parents and told them everything. They called the police immediately, and we all got there within another fifteen minutes or so."

"I mentioned earlier that we haven't been able to find a file on this at the station," Saxby said. "But yet I can't believe there wouldn't have been some sort of investigation. What can you remember about the feeling in town at the time? For example, were people accusing Ryan's friends of deliberately trying to hurt him, or of trying to cover it up? People yelling for justice, anything like that?"

"I don't believe so, Chief Saxby," Yates said. "Cape May was a lot quieter back then, and remember, it was May, so there weren't all that many tourists around yet. The whole town was stunned and saddened of course, but the general feeling was that it had been a terrible freak accident, and the other boys were just scared and didn't know what to do. Sure, there was some grumbling about how they'd behaved, and that they shouldn't have been there at all, that sort of thing. The older brother of one of the boys had bought them some beer that day, and I think he got a slap on the wrist by the police, but that's all."

"What about Ryan Dunne's family," Saxby said. "Did you know them?"

"I had met Mrs. Dunne once or twice," Yates said. "Colleen was her name. Yes, that's right, Colleen Dunne. I forget where. But aside from that, no, I wouldn't say I knew them. Now, Ryan did have a younger brother. Jim was his name. Everyone called him Jimmy. If Ryan was sixteen, Jimmy Dunne must have been five or six years younger. He was very upset about losing his big brother at such a young age. I mention him, Chief, because it was years later, when Jimmy had been out of high school himself for a year or two, that there was some fracas at a bar in town—or was it a party? Anyway, Jimmy had a few too many, and someone must have started talking about Ryan and the accident, and things got heated. Now, I wasn't there, Chief, but from what I heard from friends, he started yelling and going on about how those boys that ran away were responsible for his brother's death, and how he hated them, and on and on. The police came and he was taken away to cool off. You might find a police report about that, if you look under his name—Jimmy Dunne. That might be worth a try. It all blew over and he left town not long after. I don't remember actually seeing him after that, but I believe he was in and out of town on occasion over the years. I remember hearing that he went off to live south of the border somewhere. Mexico? Was that it? Or maybe it was Puerto Rico or another Caribbean island. I'm not sure. Anyway, that's the last I ever heard of him. My thought is that he was probably somewhat of a tortured soul. But in answer to your question, he would be the only person I can think of really coming out and yelling about those boys who ran away, and maybe even threatening them. But that must have been forty years ago or more. There was a sister too, the youngest of the three. She must have been seven or eight when Ryan died. I think her name was Shelly, short for Michelle maybe. But I don't know anything about her."

"Yes, I see what you mean," Saxby said. "If we were wondering if there was anyone who might have thought about revenge, that's a heck of a cold trail. Still, though, that's good information and we will check it out."

"Well, obviously, Chief Saxby," Yates said, "you operate in the real world, and not in the world of a mystery novel, but you must also know that what happens in the real world can be stranger than fiction. I'm sure you're also aware of the old saying: 'Revenge is a dish that people of taste prefer to eat cold.' "

13

Later that afternoon, Saxby corralled Sergeant Barstow and Deputy Connor into the conference room, where they spent most of an hour going over the developments in the Roseman and Tanner cases.

"So, I think your gut instinct about the scene at Boone Roseman's apartment was right, Vic," Saxby said. "It now looks more and more like whoever killed him took a few minutes to throw out a few false leads."

"Yes, it sure does, doesn't it?" Barstow said. "They wanted us to jump right to the most obvious thing—the drug deal gone bad. And the Somers Point case is all about revenge for that chemical spill. Not really, but you know what I mean."

"Then, if we're working with the idea that the same person killed Jeffrey Tanner," Connor said, "they did something similar to throw us off the scent, though I'm not getting what they meant for us to think. Not drugs, not revenge, but what?"

"I hear you on that, Three," Saxby said. "The blood on

the phone, the cigarette butts—if that was even them. My thought on that is that they just tossed out a few ideas to make us look in different directions. Make us look at it up and down, here and there, and not see a pattern, so we eventually come back to the idea that it was probably just an accident after all. That is, at least until we saw through that one too. I don't have everything figured out yet, but one thing I do know is, sure as I'm sitting here, someone's been playing with us."

"What's the status of the Somers Point case?" Barstow said. "Will we be working with that detective you met up there?"

"Dikko Wilkes is his name, and yes," Saxby said. "It's his territory of course, but I want us to loop him in on whatever we find, and I've asked him to do the same regarding Frankie Deutsch. I had a call with him and Dooley when I got back from my meeting with Trilby Yates earlier, and we agreed to all that. We also agreed that the most likely scenario at this point is that, first of all, Tanner was murdered. Second, with that in mind, all three cases are related to Ryan Dunne's death under the boardwalk fifty years ago.

"Shouldn't we have a file on that, Chief?" Barstow said. "I mean, seems like there must have been some level of investigation, even if it was an accident."

"Agee with you on that, Vic," Saxby said. "But there doesn't seem to be. I spent some time looking at the old files in the basement this morning, and then Doreen looked too, and we didn't find anything. It was fifty years ago, which is way before we converted over to the new system. It could have been lost in the shuffle. Frankly, back then, I wouldn't be surprised if after they decided there wouldn't be any charges, they might have just torn up the file to give the kids a break."

"Okay, so it looks like all we're going to get on that is gonna be from talking to people who were around back then, like this Trilby Yates you met with," Barstow said.

"It looks that way for now," Saxby said. "So, be that as it may, we need to switch gears to start looking at these cases as if they're all related to Ryan Dunne's death. We'll need to work out who then is a likely candidate for wanting revenge. Right now, the only name on that list is Dunne's younger brother, Jimmy, who apparently went on a tear threatening people some years after it happened. There may be others, but he's who we have at the moment."

"I can't help wondering about something, Chief," Connor said. "If this person, this killer, staged the crime scenes to throw us off, doesn't it seem like they did a really lousy job at it? Like how they found the Amtrak schedule in the woods up there in Somers Point. Have you thought about that?"

"Yes, that has occurred to me, and it's something we need to keep in mind as we go forward," Saxby said. "It may be that they tried to throw something together in a hurry and they weren't very careful. Or, it may be that they think we're dumber than we are. Or, maybe it's them who's dumber than they think. But yeah, it's something to think about.

"So, let's take a look at where we stand right now. Aside from Ryan Dunne, who will forever be sixteen years old, there were six kids with him under the boardwalk that day. Three of them are now dead. Priority number one is to locate the other three, alive or dead, wherever they may be. Doug Lawson is a local, and I've seen him at least once or twice in the past year. I don't know Bob Hallman or Manny Bowen. When I spoke with Mark Allen last night, he told me he didn't know them either. If I don't know them and Mark doesn't know them, I'm inclined to think they haven't been around Cape May since way back, but let's track that down.

"Priority number two is to find out whatever we can on this Jimmy Dunne, Ryan's little brother. Has anyone seen him, where is he, what is he doing? Three, you did most of the interviewing of Boone Roseman's friends. Let's go back and speak with them again about this new angle. Were they aware of Roseman's connection to the accident, was it something he ever talked about, was it something he worried about? Whatever else you can think of on that tack. Same with the people you spoke with about Tanner. Maybe one of these people will recall that Roseman or Tanner had been scared or threatened at some time in the past. Whoever we talk to, if we find anyone who seems to know about the accident, or the aftermath, let's remember to be on the alert for anyone who might fit the role of someone who could be after revenge."

"What about Dunne's parents?" Barstow said. "Do we know if they're even still alive?"

"That's one of the first things I plan to find out," Saxby said. "If they're alive and available, I'll try to meet with them. I figure they'd have to be in their mid-eighties by now, but we'll see.

"Well, look, it's Saturday, it's getting late, and it's been a long week. I suggest we get recharged this weekend and be ready to dive into all this Monday morning. If you want to do some weekend work, go ahead but don't overdo it. I'll be meeting Angela in the Mug when she finishes up about nine. Stop in for a drink on me if you feel like getting out. Be good to see you."

Saxby made himself dinner at home and ate it in front of the TV while channel-surfing the different news stations. After cleaning up, he spent two hours in his home office browsing through the police reports for the past week before grabbing a coat and driving over to the Ugly Mug. The place was doing a brisk business, and he found Angela helping out behind the bar. She gave him a wave and a smile, and took a minute to finish washing a tray of glasses before coming over. "I'm done anytime. What do you say we go somewhere else, just for a change of scene? Cody can handle everything here."

"Sure, that sounds fine," Saxby said. "Saturday though. Some places will be crowded. Where were you thinking?"

"How about Delaney's?" Angela said. "It's a block away and we should be able to get a table."

Saxby agreed to that idea, and a short walk down the outdoor mall brought them to Delaney's Irish Pub, where they settled into one of the high-backed booths opposite the long bar. A young waitress came right over and took their drink order.

"Have you been having a tough night?" Saxby asked.

"Oh no, it was fine," Angela said. "We were busy, but no complaints. I just thought it would be nice to get out somewhere different for a change."

"We were out somewhere different last night, you know," Saxby said. "At the winery."

"I know, and that was nice," Angela said, "but we didn't really get to sit down together and just talk. You know, hang out. You were up and out so early this morning I didn't even get to hear what happened over at Mark Allen's last night, or what else went on today. Let's hear it, Chief Saxby."

"Uh oh, well, this may not be a great time to tell you this," Saxby said. "But you should know that before I left the station today, I invited Vic and Three to come out for a drink at the Mug. They didn't say if they would or not, but I did invite them, so I should let them know that we're here instead."

Angela gave him a mock dirty look while he typed out a quick text and sent it. "Oh well, I guess this is what it's going to be like when I'm married to the chief of police. Fortunately for me, those two are good company."

"I promise not to invite anyone else next time," Saxby said. "You know what, how about just you and I go over to the winery one day soon. We can sit and relax with some good wine and pretend nobody knows us. We'll wear hats and dark glasses."

"That sounds wonderful," Angela said. "Maybe after you solve this latest murder mystery you've gotten embroiled in."

Saxby's phone gave a ping and he looked down to read the incoming text. "It's Vic. She'll be here in about fifteen minutes. How about if I use the time before she gets here to give you a condensed version of my visit with Mark last night, and what we found out today."

The waitress arrived with their drinks and a basket of fresh, hot popcorn. As they sipped their drinks and munched away on the popcorn, Saxby related the story of how he had learned about the accident under the boardwalk from Mark Allen, and then gotten more of the details from Trilby Yates, finishing up with his late-afternoon meeting with Barstow and Connor, and what he was thinking about where the investigation needed to go next.

"Amazing. I'm just stunned that this kind of thing can go on in our little town," Angela said. "It makes me wonder if it's even safe to go outside."

"Now, now," Saxby said. "I don't believe you need to be thinking like that. These crimes—these killings—are only directed at certain people for certain personal reasons. None of which means it isn't horrible, but you, along with the other townspeople, aren't in any danger. Not unless you were about to tell me that you were under the boardwalk that day too."

"Um, I doubt it, since I was probably two or three months old at the time," Angela said. "Do you really think it could be that younger brother doing this, after all these years?"

"I can't say that yet," Saxby said. "We don't have any basis to suspect him at the moment, other than circumstantial, but it makes sense that he's the first person we need to talk to. I'm told there was a sister too, but I don't know anything about her yet."

Just as the waitress stopped by to check on them, Sergeant Barstow appeared next to the booth. "I know you invited me, Chief, but before I sit down, are you sure I'm not interrupting a romantic get-together here?"

"Sit down, Vic, we're glad to see you," Angela said. "But it's nice of you to ask. Please join us."

Barstow hung her coat on the pole next to the booth and slid in next to Angela. She added her order for a glass of wine to Saxby's order for another round of the same for him and Angela.

"I haven't heard anything from Three, have you?" Saxby said.

"Yes, a half hour ago. He got involved in helping his mother with something at her house and just felt like hitting the couch after that," Barstow said. "He wanted me to be sure to thank you for the invitation, and to send his regrets. So, I figured I'd tell you he sends his 'thankrets.' What do you think? Shouldn't that be a word?"

"I think that could really come in handy," Saxby said. "Especially with me. I'll call *Webster's* first thing in the morning and demand that they add it."

"Even if they refuse, I'll still use it myself," Angela said. "So, just before you showed up, your boss here was filling me in on this latest big case you're working on."

"Oh, is it okay to talk about work a little, then?" Barstow asked. "I thought you might have had enough for today."

"It's okay, Vic, Angela knows what's going on," Saxby said. "Have you found out anything new since we talked?"

Barstow waited to answer while the waitress brought their drinks and another basket of popcorn. "Nothing earth-shattering, but we did find the other three men—or, sort of." She gave Angela a questioning look.

Angela took a look around the bar before leaning in and answering the look. "You mean the other three of the six, right? Who hopefully haven't been killed yet."

"Right, the other three boys—men—who were there that day," Barstow said.

"Good work, Vic," Saxby said. "Where do we stand with them?"

"Looks like Manny Bowen died of natural causes almost ten years ago," Barstow said. "Heart attack while hiking somewhere up in the Poconos. Shame. He didn't even make it to sixty. Bob Hallman appears to be living in the San Francisco area, for quite a few years now. I still have to confirm that's our guy, but based on what I've found so far, I think it is."

"Well, I guess that's good news then," Saxby said. "We only need to worry about Doug Lawson still here in town. I don't know him very well. What did you find on him?"

"Not a whole lot yet," Barstow said. "Lives on 3rd Avenue in West Cape May, just off Broadway. I don't know if it's his house or what, but I drove by it before I came here. There were lights on and there was a car in the driveway."

"We're certainly going to need to meet with him," Saxby said. "And also, if you can confirm that the Bob Hallman in California is our man, I'll want to check in with him as well. Assuming that's him, hopefully he's out of harm's way out there. Anything else?"

"A little. Three did some checking before he left and found a few things," Barstow said. "Both of Ryan Dunne's parents are deceased. They died within a year of each other in an assisted living place outside of Princeton. Their daughter, Shelly, lives in Moorestown with her husband. Her married name is Vance. Shelly Vance. She must be about fifty-eight or fifty-nine. Current New Jersey license, no criminal record."

"I know you've only started on all this," Saxby said, "but, anything at all on Jimmy Dunne?"

"Not a thing, Chief," Barstow said. "No Jersey license or arrest records for at least the last twenty years. I didn't look farther back than that yet, or at other states, but I'll get to that. No military service that I can see."

"With luck, when we start asking people about him," Saxby said, "somebody will know something."

"Hard to imagine we won't get some bites," Barstow said. "There's a lot of people in town who've been here forever, and the thing with Ryan Dunne would have been a big deal. What about putting out a national BOLO?"

"Okay, this might be a dumb question," Angela said. "But what exactly is a BOLO? I've heard it on TV but I don't know what it is."

"It's basically a broadcast message asking other police to keep an eye out for something or someone," Saxby said. "Stands for 'Be On the Lookout.' It could be for a suspect, or just for someone we'd like a chance to talk to. It could also be for an object, like a stolen car for example."

"Ah, thanks. Now I know," Angela said. "Now, the next time I stay up late watching *Dragnet* reruns, I'll know more about what's going on."

"Very funny, Ang," Saxby said. "Always glad to help. To answer your question, Vic, that's a good idea, but I'd like us to hold off on the BOLO for the moment. Let's see if we get anything on Dunne from talking to people around town first before we open it up to that."

"Got it. Then I think next thing I'll do is work on the

list of people we should talk to," Barstow said. "You don't care if I put in some time tomorrow, right? I don't have other plans."

"Go ahead if you like," Saxby said. "I'll probably see you there, at least for a few hours. Just please don't spend all day working. We're too small a force to have anyone burned out."

"Understood, Chief," Barstow said. She stood up and started to put on her coat. "I think I'll head home and hit the couch for a while before bed. There might be some *Dragnet* reruns on to help me sleep. Maybe I'll see you at the station tomorrow. Night, Chief, Ang—good seeing you, and thanks for the drink."

"Hey, isn't that your friend over there, on the other side of the bar?" Angela said, as Barstow was walking away. "Joanne, right? With the DEA."

Saxby looked across the bar at a tall woman standing at the bar, still wearing her coat. "You know what, yes, that is her. Joanne Belli. Homeland Security though, not DEA. I haven't seen her in a long time." Saxby stood up to wave and managed to catch the woman's eye as she looked around the bar. She motioned for him to sit and started towards their booth.

"Well, hello there, Tate, and Angela. Nice to see you. It's been too long."

"Good to see you too, Joanne," Saxby said. "Can you join us for a drink? Is Al here with you?"

"Thanks for the invite, but I'm just here to pick up take-out," Belli said. "Al didn't feel like putting on real shoes and leaving home. We're just here for a few days to start opening up the house for the season. I heard about your engagement—congratulations on that. What else is going on? Crime in Cape May keeping you busy?"

"Well, you might be surprised," Saxby said, with a chuckle. At that moment he noticed the bartender waving at them as he set a large handle bag up on the bar.

"Oh—they're calling for me," Belli said, noticing the bag as well. "I'd better pay up and get the goods back to my hubby before his onion soup gets cold. I'm here until Thursday, call me if you have time. We can do lunch and catch up. Great seeing you both." She made a "call me" sign, putting an imaginary phone up to her ear, before walking away to deal with her takeout order.

"Nice lady," Angela said, when they were alone again. "Hasn't she helped you with a case or two before?"

"Yes, she has. A few times," Saxby said. "She has access to all sorts of information that would take me much longer to dig into. Hmmm. I might just have to take her up on that lunch idea. So, what do you think, settle up here and get home to the couch? Someone told me there might be some *Dragnet* reruns on late."

14

S unday was a quiet day, both around town and at the police station. Sergeant Barstow and Deputy Connor came in to work at their desks for a few hours before joining Saxby in his office for a short meeting. The main development for the day was that Saxby had been able to contact Shelly Vance, the younger sister of Jimmy Dunne and the late Ryan Dunne. He had been candid with her on the phone, telling her that he was investigating several cases that appeared to have some connection to the accident that had killed her brother fifty years earlier. She had been surprised, but had agreed to meet with him the next day at her home in Moorestown. He had also made a courtesy call to the Moorestown Police Department, explaining that he was just looking for background information from Vance, and declining their offer of assistance.

The drive from Cape May to Moorestown the next morning was just short of two hours, with clear weather and light traffic. Roughly fifteen miles east of Philadelphia, the town, with its colonial origins, was known for quiet neighborhoods of stately homes set well back from tree-lined streets. Though he hadn't driven through the town for years, Saxby was familiar with the area, and had no trouble finding Shelly Vance's Tudor-style house. After careful consideration that morning, Saxby had decided to forego his standard "small town police chief uniform" of blue jeans and khaki shirt, opting instead for a casual but neat slacks and blazer combo. A knitted tie in a muted blue-check pattern set off his freshly pressed light-cream shirt. The blazer was cut generously enough to cover the badge and gun on his hip without the telltale bulge. He thought the outfit made him look the part of a homicide detective, if not the big-city silk-suited variety.

As he started up the brick path that paralleled the driveway, he noticed a woman off to one side using a rake to clear dead leaves out from between a group of young trees. She noticed him at the same time, dropping the rake to come over to him. She was dressed for yard work in faded jeans and an oversized flannel shirt. The heavy shirt reminded Saxby of something that Angela wore on occasion, and referred to as a "shacket."

"Good morning," she said. "May I assume you're Chief Saxby, up from Cape May?"

"Yes, ma'am, that's me," Saxby said, holding out his identification for her inspection. "Are you Shelly Vance?"

"I am her, yes," Vance said. "Apologies for my appearance. My husband and I just got home yesterday from two weeks in Washington State, and I was just trying to take advantage of the sunny day to do some catching-up on the yard."

"No apology needed, Mrs. Vance," Saxby said. "You're dressed just like I would be for yardwork, and anyway, I appreciate your making time for me today. I did check in with your local police, by the way, to let them know I'd be up here. A routine courtesy call is what we call it."

"Well, let's go inside, then," Vance said. "Give me a minute to wash up a bit and I'll put on a pot of coffee."

Ten minutes later, mugs of coffee in hand, Saxby and Mrs. Vance sat across from each other in a sunny room overlooking a small but well-manicured back yard. Several dogwood trees were showing the first hints of spring blossoms soon to come, and leaves were starting to sprout all over a massive maple.

"When we talked on the phone yesterday," Vance said, "you said you wanted to ask me about my brother Ryan and the accident. My gosh, that was fifty years ago, wasn't it? How did that all fly by so fast?"

"Fifty years is right, Mrs. Vance," Saxby said. "Within about two months. I'm sorry to have to dredge all that up. As I understand it, you were very young when it happened, seven or eight? Do I have that right?"

"That's about right, yes," Vance said. "It was May, so, I was eight, Jimmy was twelve, and Ryan was sixteen. That was so long ago. I miss him, you know. Ryan, I mean. Honestly, I don't have many memories of him, but I still feel the loss. As I've gotten older, I've noticed sometimes that it's hard for me to picture his face. I try to concentrate but it doesn't always come to me. I have some old pictures of course, but it makes me angry sometimes that I have to dig out a photo album to remind me of my brother's face."

"I can imagine that could be very upsetting," Saxby said. "But it's a good thing you have the photos for when you need them."

"You're absolutely right, Chief Saxby," Vance said. "I'm glad to have them. Sorry about all that. Funny how it can all come flooding back when I least expect it. So why is this coming up again all of a sudden? Ryan's death was an accident. Is the case being re-opened for some reason?"

"No, no, it's nothing like that," Saxby said. "There's no doubt, as far as I'm aware, that your brother's death was an accident. But some recent events have caused me—the police, I mean—to need to look again at what happened back then. This is going to sound strange, so please bear with me." Saxby paused to take a sip of coffee and think about how best to proceed. "In the last week or so, in Cape May, we've had two suspicious deaths. Well, murders, frankly. There's also a similar case in Somers Point. Again, clearly a murder as well. We believe that all three are connected in a way that's related to your brother's death back in 1972."

"Oh my God, that's ... that's just ... I mean, really?" Vance said. "How could that even be, after all this time?"

"Well, Mrs. Vance, I did tell you this was going to sound strange," Saxby said. "The thing is, you may remember that Ryan was under the boardwalk that day with six other boys. Six of his friends. They were all sixteen or close, and all from the high school class of 1974."

"Yes, sure, I remember that," Vance said. "I mean, I'm not sure I understood it at the time, but in the years that came after, everybody knew that he'd been there with six of his friends."

"Right, so that's the thing," Saxby said. "Those three men I mentioned, the two in Cape May and the one in Somers Point? They were three of the six. They were all under the boardwalk that day with your brother."

Mrs. Vance set down her coffee cup almost hard enough to break it, and did a sharp intake of breath. She looked around the room, and Saxby was struck by the idea that she was looking for a ghost that had just rapped sharply on the paneling.

"Now I'm trying to remember who those six boys were," Vance said, after taking a moment to compose herself. "I knew them, or most of them anyway, at least a little bit, when I got older. One of them was named 'Roseman,' with a funny first name. Boyd? Something like that. I remember John Hallman, and everybody knew Frankie Deutsch."

"You're on the right track," Saxby said. "It was Boone Roseman, and not John but Bob Hallman. We found Boone Roseman first, a week ago. We later learned that Frankie Deutsch had been killed in Somers Point a few days before that. We believe Bob Hallman to be alive and well in California."

"This is just incredible," Vance said. "Boone and Frankie are both dead, then? Can you tell me who the other one is? The third one?"

"That would be Jeffrey Tanner," Saxby said. "The circumstances of his case are less clear, but we're treating it as a likely homicide. We started to suspect that the cases were connected before we had any idea what that connection might be. I'm sure you can understand why we need to take a hard look at the circumstances around the accident."

"I think I remember one of them named Jeff," Vance said. "This is so incredible. Are you thinking that someone is punishing those boys? Everyone knew it was an accident, right?"

"That is my understanding, yes," Saxby said. "It was ruled an accident and none of the six boys were charged. But now we have to consider that there may be someone out there who holds them responsible. Mrs. Vance, I realize I've already upset you by bringing this all up again, but I'm afraid I may upset you even more. We've learned about an incident involving your brother Jimmy that happened some years after Ryan's death, when Jimmy was twenty or twenty-one. There was a scuffle in a local bar, no doubt some alcohol had been consumed, and he apparently started going on about how the six boys were responsible because they had run away—something like that. One of the six boys was there that night, and witnesses recall your brother yelling at him, threatening him, and eventually punching him. That's as far as it went, and the whole situation was defused when the police arrived. I don't believe your brother or anyone was charged."

"I remember hearing that he had gotten into trouble at a bar one night," Vance said, "but I never knew that it was about that. Are you suggesting that Jimmy could be attacking these men now, after all these years? You know that sounds crazy, right?"

"Yes, I do know it sounds crazy," Saxby said. "The whole situation sounds crazy, Mrs. Vance. But at the moment, Jimmy is the only person we know of who's known to have threatened revenge—if I can put it that way—for Ryan's accident. Understand, I'm not accusing him of anything at this point, but you can see how we would need to talk with him. Are you in touch with him?"

Mrs. Vance had gotten up to stand at one of the windows, where she was looking out into the back yard. "Looks like the dogwoods will be blooming soon." Saxby waited in silence while she looked out at the trees a while longer before coming back to her chair. She picked up her coffee cup, looking down into it for a few seconds before setting it down again without drinking. "No. I haven't heard from him for ten or fifteen years. Back then, I know he had been in and out of the country quite a bit. He lived in Cuba for two or three years. I believe he met some people from there when he was in Costa Rica. He hit it off with them, followed them home, and got some kind of work and a place to live. Anyway, as I said, that was more than ten years ago, and I don't know what he's been up to since then. He was always what people might have called 'a troubled kid,' and then later, somewhat of a troubled man. I remember my parents as good parents, and they tried to do what they could with him. I wasn't any help, you know —I was always just the little sister. Thinking about it now, it shouldn't be a mystery that he was affected by Ryan's death. Jimmy looked up to him a lot, and then suddenly he was gone. He must have looked everywhere for a place to put his anger. That's probably what that bar fight was about."

"So, you haven't heard from him in ten or fifteen years, then," Saxby said. "Can you think of anyone else who might have been in contact with him after that? For example, would one of your kids have contacted 'Uncle Jimmy?' "

"No. I can't see that as a possibility," Vance said. "They knew him when they were little, but he wasn't exactly a warm and fuzzy person to be around, you know? We gradually started contacting each other less and less—it went both ways, until finally a few years had gone by. He sent cards when our parents died, but he didn't show up. I've always figured that he probably went back to Costa Rica, or maybe even Cuba again, but I don't really know that."

"From what you remember about Jimmy," Saxby said, "is it your sense that he carried anger about Ryan's death for a long time? How to put this ... was he haunted by it? Was he obsessed with getting even with someone over it?"

"Hmmm. Haunted? Maybe. That might be a word to describe how he was," Vance said. "I think obsessed is too strong a word. I mean, the situation you mentioned at the bar that night, I'm not very surprised about that. I'm sure the beer, or whatever he was drinking, had something to do with it too. He could have a short fuse."

"Mrs. Vance, what we're dealing with here is strange stuff," Saxby said. "Believe me when I tell you that I get that. With that in mind, I have to ask—do you think your brother Jimmy is capable of physical violence? Related to Ryan's death or otherwise?"

"Oh wow. Okay. I guess I understand that you have to ask that," Vance said. "I haven't really known him for so long, but yes, I'd have to say that he's capable of violence, if that's the question. He definitely has a dark side. If the question is 'Do I think he did these things,' then I'd have to say no, I don't. I can't see it. But somebody did, right? And you have a job to do. Oh my God. My poor brothers. How different things could have been if those boys had just gone fishing that day instead of drinking and smoking pot. Damn it. There I go again, Chief Saxby. I'm sorry."

"There's no need to be sorry, Mrs. Vance," Saxby said. "I didn't just drive up here to find out where Jimmy is. I came up here also to hear your thoughts on the situation, and I'm grateful that you've been willing to share them so openly. Can you think of anyone else who might be able to help us find him? Maybe some old friend of his in Cape May?"

"I've thought about that off and on while we've been talking," Vance said. "And I'm afraid I really can't help you there. We didn't have the same circle of friends at all, and then he was in and out of town a number of times, until finally leaving for good. No, I'm sorry, nobody comes to mind. I'll be happy to let you know if I think of anything."

"Thanks, I appreciate that," Saxby said. "Two more things, if I may. Could you spare a photo of him, as recent as possible? I'm happy to make a copy and get it back to you if you don't have one to spare."

"Sure. I can get you a pretty good picture that you can keep," Vance said. "I have some saved and I can always print out another. What was the other thing?"

"In the event that we're able to find Jimmy," Saxby said, "can you tell me something about your childhood that he would remember, but people outside the family wouldn't know? Just to help make sure we're talking to the right person?"

"You mean like a sort of codeword? Something like that?" Vance said. She thought for a moment. "We had a dog when we were little, that was mostly Jimmy's dog. Her name was Cleopatra. We called her Cleo. We had that dog for years and Jimmy was very fond of her. She was a beagle. There's no way he'd forget about Cleo."

Forty-five minutes later, Saxby was cruising down the Atlantic City Expressway, eastbound towards the junction with the Garden State Parkway and points south. The meeting with Shelly Vance had been interesting, but not conclusive in any way. In fact, he thought to himself, he might even have more unanswered questions than he had yesterday. She had been clear that she didn't believe her brother Jimmy was the killer, but at the same time she admitted that she couldn't rule it out. He was fully capable of great anger and violence. In the end though, she had been open with Saxby in saying that she didn't really know him, at least not as an adult in recent years.

He was lost in thought and trying to square up all the different angles in his head, when his cell phone rang, sending its loud buzz through the car's speakers. He hit the button to take a call from Sergeant Barstow. "Afternoon, Vic. What's going on? Are you calling to tell me you've solved all our recent crimes?"

"Ah … I'm sorry I can't tell you that, Chief," Barstow said, "but I'm working on it. Are you on your way back?"

"Yes. I'm on the expressway and I just passed the service plaza," Saxby said. "ETA Cape May Police Station about fifty-six minutes." He knew that Barstow loved to rib him about his uncanny ability to say exactly what time he would arrive somewhere.

"Fifty-six minutes, okay then. I'll set my watch," Barstow said. "How did it go with Mrs. Vance?"

"It went well, I guess," Saxby said. "Very nice lady and happy to help, but the bottom line is that she hasn't seen Jimmy Dunne in years and doesn't feel like she's known him very well since way back when. I'll fill you in on the rest later, but no real answers. How about from your end?"

"Interesting development down here today," Barstow said. "I was planning to call Doug Lawson this morning, but he beat me to it. He actually called in to the station to make a report, and talked to Doreen, and then I drove over to see him. Somebody attacked him late Friday night outside his house. He was walking out to his back shed and somebody jumped out of the hedge and tried to club him. He was able to duck in time to just get a whack on a shoulder. The guy ran off pretty fast and Lawson said he thinks it was probably because a car had pulled up on the side street and the lights scared him away. Lucky timing for him, I guess. He's shook up, but okay. He's going to get a friend to come stay with him for a few days."

"Wait a minute," Saxby said. "He says somebody attacked him Friday night, and he's just getting around to telling us on Monday?"

"Looks that way, Chief," Barstow said. "And I asked him about that. He said he wasn't really hurt and was back and forth about it until a friend of his basically demanded that he report it."

"All right, sounds pretty dumb, but it is what it is," Saxby said. "That just about puts a bow on the whole thing, doesn't it? That's four of them attacked now. Was he able to give you a description, or did he have any idea who it was?"

"He did give me a general description," Barstow said. "But also, he thinks he knows who it was. Here's where I would ask if you're sitting down, but I already know you're driving."

"Lay it on me, Vic," Saxby said. "Who does he think it was?"

"He thinks it was the guy who threatened him and punched him in the Anchorage Bar about forty years ago," Barstow said. "He thinks it was Jimmy Dunne."

"What? Are you...? Hang on a minute, Vic," Saxby said. He was quiet for half a minute as he took the exit for Parkway south towards Cape May and the other shore towns, merging back into traffic as he came up the ramp. "So, you're saying we have a possible Jimmy Dunne sighting in Cape May. How sure did he seem about it? Did he see the guy's face?"

"My guess is that he was a little more than half sure," Barstow said. "Three-quarters maybe. He says he only caught a quick glance of the man's face in the flash of head-lights when the car was parking nearby, but the more he thought about it, the more he thought it was Dunne. There's something else though. When Lawson started thinking the guy was Dunne, he remembered that he thought he saw him leaving the Acme early last week. He said a man walking out with a bag of groceries looked familiar, but he couldn't remember from where. After last night, he remembered the guy at the Acme and started to put it together. I checked with the Acme, and unfortu-nately, they've already deleted the footage from the day

Lawson was there."

"Oh, that's too bad, but okay then. If he's right about all that," Saxby said, "it could mean that Dunne's been in the area for a while, stalking all these guys. Lawson could be wrong though, so let's proceed with that in mind. How are we doing with going back to the folks we talked to last week about Roseman and Tanner?"

"Three spent most of the day on that," Barstow said. "And I talked to a few people too. Several of them—the older people, mainly—remember the accident, but nobody would say they were aware of Roseman or Tanner being threatened or worried about anything related to it."

"I'll be there in less than forty-five minutes," Saxby said. "How about if you save the rest and let's get together in my office when we get back. Grab Three, too, if he's available."

"Will do, Chief," Barstow said. "Drive safe and we'll see you back at the ranch when you get here."

It was almost three when Saxby, back in the station and fortified with a Wawa sandwich, called Sergeant Barstow and Deputy Connor into his office.

"Have a seat, guys," Saxby said. "This shouldn't take very long, but I wanted to hear how it went with your recent interviews. Vic told me earlier that Doug Lawson believes he was attacked by Jimmy Dunne last Friday night, but let's set that on a shelf for the moment. Aside from Lawson, when is the last time anyone saw Jimmy Dunne and does anyone think they know where he could be? Also, what, if anything, are people saying about Ryan

Dunne's accident and who might still be upset about that?"

"I got to speak with five people that I had talked to about Boone Roseman recently," Connor said, "including two who might be old enough to remember the accident. Three of them, including the older two, were aware that Roseman had been one of the six friends of Ryan Dunne, but none of them had any sense that it was something that he ever talked about, or that it was something he was worried about. When I framed it like … 'Could they think of anyone who might be out there trying to get even in some way', nobody went for that idea. The one man, Keith Hopkins, told me that he'd been in the Anchorage that night when Jimmy Dunne was yelling at Doug Lawson and others, but he also remembered seeing Dunne over the years after that, and thinking that he'd gotten over it, like, made peace with it. I guess in summary, Chief, nothing much useful from the Roseman contacts. Oh—that same man—Hopkins—is the only one who remembers seeing Dunne in town. He's pretty sure it was almost fifteen years ago, and that Dunne said he'd been in Cuba, and was headed back there to live. He hasn't seen or heard from him since."

"Interesting. That's the second mention I've heard today about Dunne spending time in Cuba," Saxby said. "His sister told me he had lived there for a few years. That could be important, but I don't see why yet."

"I have a third, Chief," Barstow said. "Speaking of older people in town. I took a break earlier and walked over to Starla's, where I bumped into Bob Neville. He was having coffee and a muffin at one of the tables and I sat down with him for a few minutes. You know, he's been here since before I was born. I figured he'd be a good person to chat up. He remembered the accident, and he also was aware that—as he put it—'there was a pissed-off younger brother.' Neville's daughter dated Jimmy Dunne for a while, apparently, and they remained friends for some time after. Unfortunately, we don't get to talk to her because she passed away a few years ago, but Neville remembered that Dunne had traveled out of the country a lot. Central America, he thought, but also Cuba. For what it's worth, he was skeptical of the whole revenge idea, but admitted that Dunne had been very angry, at least for a time. Neville thought it's been twenty years or more since he's seen Dunne or heard anything about him, until today."

"Okay, well, nothing conclusive yet, but good information," Saxby said. "I get the general picture that people who know at least a little bit about the accident or have had dealings with Jimmy Dunne don't put much stock in the revenge idea, but at the same time nominate him as the most likely candidate if there was something to it. Is that a fair way to put it?"

"I think so, Chief," Connor said. "Pretty vague stuff so far, unfortunately, but we'll keep plugging at it."

"What about the Tanner family?" Saxby asked. "Have we spoken with either Paul Tanner or his mother?"

"Paul Tanner was next on my to-do list," Barstow said. "I called his office earlier and was told that he'd be in all day and I could stop by whenever."

"You know what, Vic," Saxby said, "let me take Tanner please. I've been meaning to check in with him anyway. I think it's time he knew about our change of direction regarding his father's death. Since you've already got a little rapport going with his mother, you can do the same with her. Maybe one of them will know what Jeff Tanner thought about the accident, or if he had ever been threatened." Saxby looked at his watch. "It isn't even four yet. I think I'll jump in the car and go see if I can catch Tanner at his office. Another day of good work so far, Vic and Three. We'll get there."

The headquarters of Tanner Construction, a few short blocks away off of the center of town, was the only building in Cape May that most people would refer to as an "office building." Saxby knew that many in the contracting business worked early shifts, so was not surprised to see, at four-thirty, that the parking lot had already started to empty out. Finding a spot near the main entrance, he went in and easily found the reception area, where a professionally dressed woman sat at a large desk that held several neat stacks of papers and folders along with other expected tools of office life.

"Good afternoon," Saxby said. "Chief Tate Saxby for Paul Tanner please."

"Hello, Chief Saxby," she said. "Yes, I believe Mr. Tanner has been expecting someone from your office today. Let me just give him a quick buzz." It occurred to Saxby that the phone system she used to call Tanner had more buttons on it than any phone he'd ever seen. Certainly, more than the system at the police station. He wondered to himself how they could possibly all be needed.

"You can head on back, Chief Saxby," she said, setting the phone back into its cradle. "End of the hall, last door on the left."

Saxby nodded his thanks and went down the carpeted corridor, finding Tanner's office door open. His knock on the doorframe was answered with a somewhat muffled voice coming from the other side of a partly open door across the spacious office. Saxby crossed the office as he answered. "Is that you, Mr. Tanner? I couldn't quite hear you."

"I'm sorry, I'm just finishing up," Tanner said, after he pushed the door open revealing the small room he was in to be a brightly lit and well-appointed bathroom, complete with a stall shower. Tanner finished drying his hands with a small towel and stepped back into the office, buttoning up his shirtsleeves. "Pardon me, Chief Saxby. My father had the full bath installed when this was originally his office years ago. I've gotten into the habit of doing a 'freshen-up' most days in the late afternoon. Gives me a little break and something of a second wind to tackle the last tasks of the day, which sometimes go well into the evening. Good to see you, though I was expecting your Sergeant Barstow. Is she okay?"

"She's fine, Mr. Tanner," Saxby said. "I just felt like it was time I checked in with you. Overdue, in fact. How are you and the family holding up?"

"Oh, we're fine, for the most part," Tanner said. "Life goes on, and I suppose it's good for me that I have this business to run. Keeps me moving around and occupied." He gestured to a sitting area with several chairs around a low table. There was a stack of newspaper on the table that he squared up and pushed to one side as they sat down.

"Ah, *The New York Times*," Saxby said. "So, you're a puzzle man like me. Looks like you're almost done. Impressive."

"My father got me hooked on that years ago," Tanner said. "Even though it's 'brain work,' I find the focus can be very relaxing when I need a short break. I do the puzzle for twenty minutes, and then I'm ready for the next call with an angry supplier. You must have similar situations in your line of work."

"Oh yes, I sure do," Saxby said. "I might have to take your advice and try that. Could be just the thing for right after a meeting with the town council."

"You called this meeting, Chief," Tanner said, "but let me ask you, have you come to the conclusion that my father's death was other than an accident?"

"Yes, I'm afraid so," Saxby said. "That's why I mentioned that my coming to see you was overdue. I can tell you that right now, we, along with the county, are treating your father's death as a homicide. A number of things have come to light over these past few days that have led us to that decision."

Tanner took a few deep breaths and shook his head a few times before looking back at Saxby. "My God. It's come to this, then. I think you may have known I had a feeling that something was off. Are there ... I mean why? Do you have any suspects?"

"Let's not rush ahead too much, Mr. Tanner," Saxby said, "but I'll tell you what I can. It's been an interesting few days, with some developments that are quite strange, frankly. And that's probably putting it mildly. Anyway, we now believe that your father's death, along with the recent deaths of two other local men, is related to the accidental death of a teenage boy in Cape May almost fifty years ago. Were you aware of the circumstances around the death of Ryan Dunne, back in May of 1972?"

"Yes, I know about that from my father," Tanner said. "It was before I was even born, but he told me about it. He talked about it a few times."

"Okay, so you know that your father, when he was sixteen, was one of Ryan Dunne's friends under the boardwalk that day," Saxby said. "Your father and five other kids, all about the same age."

"Yes, again, I don't want to say that he talked about it a lot," Tanner said. "There wasn't any reason to. But he told me about it. I think it was one of the regrets of his life. I mean, you probably know that they all caught some flak for running away, until one of them told their parents. But there was no question that it was an accident. Somebody told me ages ago that the boy died almost instantly."

"That fits with how I understand it," Saxby said. "Can I assume that you knew about the death of Boone Roseman about ten nights ago? Not last night, but the Sunday prior?"

"Sure, I heard about it. Hard to think there's anybody in town who didn't," Tanner said. "He was attacked in his apartment on Columbia, right? Or was it Washington Street?"

"That's right, Columbia," Saxby said. "Someone killed him in his apartment. At first, we thought it was drug-related, like so much crime is, but we've come to think differently about it. There was another fatal attack, with some similarities, that Cape May people may not have heard about, because it happened up in Somers Point several days before."

"No, you're right, I hadn't heard about that," Tanner said. "That's obviously terrible, but how is that related to my father? Or Boone Roseman, for that matter?"

"Your father," Saxby said, "along with Boone Roseman, and the man up in Somers Point, whose name was Frankie Deutsch, make up three of the six boys who were under the boardwalk that day, and, as you put it, ran away. With some great reluctance, and skepticism, I've had to come around to believing that somebody is targeting these men because of the way they behaved on that day."

Tanner's eyes went wide and his mouth fell open for a few seconds before he managed to speak. "Whoa. You knocked the words out of me for a second there. Is that even really possible? That's some incredible stuff you're suggesting. Some kind of revenge, then. Wow."

"It is incredible, yes," Saxby said. "And it took us some time to get to it , but that's where the evidence leads us, if only circumstantial so far."

"What about the other three men, then?" Tanner said. "You must have looked for them, right? Are they still in town?"

"We have tracked them down, yes," Saxby said. "One is deceased years ago, another is alive and well in California, but the last one, Doug Lawson, is still here in town. He has reported that someone tried to attack him outside his home a few nights ago, but he wasn't seriously hurt. Part of the reason I'm telling you all this, Mr. Tanner, is that we're looking for anyone who might have some idea about who would have a motive to hurt these men. We're talking to other people also. Mind you—we have our own ideas, but right now I'm asking if you have any thoughts on the matter."

"Hmmm. Yes, I see," Tanner said. "I can't say it's anything I've ever had to think about, so this is all new to me. I might need some time to mull it over. One thing I remember my father telling me is that Ryan Dunne had a younger brother. Jim, or Jimmy was his name, I think. My father told me that he had run into this guy once, this Jimmy, and he'd yelled at my father. 'You assholes could have saved him,' or something like that. It was just some yelling, according to my father, not any kind of fight. I think that was the last my father ever heard from him."

"Was there any time after that," Saxby said, "that you got the sense that your father felt threatened, or was threatened? Worried about Dunne coming after him or the others? Anything at all like that?"

Tanner seemed to think carefully before speaking. "No. Not that I can think of. That time I just mentioned was the last time my father had any contact with him. If it was something he worried about but kept to himself, I guess I can't rule that out, but I doubt it."

"Are you aware of your father being friends with Boone Roseman?" Saxby said. "Same question for Frankie Deutsch in Somers Point."

"Well, we know they were friends on some level back when they were teenagers," Tanner said. "But as far as I can recall, they didn't stay close later in life. I knew Boone from around town, same as my father, but they didn't cross paths very often. So, friendly yes, but friends—I wouldn't say that. And the Somers Point guy doesn't ring a bell to me at all."

"Well, okay, then," Saxby said. "Oh, just so you're aware, in case your mother mentions it, Sergeant Barstow was going over to have a similar conversation with her. If either of you think of anything, please let us know."

Both men stood up and Saxby started towards the door. "By the way, how are things going over at the Doyle house? No more break-ins, I hope."

"No, I'm glad to say no more trouble over there," Tanner said. "The work should be done in a week or so. We lost several days after … well, you know. There was a lot of paperwork. You know how it is when lawyers get involved."

"Oh yes, I'm familiar with that," Saxby said. "Thanks for your time, Mr. Tanner. I'm sure you'll be hearing from me again soon, but please don't hesitate to call if you think of anything else. We'll get to the bottom of this eventually."

After the meeting with Paul Tanner, Saxby drove along the beachfront, stopping the car at the west end of Beach Avenue to get out for a little fresh air. He looked out across the long curve of empty sand, where the tiny town of South Cape May had stood before much of it was washed away by a hurricane almost eighty years ago. He looked at the spot on the beach about two hundred feet out where, three years before and in the dead of winter, an early morning fisherman had come upon the body of an inno-cent young woman. That had kicked off an incredible investigation into a string of killings with a chilling back-story that he probably wouldn't believe if he hadn't lived through it personally. Farther down the beach, he could see the ruins of the old WWII bunker, with the nearby light-house and the enormous bulk of St. Mary's by the Sea, empty now, but for many years a nun's retreat house. With the ocean air blowing in his face, he closed his eyes for a moment, remembering a more recent multiple-murder case that had ended with a deadly shootout in the street on a dark, rainy night. The memory brought a sudden pang of pain to the wound in his side where a bullet had grazed him that night. A phantom pain, but a pain nonetheless, that came back to visit him every now and then. *And now it looks like we're at it again,* he thought to himself. *What the hell is it all about this time? And how many more will die?*

The ring of his phone brought him out of his reverie, and he turned back to the car as he hit the button to take the call from his friend Joanne Belli.

"Well, hello, Mrs. Belli," Saxby said. "How nice to hear from you again in such a short time. Were you thinking of getting together before you have to head back up north?"

"Yeah, why don't we?" Belli said. "Al has to go up the road for some appointments tomorrow, and I wouldn't mind an excuse to get out of the house. What do you think of lunch tomorrow?"

They chatted back and forth for a few minutes, agreeing to meet at the C-View Inn the next day, before ending the call.

Saxby turned back to the beach, taking in a long last look up across the sand and the waves to a sunset painted in brilliant hues of yellow, orange, and red. He waited for the lighthouse beacon to come around again, sending its beam out across the water, before getting back into his car. *It may take me some time, but whoever you are, I'm going to find you*, he said aloud to himself under his breath, as he drove away.

15

Saxby found the lunch with Joanne Belli to be a very pleasant interlude, even if they were interrupted several times by local people who hadn't seen her in a long time and wanted to say hello. After their plates were cleared away, Joanne ordered coffee while Saxby opted instead for a refill of his iced tea.

"That case you're working on makes for quite a story," Belli said. "You've had a hell of a run over the past few years. Makes my job seem like watching paint dry."

"It has been a heck of a few years, hasn't it?" Saxby said. "My team hardly has any time at all to write up parking tickets. Anyway, you're exaggerating. I'm sure you get to work on all kinds of exciting things. Jetting all over the country and meeting all sorts of interesting criminals and all that."

"I don't know, Tate," Belli said. "The most interesting criminals I've heard about lately seem to pop up right here in town. At least it keeps you on your toes, right?"

"Yeah, it does," Saxby said. "I'm just not convinced it's a good thing. There is something you could help me with—if I haven't worn out my supply of favors, that is. I don't want to ask you to do anything you're not supposed to do."

"Thanks for that," Belli said, "but I actually have a lot of leeway when it comes to helping law enforcement. If I can help you, I will. What do you need?"

"That man I told you about—Jimmy Dunne," Saxby said, "we've heard from several people that he has some history in both Costa Rica and Cuba. Cuba most recently, and apparently, he's actually lived there off and on. Like for years, is what people have said. Are you able to put out some kind of request to see if there's any record of him coming in or going out of the country recently? Costa Rica or Cuba, in particular, but I'll take what I can get."

"Sure, I can do that," Belli said. "Since we're thinking that Cuba is a possibility, I'll make it a joint request with Canada. U.S. citizens can travel to Cuba, but only for certain reasons and only with the right paperwork. If it were me, and I wanted to go on the lam to Cuba, I'd go up to Canada and leave from there, where it's much easier. Other than that, I'm sure plenty of people go down to Florida and get on some boat or other. Havana's only about ninety miles from Key West. But if your guy isn't inclined towards boats, then I would say Canada is the way to go. I can put that in this afternoon. Shouldn't take more than a few hours to get results, if there are any."

"That sounds great, Joanne," Saxby said. "I want to be clear though, that I'm not asking for any action to be taken —just for any info you can find. All he really is at the moment is a person of interest. It's funny, because he almost seems like a ghost. A number of people have said they saw him ten years ago, or twelve years ago. They heard he said this or that, or they thought he did so and so. Or 'my friend told me they saw him'—that sort of thing. There's a part of me that wouldn't be surprised if he turned out to not even be real. I don't know. I guess I'm just tired and could really use a break with this. One thing is, if he turns out to be 'the guy,' I have a feeling that he may be done with what he was doing here. That's why I'm thinking it's possible that he's left the country."

"On that, there's something you should bear in mind," Belli said. "If this Jimmy Dunne is your guy, and he really has left the country for Cuba, there probably isn't much you can do about it. It's a crummy situation, I know, but if he's back in Havana, it's likely that he's safe there. With or without the State Department getting involved, I can't imagine the Cubans handing him over."

"Yeah, I understand," Saxby said. "And likewise, I doubt the State Department would take it up. If that's how it turns out, we'll deal with it, but let's see if we can figure out where he is and take it from there."

"That's a good plan. Anyway, I'm glad to help. We'll see what we find," Belli said. "And I'll let you get lunch."

Saxby laughed and signaled for the check.

Outside on the sidewalk, as they stood talking for a few minutes, Saxby noticed the pair of surveillance cameras mounted on the building just under the eaves.

"Remember I told you about how we spent all that time looking at the footage from the camera in the Wawa parking lot?" Saxby said.

"It turned out to be a dead end, right?" Belli said. "With

the potato chip truck and the long songs playing on the radio." She was looking at one of the cameras, and turned to follow a sightline across the street and down a hundred feet or so towards the Wawa market. "You'd have to check, but that one camera on the right might give you a good, wide view of the whole area. Hopefully it's a recent hi-res unit."

"I think we're going to have to look into that," Saxby said. "I'll get one of my deputies on it."

"I'll be in touch as soon as I can. Probably tomorrow morning, but possibly late tonight," Belli said, before getting into her car and driving away.

As soon as Saxby got back to the station, he took a walk around, checking in with all the officers he could find. He saved the stop at Sergeant Barstow's desk for last, telling her about his lunch meeting with Agent Belli and how she was going to check on border crossings. "As long as we're doing that, I'd like you to go ahead and put in that national BOLO. We need to get to the bottom of where this Jimmy Dunne is, or if he's even still in the country. Last thing—do you know where Three is?"

"He's out on patrol, Chief," Barstow said. "There was a fender-bender outside the Mad Batter on Jackson Street. He's there with Brody and one or two of the others."

"Fine. No need to interrupt him," Saxby said. "Okay, then. I should be at my desk for the next few hours. Thanks, Vic."

He left Barstow to continue her work, heading back to his desk, where he put in a call to Detective Dooley. They talked back and forth for twenty minutes, going over the combined cases and catching each other up on recent developments.

"I agree that it's time to put our foot on the pedal and find Dunne," Dooley said. "The thing is, if he isn't our guy, I'm not sure where to go next. We'll have to recalibrate."

"Agree with you on that, Tom," Saxby said. "But I'm sure we'll figure it out. I'll be in touch."

Shortly after nine that evening, while Saxby was at home helping Angela unpack boxes and move things around the kitchen, Agent Belli called. He rushed to find his phone amongst the boxes and bubble wrap.

"Sorry for the delay there, Joanne," Saxby said. "You caught us rearranging the kitchen and I had to rummage around for my phone. Are you calling to tell me you've already gotten a hit on the border crossing?"

"As a matter of fact, I am," Belli said. "Sometimes things happen fast. I don't have much, but I can tell you that a U.S. citizen by the name of James Dunne boarded Air Canada flight 108 at 6:30 Sunday evening, in Toronto. I'll give you three guesses where it was going, and the first two don't count."

"Hmmm, let me see, then," Saxby said. "The only guess I have is Cuba. Toronto to Havana."

"Bingo. As you suspected," Belli said. "The traveler was

a white male, sixty-two years old, with a home address in Falcon Heights, Minnesota, which is a suburb between Minneapolis and St. Paul. The passport number is valid in our system, and I've emailed you the photo. Before you ask, that's about as far as I get with Canadian records without putting in a further inquiry, so I don't have any travel history for you. The other thing, Tate, is for now I want you to take all this with a grain of salt, because there's something strange that I need to track down. The record of this border crossing had a flag attached to it, and I don't know yet what that means. I have a call in to a tech guy I know who I'm sure will be able to explain it to me. I'll try to get with him in the morning."

"A flag you say, hmmm," Saxby said. "You mean like there was some kind of violation, or something wrong with the passport?"

"That could be it," Belli said. "Or it could just be a remark, or memo, that was put in manually. It may be nothing at all—I don't know yet. It's something I haven't seen before. I'll find out as soon as I can and report back to you."

"Okay, I got it. I'll wait to hear what you find out tomorrow," Saxby said. "Aside from that, he sounds like the right age. I don't recall Minnesota coming up when I met with his sister the other day, but I'll check with her on that. Thanks, Joanne. Anything else?"

"That's all for now," Belli said. "I see if I can get anything else tomorrow and let you know."

"So, Joanne found the guy you were looking for?" Angela said, after Saxby ended the call. "Jimmy Dunne?"

"I can't say she found him," Saxby said. "Because it looks

like he's flown the coop back to Cuba. If that's the case, then we'll have to see where we go next. The fact is, really, we don't have anything on him that isn't circumstantial or hearsay, but man, if it's him, I hope he doesn't get away clean. Cuba would never turn him over to us."

16

Saxby made it another early morning in the office, and by the time Sergeant Barstow appeared in the doorway at nine, he'd already cleared out his inbox for the day, and had just clicked "Send" on the last of several city email chains that had been waiting for his comment.

"Morning, Chief. Good time to interrupt?" Barstow said.

"It's a great time, Vic," Saxby said. "I've been plowing through paperwork like a white tornado since seven, and I'm ready to do something else. Not to mention that my coffee's cold and bitter. Follow me to the kitchen and I'll tell you about the call I got at home last night."

They walked together to the kitchen, where Saxby fixed himself a fresh coffee and related the details of the call from Agent Belli.

"So, depending on what your friend finds out about this 'flag' on the record, it looks like Jimmy Dunne may have gone back to Cuba," Barstow said. She had a skeptical look on her face that Saxby had seen before. "That's very interesting, because about ten minutes ago we got a hit on the BOLO."

"Really, now," Saxby said. "I didn't see that coming. What did we get?"

"It came from a county sheriff in Minnesota by the name of Bill Ambrose," Barstow said. "He's got a man named Jimmy Dunne in his lockup, moving to a state prison in a few days. The guy was an accessory to some small-time robbery. A jewelry store smash and grab I think it was. He seems to fit our description, though we don't have a photo yet."

"Well, I sure don't know everything," Saxby said, "but I'm damn sure that Jimmy Dunne can't be in both places at once. Clearly, one of these reports is wrong, but which one? Or is it both? We've got some work to do, Vic."

The next two hours were busy ones, filled with a flurry of emails and phone calls. Saxby printed out the passport photo of Jimmy Dunne that Agent Belli had sent him, while Barstow was able to obtain a copy of the recent mugshot from the Hennepin County Sheriff's Department in Minnesota. They compared both to the photo that Dunne's sister Shelly Vance had given to Saxby during his meeting with her, agreeing that the three photos appeared to be of the same man. As an extra check, Saxby was able to contact Vance to ask her to look at the passport and mugshot photos, with her agreeing that they appeared to be her brother. They all agreed that Vance's photo of

Dunne was the oldest, with the next being the passport photo and the mugshot the most recent.

"Which makes sense," Saxby said, talking it over with Barstow in his office. "The one his sister gave me shows him about fifteen years ago, and the mugshot was taken inside the last six months or so. The one on the passport could be five years or more old, from whenever he last renewed it."

"I started off the day thinking I knew which way was up," Barstow said, "but now I'm not so sure. These both seem like such reliable sources."

Saxby held up his hand as his cell phone buzzed, and he looked at the screen, seeing the call was from Agent Belli. He tapped the screen to take the call. "A good late morning to my favorite Homeland Security agent."

"Morning to you, Tate," Belli said. "I've got some interesting information for you on that customs record. As a matter of fact, I have a friend of mine, Vijay Bassavarra, from our technical support team on the line. Vijay's been looking at that customs flag for me. I thought it would be easier if we just got on a call so you can hear it right from him."

"Okay, got it. Sounds like a great idea," Saxby said. "And if nobody objects, I'm going to put you on speaker, because I have Sergeant Vicki Barstow in my office with me. I'd like her to hear this also." No objections followed and Saxby tapped his screen to make the change.

"Alright, then. From what we've learned this morning," Belli said, "it looks like we do not actually have a record of Jimmy Dunne leaving the country. Vijay, would you mind telling us what you found please?"

"Certainly, no problem," Vijay said. "Hello, everyone. So, Joanne—Agent Belli—put in a standard trace yesterday afternoon, which returned a result about four hours later. Only thing is, she noticed that the record had what we call a 'flag.' To a user, it's like you're looking at the form on your screen, and one of the fields is highlighted in a different color, but there isn't any visible key that tells you what it means. See, it's the different colors that point to the various arrays in the database, and once you—"

"Excuse me, Vijay, these folks are really smart," Belli said, "but you're the only master programmer here. Can you just tell us what it means, please?"

"Right, yes. I'm sorry," Vijay said. "Joanne yelled at me earlier for going on about this, and it's just that, well, it's interesting. Anyway, sorry. It took me a while to dig into it, and I had to go to another team member, but basically it looks like the record was cloned from the last record for that same person and passport, which was about five years ago. It was copied from an existing prior record."

"So, just so I'm understanding you," Saxby said, "you're saying that this person, Jimmy Dunne, legitimately flew from Toronto to Havana five years ago, and that just yesterday somebody duplicated that record to make it look like he made the same trip again? Is that what I'm hearing?"

"That's it, Mr. Saxby," Vijay said. "I don't want Joanne to yell at me again, but what it looks like to me, in a clamshell, is that someone changed the time stamp, which then made the old record sort to yesterday's date as if it was current."

"In a clamshell? Oh—right. In a nutshell you mean," Belli said. "Who could have done that though?"

"Nutshell, right, thanks," Vijay said. "Ah, I think just

about anyone with level 4 access and a good knowledge of our system could have done it. Your access would let you do it, if you knew how."

"That's got to be a flaw in your system, right?" Saxby said. "That seems like something that people shouldn't be allowed to do."

"You are right, Mr. Chief Saxby," Vijay said. "And you will be glad to know that I have already put in a request to fix that part of the code. We call that an 'SER' —a 'system enhancement request.' That should be fixed over the weekend."

"Have you been able to tell who did this?" Saxby said. "Who altered the record?"

"Unfortunately, we can't see that now," Vijay said. "The field that should have a user ID in it is blank. That is part of what we are going to fix. Nobody should be able to make a change without leaving a, how do you say...a trail."

"Okay, well, I guess it is what it is, then," Saxby said. "You know what to do to fix your system so this isn't an ongoing issue, but for me at the moment I have two take-aways. One ... Jimmy Dunne has not left the country, and two ... there appears to be someone with a long reach who wanted us to think that he had."

"Chief, I would just clarify," Barstow said, "that we can't accurately say that he hasn't left the country, just that he hasn't done it by flying from Toronto to Havana, or prob-ably flying from any U.S. or Canadian airport."

"Fair point, Vic, and you're right," Saxby said. "That's accurate, but for the moment, my money is on the idea that he's still around somewhere. That is, if he even has anything to do with all this. Anyway, Vijay, thank you very much for your help with this. You too, Joanne, thanks to you both. Much appreciated."

After the call was ended, Saxby and Barstow sat in silence for a moment.

"Where do you think from here now, Chief?" Barstow said. "What are you thinking?"

"I'm thinking that we need to know if this guy is just a ghost, or a memory, or what," Saxby said. "Which means that the next step for me is to get on one of the next flights out to Minneapolis. If our friends in Hennepin County actually have Jimmy Dunne in a cell, that'll be a good, solid piece of information. Who knows? If it's him, and if he'll talk to me, he might have some useful ideas."

"I had a feeling you might say that. Which is why, before I saw you this morning," Barstow said, "I took the liberty of looking at flights, and I saw that they have direct flights now from Atlantic City International to Minneapolis."

"Ah, that's a lucky break," Saxby said. "I'm going to ask Doreen to get me on a flight out there tonight. You can help by contacting Sheriff Ambrose and see if he can get me in to see their version of Jimmy Dunne tomorrow. Find out where I need to go and all that."

"Sure thing, Chief. I'll get on it," Barstow said. "You know, if it turns out that Jimmy Dunne actually is in jail in Minnesota, then Doug Lawson must have been wrong about who attacked him Friday night. I was planning to drive by there today to check up on him. Should I bring that up?"

"Hmmm. You know what, I have an idea," Saxby said. "Because there's another possibility, and that is Lawson's lying. Why he would be, or if, I don't know yet. I'm just saying between you and I that could also be what's going on. Go ahead and check in with him. Legitimate concern for his safety, all that. Take a copy of the passport picture with you. No reason you can't say it's a passport picture of Jimmy Dunne from five years ago. See if he still thinks that's the guy he saw in the Acme and who attacked him. You're just following up now that we've gotten a picture. Other than that, don't mention anything else about all this we've talked about today. Wait till I see what I can do tomorrow, and we'll take it from there, okay? Now, I'd better talk with Doreen and then wrap up a few things here before I go home and pack my toothbrush."

An hour later, while Saxby was at his house throwing an overnight bag together, Sergeant Barstow drove over to Doug Lawson's house again to check in with him. As she made the turn onto his street, she noticed a white pickup truck parked in front of his driveway that hadn't been there earlier. The brake lights were on, and as she came up behind the vehicle, she saw the reverse lights flash as though the driver had just shifted into gear.

She felt an adrenaline boost go through her body as she swerved out to pass and then quickly back to block the pickup with her cruiser. Hitting the switch to turn on the light bar, she got out of the car and started towards the driver's side, with her left hand up in a "Stop" gesture and her right hand resting on the butt of her pistol. The window came down, and the man inside held his hands up in plain view.

"I'm just checking on Doug, Officer," the man said. He was clean-cut and middle-aged, maybe fifty. He wore a clean chambray shirt, and a baseball-style cap in light blue with an embroidered emblem that Barstow didn't recognize. The pickup was free of any markings. "He's my cousin. You can ask him."

"I'll do that, sir," Barstow said, relieved, but still suspicious. "Can I get you to switch off the ignition and step out of the vehicle please?"

"Sure, no problem at all," the man said. He opened the door and stepped out after turning the car off.

At that moment, the front door of the house opened and a man appeared. Barstow heard the door and was further relieved to see that it was Doug Lawson on the porch.

"It's okay, Sergeant," Lawson said. "That's just my cousin, Peter. He dropped off some things I needed."

"Okay, that's good," Barstow said. She turned back to the man with the pickup truck. "So, you've been checking up on Mr. Lawson?"

"A few times, yes," the man said. He pulled out a wallet and dug into it. "The name's Peter Franks. Would you like to see my ID?"

"Sure, thank you," Barstow said. She took a moment to look over the driver's license he handed her before handing it back. "Thank you, Mr. Franks. I'm sorry if I startled you there. We're just very concerned about Mr. Lawson's safety and I didn't recognize your truck. Will you be coming back today?"

"I plan to, yes," Franks said. "I was just dropping off some groceries and other stuff. Now I have an appointment, but I should be back around dinnertime. I was going to pick up Chinese."

"That sounds like a good plan, then," Barstow said. "Will you be in this same truck when you come back? Just so I know who it is and I don't have to cut you off again?"

"Sure, Sergeant, I can do that," Franks said. "I'll make sure I only drive this for the time being."

"And my friend Bernie is here with me, Sergeant," Lawson said. "He'll make sure I'm not alone, and then when Pete comes back there'll be three of us." As he finished speaking, another man of about Lawson's age came out of the house and stood beside him on the porch. He gave Barstow a friendly wave.

"And this blue Chevy here," Barstow said, "is that Bernie's car? In back of your Camry?"

"That's right," Lawson said. "That's Bernie's Malibu, and my Camry in front of that."

"All right, then. I'll make sure the other officers have that information, and I think we have a plan," Barstow said. "You're certainly clear to go, Mr. Franks. Thanks for your cooperation."

Franks got back into his pickup and left, first backing up to maneuver around the police car.

As he drove away, Barstow climbed the steps up to the porch, unfolding the copy of Jimmy Dunne's passport photo. "I almost forgot, Mr. Lawson, we were able to get a copy of Jimmy Dunne's passport picture from about five years ago. Do you think this could be the man who attacked you the other night? And who you thought you saw in the Acme?" She handed the paper to Lawson, who studied it carefully.

"Well, it was dark," Lawson said. "And the whole thing scared the heck out of me, but yes. I'm pretty sure that's him."

"Seventy percent? Ninety percent?" Barstow said.

"How about eighty-five percent?" Lawson said. "Yeah, that's about it. I can't say for certain, but yeah, I'm pretty sure that's him."

"Okay. That's good enough for now, then. Thanks," Barstow said. "Please call me if anything changes. If anything strange happens, or if you need to leave the house, anything at all. I'll drop in on you later this evening for a quick check, and also, we'll be doing regular patrols down the street and through the neighborhood. Let's have a good and uneventful day."

Back at City Hall, Barstow sat in the cruiser for a few minutes before going inside. She scrolled through the dashcam recording of the encounter in front of Doug Lawson's house several times, making a few notes on a small pad. Sergeant Brody and the other patrol officers would need to be made aware of what visitors and vehicles they might encounter over at Lawson's house. She looked at her watch, thinking that Saxby would probably be driving up the Parkway at this point, on his way to the airport outside Atlantic City.

∼

It was a long day for Saxby, but his flight to Minneapolis had all the key ingredients of a pleasant trip. It took off on time, it was a very smooth flight, and the plane was only about a third full, giving him a row to himself. Despite this run of good luck, it was after ten o'clock when he finally was able to drive out of the airport. Forty minutes later, after a stop at a Five Guys and Fries for some takeout food, followed by a package store for a half-bottle of Maker's Mark bourbon, he was settled into a comfortable hotel room a few miles to the south of the city. In between bites of burger and sips of bourbon, he made a short call to Angela to let her know he had arrived in one piece, and a second call to Sergeant Barstow for a general catch-up on the day.

After he had finished the calls and cleared away the remnants of his late dinner, he set the TV to a quiet music station and readied himself for bed. Before switching off the light, he refilled his glass and took fifteen minutes to mull over his plans and expectations for the next day.

17

During breakfast in the hotel restaurant the next morning, Saxby read over the communication that Sergeant Barstow had forwarded to him from the Hennepin County Sheriff's Office. He recalled prior trips to the Twin Cities and consulted a map to refresh his memory of downtown Minneapolis. He was anxious to confirm that the Jimmy Dunne in the county jail was in fact the person of that name who had grown up in Cape May, though at the same time apprehensive about where he'd be left if it turned out that their main suspect couldn't possibly have done the crimes he was suspected of. *Well, if that's how it goes,* he thought to himself, over his last cup of coffee, *we'll just keep going back to the facts and follow them wherever they take us.*

After parking the rental car in a municipal lot across from the main county complex, he walked the few blocks to the law enforcement entrance of the jail building, where he was greeted by a uniformed officer who identified himself as Officer Garrison.

"And you must be Chief Saxby, in from New Jersey," Garrison said, as they shook hands. "Sheriff Ambrose asked me to meet you here and see that you have everything you need."

"I appreciate that," Saxby said. "Please pass on my thanks to Sheriff Ambrose for putting this together so quickly. Is Mr. Dunne aware that I'm here, and willing to meet with me?"

"He is, yes," Garrison said. "I spoke with him late yesterday, after we confirmed that you were on your way. He was surprised, but didn't put up any fuss about meeting with you. I think it was the mention of Cape May that piqued his interest. I was there once, you know, many years ago, for an overnight when my family made a road trip down the East Coast. Beautiful little town as I recall. I mean, through the eyes of an eight-year-old kid."

"I thought that when I was eight too, and it's still beautiful," Saxby said. "Let me know if you ever get there again and I'll be glad to meet up with you and show you around."

Garrison waited while Saxby talked with an officer on the other side of a glass half-wall, signing in and handing over his pistol. He was given an adhesive "Visitor" sticker with his name on it, which he stuck onto the lapel of his blazer. They then went down a short hallway, where they entered a large, stark room which was empty aside from a half-dozen small round tables, each with four chairs around them.

"There isn't anyone else expected for a while," Garrison said, "so pick whichever table you like and I'll go get him. It shouldn't take me much more than about five minutes. Oh —cuffs on or cuffs off is up to you. He's not violent, as far as we know. He was the getaway driver for a smash and grab. He seems to really regret getting mixed up in it, but that's tough luck I guess. He's very intelligent."

Saxby nodded, and sat down at one of the tables to wait as Garrison went out. He returned in less than ten minutes, leading a handcuffed man by the elbow. The man wore khaki slacks with a neatly tucked shirt in a matching color. He was smaller than Saxby by two or three inches, and appeared to be in good shape, if with an extra ten pounds around his midsection. He was clean shaven and showing a recent haircut. *Yep, he sure does look like the guy in the pictures,* Saxby thought to himself, standing up as Garrison brought the man over to the table.

"Thank you for agreeing to meet with me, Mr. Dunne," Saxby said. "My name is Tate Saxby, and I am the police chief of Cape May, New Jersey."

"Is my sister and her family okay?" Dunne asked.

"If you mean Shelly Vance, of Moorestown, New Jersey —yes. I met with her at their home in New Jersey just the other day. She and her husband and their kids are fine."

Saxby could see right away that Dunne was relieved by that news, and appeared to relax visibly. He gestured to Garrison to remove the handcuffs.

"You take your time," Garrison said. "I have to stay in the room, but I'll be over there by the door."

"Thanks for that," Dunne said, holding up his uncuffed hands. "It's good to feel a little bit less like an animal now and then." He and Saxby sat down across from each other. "I don't know why you came all the way out here to see me, Chief Saxby. I can't see how this can have anything to do with the robbery."

"No, you're right," Saxby said. "My visit has nothing at all to do with that. As a matter of fact, I don't know much about it, and it isn't my business."

"Okay. Why are you here, then?" Dunne asked. "And why do you know about my sister Shelly?"

"I'll explain all of it, Mr. Dunne," Saxby said. "It's strange though, because, if you are who I think you are, you've already answered my biggest question."

"That's interesting, because I've hardly said anything," Dunne said. "I hope you'll be getting to the point soon, because I've got all sorts of exciting things to do back in my cell."

"Fair enough," Saxby said. "I'll get right to it, then. I'm here because my department is investigating several cases that appear to be related to the accidental death of a Cape May teenager about fifty years ago. A group of boys were horsing around under the boardwalk and one of them sustained a fatal injury when he hit his head on a jagged piece of metal."

"You've got to be talking about my brother, Ryan," Dunne said. "Are you testing me for some reason? Why bring that up now?" Saxby felt like he could sense the memories flooding through Dunne's head, and could see that his eyes filled with emotion.

"First, yes, I am talking about your late brother, Ryan," Saxby said. "And I'm sorry that I needed to bring up the past like that."

"You said that I've already answered one of your questions, or something like that," Dunne said. "What did you mean by that?"

"I said we're investigating several crimes," Saxby said.

"Murders in fact—three of them, that appear to be related. Do you remember the names of the other boys who were with your brother when he died?"

"Sure, how can I ever forget them?" Dunne said. He proceeded to accurately rattle off the six names.

"Yeah, that's them," Saxby said. "Like your brother, they were all sixteen at the time, high school class of 1974. They would all be sixty-six this year. But there's been some recent developments. Over the course of the last two weeks, three of those men have been killed. Another of them was attacked, but managed to escape serious injury."

Dunne drew in a sharp breath through his teeth, shaking his head slowly. "That's pretty ... I don't know. That's ... wow. Something tells me you aren't kidding. I mean, how could that even be? Could they have been accidents?"

"We believe one of them was made to look like an accident," Saxby said. "But otherwise, no, we've got three murders on our hands—Roseman, Deutsch, and Tanner. Doug Lawson was attacked the other day, but managed to get away safely."

"I remember Doug Lawson," Dunne said. "I got in trouble for yelling at him and punching him in a bar. *Whew*, that was a long time ago. I was twenty-one. I left town not long after that and haven't been back much."

"That was at the Anchorage, wasn't it?" Saxby said. "Somebody told me about that night. An older person who was in town back then. They said you had yelled at a couple of people and threatened to get revenge on those other six boys. I'd like to hear your take on that, if you don't mind going through it."

"My take on it? Okay, sure. I'll give you my take on it," Dunne said. "My take on it is that I was younger, dumber, and drunk. Look, it's true that I blamed Boone, and Frankie, and the others for Ryan's death for a long time. I mean, I used to think maybe they could have helped him somehow, or saved him, if they hadn't run away. I remember that night in the bar, I'd already had a few shots and beers, and I saw one of them—Boone, I think. I didn't talk to him, but seeing him made me think about Ryan, and I started to get pissed off at him and everyone else in the world. And then another of them came in, and that was Doug. I don't even remember what I said, but I started yelling at him and ended up punching him. That's when I got thrown out and the bartender called the police. I apologized to everyone the next day, and I felt like an idiot. The police never charged me."

"That's consistent with the version I was told," Saxby said. "Was there a time that you really felt like getting back at those boys? Those men?"

"Oh, I guess so, sure," Dunne said. "But only when I was around that age, and younger. I was a kid, you know? Missing my brother and trying to find someone to blame. As I got older, and smarter, I understood that it was just an accident. That night at the Anchorage, when I took it out on Doug Lawson—or, I should say, the morning after—was when I really started to move on. I guess the short answer, Chief Saxby, is no. Aside from the fantasies of an angry young kid, no, I never seriously thought about getting revenge on them. And by the way, I can't be a suspect anyway, right? I've been here in this county jail for six months."

"I have to agree with you on that, Mr. Dunne," Saxby said. "It's clear to me that you couldn't have committed these recent crimes back in New Jersey. That's what I meant when I commented earlier that you had already answered some of my questions. I flew out here to learn as much as I could about the history of this case, but also to see for myself if you were really you. I had even asked your sister Shelly to tell me something that could help me confirm that. She told me something about a favorite childhood pet of yours. A Basset Hound."

"Nope. We never had a Basset Hound," Dunne said. "Cleo was a beagle. She was a good friend to me. That was awkward, about my dog, but you got it out. Do you believe that I'm me now? It must be disappointing for you. You find your main suspect, but oh wait, he's been in jail out in Minnesota for months. Sorry about that, Chief. Back to square one."

"It's okay with me if you aren't our killer," Saxby said. "You've got enough to deal with, it seems. It's also true that I'd like to resolve these cases as quickly as possible, ideally with nobody else getting hurt. I said before how I don't know much about this robbery that you're going up for, and how it isn't my business, but one little thing I can do is to put a note in your file saying that you were willing to meet with me and that you were cooperative and tried to be helpful. It's not a lot, but it's something I can do that could conceivably help you in a parole hearing down the road. I'll do that for you. In that spirit, can you think of anyone else who maybe we should look at? Anyone at all?"

Dunne clasped his hands behind his head and stretched, looking up at the ceiling for a moment before answering.

"Hmmm. You know, that isn't a question I've ever thought of. I bet if you could find ten people who were around in town back then, and asked them who was most likely to want to hurt those six guys, probably everyone would point to me. Part of my lot in life, but hey, it makes sense. A lot of people were upset. My mother and father were very upset that they had run away and not tried to do anything to help Ryan. Shelly was too, of course, but she wasn't even ten years old. No, I'm sorry to disappoint again. I can't think of anyone who would have wanted to do anything to them. And after all this time even. What's up with that? That was fifty years ago. Man, whoever's out there, give it a rest already."

"I couldn't agree with you more on that," Saxby said. "Switching gears for a minute, do you have an active passport?"

"Hmmm, that's an interesting question," Dunne said. "Yes. I've had a passport for almost thirty years, I guess. Something like that, because I was in my early twenties when I first went all over Central America. Why are you asking about that? Lots of people have passports."

"You're right about that, there's nothing wrong with having a passport," Saxby said. "I bring that up because of something strange I learned less than forty-eight hours ago. We found a record of a man named James Dunne getting on a plane from Toronto to Havana, Cuba, this past Sunday night." Saxby slid a copy of the passport photo Agent Belli had given him across the table to Dunne, who picked it up and looked at it. "That's the photo on record for the passport that was scanned. The address is in Falcon

Heights, Minnesota, which is roughly between here and St. Paul. Do you know the place?"

"Of course I know it," Dunne said. "I've had an apartment there ever since I came out this way. A friend took the place over for me, while I'm, you know, while I'm away. What does all that mean? I obviously haven't left the country in the last week."

"You know, your last comment is one of the plainer things I've heard recently," Saxby said. "So, today is Thursday. Tuesday evening, I got this report about you having left the country. Not twelve hours later, we learned that the report had somehow been faked. We don't yet know who pulled that off, or how, but the point is, someone has gone to some trouble to create the illusion that you fled the country to Cuba."

"Is someone trying to frame me?" Dunne said. "Is that still what you call it? You know, set me up to take the fall for killing those guys?"

"I gotta say, Mr. Dunne," Saxby said. "It's looking that way at the moment. As you said yourself a few minutes ago, if we accept that these killings are related in the way they appear to be—to your brother Ryan's accident—then it probably makes sense that you would be the default suspect."

"Sure looks that way, doesn't it?" Dunne said. "I guess I'd suspect me myself. But if it isn't me killing them, who else would it be? You already know I went through a period of talking shit about revenge way back then—I've admitted it. But I grew out of all that a long time ago. I never knew anyone else who talked about stuff like that.

Not even my parents. I was the hothead, and it isn't me. You don't suspect my sister Shelly, do you?"

"No, I don't think your sister has anything to do with it," Saxby said. "In fact, it turns out that she and her husband were out on the West Coast during the time that these recent crimes were committed. We checked, just to make sure. Back to your passport for a minute—do you know where that is?"

"I do, unless it's been stolen," Dunne said. "The friend I mentioned—Valerie—who took over my apartment in Falcon Heights, has it. I mean, she has one of those fire-proof safes with some of my important papers in it. She's always home, and I know the number if you want to call her and see if it's still there."

"Why don't we do that," Saxby said. "Just to cross that item off the list. When you speak with her, get her to read you the passport number, and write it down for me please." He passed a small notepad and a pen across the table.

Saxby dialed the number that Dunne gave him and a woman answered after a few rings. Saxby let the two friends have a brief back and forth before Dunne asked her to check for his passport. They waited a few minutes while she put down the phone and went off to open the safe and check.

"Yeah, Jimmy, your passport's here, right in that big envelope with your other stuff," she said. "Looks like it's valid for two more years."

"Oh, great. Thanks, Val." Dunne said. "So, there's enough time on it for me to take you on a trip when I get out. Can you read the number on it for me please, so I can write it down?" He wrote the number down on the pad as she read it to him, repeating it back before pushing the pad and pen back to Saxby.

"Listen, Val, I've got to go right now," Dunne said. "But I'll call you as soon as I get to my new digs and we can catch up. Lock that up again please, and thanks for your help."

They said their goodbyes and Saxby ended the call. He took a minute to carefully compare what Dunne had written down to a note of his own. "Yep, that's the passport number that was used."

"My last trip to Cuba was a little over five years ago," Dunne said. "I wonder if somehow the entry from that trip could have been copied or cloned somehow? Is that a possibility?"

"In fact, we think that's probably what was done," Saxby said. "I spoke with people at Homeland Security, and they're going to be looking into that. With luck, they'll be able to tell who did it and fix the hole in their system, but that's out of my hands."

"Seems like someone's been going to a lot of trouble to get me to take the fall for this," Dunne said. "Are you thinking they're out to get me for some reason, or am I just a convenient patsy?"

"Right now, I'm thinking that the most likely scenario is that this really has nothing to do with you," Saxby said. "I don't know—yet—why these men were killed. Revenge? Hmmm. I doubt it. I'm leaning towards some other reason that I haven't seen yet, and somebody who knew about, or heard about your past has tried to point it all to you. I think that making the police believe that you had fled the country was a key part of their plan."

"And it sounds like it might have worked if you hadn't found me sitting here in jail," Dunne said. "At least I gave you an excuse to visit the wonderful Land of 10,000 Lakes."

"You've been a help, Mr. Dunne," Saxby said. "I appreciate it, and I will put that note into your file before I leave."

"Thanks for that, Chief," Dunne said. "Can I ask you one more thing, since I've been dragged into this—or they tried, anyway? Could you let me know when you settle it? When you figure it all out? I'm guilty of some stuff, but not that. I'd like to know when my name is in the clear."

"I'll be sure to do that, no problem. When we get it figured out," Saxby said.

When he returned from taking Dunne back inside, Officer Garrison escorted Saxby out to the reception area, where he waited while Saxby signed out and retrieved his pistol. Before leaving the facility, Saxby took a few minutes to write out a note on the visitor report to be added to Dunne's file.

"See that gets into his file for me, would you," Saxby said, handing the paper to Garrison.

"Will do, Chief," Garrison said. "Do you think you found out what you needed to know?"

"I found a few answers, that led to as many questions," Saxby said. "He clearly can't be our killer, so the question for the day is ... who in hell is trying so hard to make us think he is?"

18

I t was Manny who spoke first. "Oh my God—what happened? Is he still alive? We have to check if he's alive."

"Who knows how to tell?" Doug said, before kneeling down and throwing up into the sand.

"I don't think he is. Look, he isn't moving at all," Boone said. He spoke haltingly, between short, fast breaths.

"But his eyes are open. He can't be dead, right?" Manny said.

"A lot of people die with their eyes open," Jeff said. "That's what happened to my grandmother. He has to be dead. Look, he's stuck there. He's stuck on that thing. We've gotta get out of here."

"What you mean?" Doug said, having recovered some-what. "We've got to call the police, or the rescue squad. That's what we've got to do."

"Oh, great idea, dope," Jeff said. "And they'll think we all did it."

"You're the dope, you dope," Doug said. "It was an accident. He must have tripped on something. I saw him push you and then you pushed him back."

"I only pushed him because he pushed me first," Jeff said. "And anyway, we were just messing around. You were wrestling with him yourself. I saw you shove him."

"All of you, stop. Just cut it out," Manny said. "Even if it was an accident, we're still going to get in trouble for drinking beer and smoking pot. We need to get out of here, fast."

"Let's go somewhere else where we can figure out who to call or whatever. But where?" Bobby said.

"I know where," Manny said. "The Crow's Nest. It's a guesthouse my parents bought on Madison. My dad's been fixing it up to rent for the summer, but he's out of town this week and I have a key. It's on the corner of Madison and New Jersey. Big blue house with a white swing on the porch. Let's go there."

"Okay. Okay. That sounds good. Let's do that," Jeff said. "Let's meet up there. We can't go home just yet."

By the time Manny arrived with the key about ten minutes later, three of the boys were already there at the house, crouched down on the porch. The last two arrived within another five minutes, and they all gathered in the half-painted front room, stepping between paint cans, piles of sawdust, and assorted tools. The combined smells of paint thinner and carpenter's glue hung in the air.

Frankie went into the nearby bathroom after indicating

that it was his turn to throw up. Boone had been crying off and on since arriving at the house.

Jeff came right up to Doug, who was standing beside one of the windows, looking out towards the beach. "You and Ryan were playing tackle. You shoved him and he fell back on that spike. This is your fault."

Doug stepped back, furious, and with fists balled up. "I did not shove him. We were messing around, but then he was just fine. He tripped after you ran into him. You're a jerkoff."

"But you started the whole thing," Jeff said. "We were all fine until you started running around like a spaz. You can't even handle two little beers. And anyway, you're the jerkoff."

"Stop it, you guys," Manny said, almost yelling from the other side of the room. "We all better start agreeing it was an accident, or we're going to be up shit's creek."

"It was an accident," Doug said. "I mean, it really was. We don't have to lie about it."

"Doug is right," Boone said. "Everyone was messing around. He tripped or whatever and fell backwards. That's what happened. Hey, has anyone seen Bobby?"

"I just saw him going out the back door," Frankie said, having returned from throwing up in the bathroom. "He said he was going home to tell his parents. I tried to stop him but he ran away."

"Shit. We are so screwed," Jeff said. "We're probably going to get reform school or something like that. Our summer is going to be ruined. There goes my chance with Lisa Shea."

"I told you, it really was an accident," Doug said. "That's

what you boneheads need to say. All of us I mean. Just tell the police what really happened. We'll be okay."

A couple of the others nodded silently, resigning themselves. Boone tried hard not to cry again.

"I agree with Doug," Manny said. "It was an accident. We just tell the truth and we'll be okay."

Within another twenty minutes, they all started drifting back to their homes, as the ominous wailing of sirens in the distance grew louder.

19

It was the morning after his return from Minnesota, and Saxby picked up a marker and stood in front of the conference room whiteboard, deep in thought. Barstow and Connor waited patiently to see what he might write. Twice, he reached out as if to start, but both times lowered his arm without writing. Shaking his head as if to clear it and make room for new thoughts, he turned back towards the table and put the marker down.

"Remember when we were here in this room on Saturday, and we talked about how the three crime scenes appeared to have been staged in some way or other?"

"Sure, Chief," Connor said. "And we talked about how it kinda looked like whoever did that had done a crappy job."

"Right. Exactly," Saxby said. "They did a crappy job at trying to point us to a drug deal, or an Indonesian killer bent on revenge for a deadly chemical spill. I'm slapping myself for not seeing through it all. There's something I read once—'Oh what a tangled web we weave, when first we practice to deceive.' "

"You're getting Shakespearean on us now, Chief?" Barstow said.

Saxby laughed. "Sounds like Shakespeare, doesn't it? You're not alone. Actually, it's from Sir Walter Scott, a few hundred years later. Scottish writer. He was talking about how things can tend to spiral out of control when you're lying and trying to deliberately mislead. The life lesson there would be something like … speak the truth, or as close to the truth as you can, because when you start to lie, that leads to another lie, and another, until you're in too deep. So, bear with me a minute. I'm going to ask a few questions, and I want you to tell me the simple answer that comes to mind. I'm not tricking you and this isn't a test.

"Now then, I'm sure we can all agree that most killers don't want to be caught, and sometimes they do things to hide what they've done or who they are, right? So, for example, if, for some reason or other you wanted to kill somebody, it would be to your advantage to disguise that reason, right? Because the motive frequently gives away the killer. If you wanted to kill Boone Roseman for example, what might you do to disguise the motive? What do you think, Three?"

"I guess the first thing that jumps to my mind," Connor said, "is exactly what we think was done with Roseman. Try to make it look like a drug deal gone south. Aside from that, maybe just make it look like some kind of robbery."

"Good work. That's exactly what I was thinking," Saxby said. "But what if you did a lousy job at disguising the motive? Vic? Don't overthink it."

Barstow hesitated, looking back and forth between the other two. "If I did a lousy job, the idea wouldn't work and police wouldn't fall for it. They would look for the real motive. Is that what you're getting at?"

"Exactly right, Vic," Saxby said. "If you did a crappy job at covering up the motive, we cops could see through it and start looking for what the real motive is. I'm going to throw out an idea. My idea is this: yes, our killer tried to hide his motive, but not because he expected it to work. No. All those things he did, the Amtrak schedule, the ceremonial dagger, putting cocaine on Boone Roseman's nose, deleting the texts—what else? Oh, blood on the phone, the cigarette butts—we weren't really meant to fall for that nonsense. On the contrary, he meant for us to see through all of it. We've been saying that he did a crappy job at hiding the motive, but I don't think that's really it. I think he did a good job at making it look like he did a crappy job at hiding the motive. But not good enough."

"I think I'm following you, Chief," Connor said, "but why? Why would he go to all that trouble if he really wanted us to cut through it so easily?"

"You're asking the right question," Saxby said. "And the answer is … because, what he really wanted was to give us an 'aha moment'. A 'eureka moment'. We were supposed to be distracted by all the fluff with those three cases for just long enough until we finally stepped back and said 'Wait a minute—now I get it—these men were all there under the boardwalk. They're three of the six. This is all about someone getting revenge for Ryan Dunne'. See, he wanted us to be high-fiving each other when we finally got to that. Make sense?"

"I think so, Chief," Connor said. "And that's pretty much what happened, right? We did the legwork on each case as much as we could, until we finally realized how Roseman, Tanner, and Deutsch were related. And then there's the attack on Doug Lawson. Only thing is, now we find out that Jimmy Dunne has been in a jail cell out in East Jabip all this time, and the whole revenge idea doesn't look so good anymore."

"Exactly. Which leads me to the next idea I want to throw out," Saxby said. "But first, here's what we have so far. Somebody kills these three men. They do a half-assed job of making it look like a drug deal or whatever so that we see through it fairly quickly and feel sure that we've arrived at the true motive—revenge. They even went so far as to try to make it look like Jimmy Dunne did all this and then fled to Cuba. My theory on that is that they assumed he was already in Cuba or some other faraway place and wouldn't interfere. At least for long enough for them to completely cover their tracks. Risky as all hell, but on the other hand, everyone we talk to who knew him seems to think he's off in Cuba or somewhere else anyway."

"So, what do you think it comes down to then, Chief?" Barstow said. "What's your idea?"

"It's this … Jimmy Dunne couldn't have done it—and by the way—we can't find anyone else who fits in as the patsy in the revenge scenario. No, he has nothing to do with it, because revenge for Ryan Dunne isn't the true motive at all. It's just another misdirection, and one that we weren't supposed to get past."

"Are you saying that we need to start looking at a completely different motive for killing those three guys?" Barstow said.

"Well, sort of," Saxby said. "I doubt we're going to find

another motive for killing those three men. What we need to look for is a motive for killing one of them. Which leads me to my second literary reference for the day. On the flight home yesterday afternoon, I happened to mention to the flight attendant that I wished I had brought a book to read or a puzzle or something. She surprised me a few minutes later when she came back with one of those airline magazines that had a crossword puzzle in the back, along with a little paperback of mystery stories. Are you familiar with the short story *The Purloined Letter*, by Edgar Allen Poe?"

"It's been some years since I read Poe," Connor said, "but I think the basic idea is that police are searching up and down for some really important letter that was being used to blackmail some bigwig. They look in every possible intricate hiding place and can't find it, until the detective realizes that it's just been sitting out in a little pile of other letters."

"You're right, Three, that's about it," Saxby said. "It's the classic story about something that nobody sees because it's right there in plain sight."

"I think I know what you're getting at, Chief," Barstow said. "You're suggesting that one of those guys was killed for some specific reason, and the others were killed just to make it look like revenge on the group. Wow, that's some pretty brutal stuff, if that's really what's going on."

"It sure is, Vic," Saxby said. "If I'm right about this, we're dealing with a real sicko, and a very dangerous one at that."

"That's some heavy stuff, Chief," Connor said. "I almost hate to say it, but the whole thing makes a lot of sense. We just need to figure which of the three dead guys was the real target."

"Right. I haven't got that all sorted out yet, but I have some ideas," Saxby said.

"Follow the money. This isn't a crime of passion," Barstow said. "Something this cold-blooded has to be about who benefits. Who benefits the most? To me that spells money."

"Well, with his father out of the way, Paul Tanner stands to take over Tanner Construction," Connor said. "His mother and sister are still around, though neither of them appears to be involved with the business very much. Boone Roseman had a small inheritance and a few assets that I assume will go to the niece and nephew, but I don't think that money adds up to the killing kind."

"Frankie Deutsch was a wealthy man," Barstow said. "Probably as much as a few million there. I don't know where that will go, but he does have a surviving brother. I think a lot of people would off someone for a million or two. Especially if you didn't like the person. What are you thinking, Chief?"

"I'm thinking that you both have good ideas," Saxby said. "It's true that Frankie Deutsch was a wealthy man, so that's worth looking at. There's something else though. I mentioned that the flight attendant had loaned me a book of mystery stories yesterday, and also a crossword puzzle— which I completed, by the way. I've always loved crossword puzzles. That's actually one of the main reasons I get the *New York Times* every Sunday—for the puzzles at the back of the magazine section. I've gotten to the point that I can complete the main puzzle more often than not. Anyway, when I was doing the puzzle on the plane yesterday, it reminded me of something. When I went to see Paul Tanner at his office the other day, I saw that he also had the *Sunday Times*, and had been working on one of the puzzles. He told me he was almost finished, and how it relaxed him, and so on. But here's the thing that didn't register at the time—it wasn't the main Sunday puzzle he was almost finished with—it was the 'Cryptic Crossword' on the page before."

"I don't get it, Chief," Barstow said. "Is there something special about this 'Cryptic Crossword?' "

"Sorry, guys, I shouldn't expect everyone to know that," Saxby said. "Whether you do crosswords or not, you know basically how they work, right? Let's say you need a four-letter word and the clue is 'Nick and Nora's furry friend.' The fictional detective in *The Thin Man* series was Nick Charles, and his dog's name was 'Asta.' That shows up in crosswords all the time. Or you need a six-letter word, and the clue is 'Largest Bahama island.' Well, that's obviously 'Andros,' so you fill that in. It isn't always as easy as that, but that's how it works. In a 'Cryptic Crossword' though, the clues themselves are part of the puzzle, and they don't seem to make sense when you first read them. You have to figure out what the clue is asking for before you can even think about what the answer is. I can't give you an example because I've never been able to get it myself. I can complete some tough crossword puzzles, but a cryptic crossword? I don't even try."

"So, what are you thinking about Paul Tanner," Barstow said. "Are you saying he's some kind of super genius?"

Saxby laughed at that. "I'm not sure about that, though

he may be. This whole thing, with these killings and the staged scenes, it seems like a puzzle within a puzzle. We first thought it was one layer, until we thought it was two layers. Now it looks like it's three layers. That's why I can't help but think that we're dealing with someone who really loves puzzles. It's almost like, if you equate a tough but conventional crossword to a chess game, then the cryptic crossword might be a three-dimensional chess game. Someone who can do that has a mind that works on a higher level than most of us. I'm saying it's someone like that who's been killing these people."

"Seems like one thing we need to do is to have another chat with Doug Lawson," Barstow said. "Seeing as how we now know it couldn't have been Jimmy Dunne who attacked him."

"You're right, Vic, that does need to be one of our next steps. I've been thinking about Lawson, and I don't yet see what his connection is to all this," Saxby said. "But I'm leaning towards it being more than that he's one of the six. I'm meeting with Tom Dooley later this afternoon to bring him up to speed on my trip and everything else, and I'll get his take on it. Let me see where he stands first, and then maybe you and I can plan to see Lawson in the morning. By the way, how did it go the other day when you went by to check on him?"

"Just fine. Very quick visit," Barstow said. "There's a friend by the name of Bernie Welles staying with him for a few days. Local man. About Lawson's age. Just as I pulled up, I ran into another man as he was just leaving. I got the impression that he was some sort of contractor, with the way he was dressed and a new pickup truck, but that's just a guess. I spoke with him for a minute before Lawson came out of the house and told me the guy was his cousin, and he would be stopping by again to check up on Lawson. Seemed like a nice enough guy. Peter Franks was his name."

"Sounds good, then, Vic," Saxby said, standing up. "Let's break this up for now, then. Lots to do. Let's try to have a meeting like this each afternoon for a while, even if it's just a brief check-in."

Barstow gathered her papers and was the first to leave the room.

"Oh, Three, by the way, before you go," Saxby said. "Something I meant to talk to you about before my trip, but I got caught up in everything else. Last week, when we were all working on Boone Roseman, you spent some time looking around for any cameras in that part of town that might have caught footage of the traffic in the area on Sunday night into early Monday. Wasn't that you?"

"Yes. That was me," Connor said. "But it turned out that there wasn't really much to look at. No banks or hotels in that area, and what we did find, closer to the marina, just had too much generic traffic in and out to be useful."

"Right. I remember you saying that," Saxby said. "It was a good thing to try though. Here's why I bring it up, and I'm switching gears from Boone Roseman on Sunday to Jeff Tanner on Wednesday night. I had lunch with a friend at the C-View the other day, and I noticed the two cameras up high on the building. Weren't you looking at some footage from them?"

"I was, yes. They're pretty good cameras," Connor said. "I looked at some of the footage for Sunday but didn't see anything helpful. But if you're switching gears over to Jeff Tanner, are you saying what I think you're saying?"

"I am," Saxby said. "I'd like you to get back to them, at the C-View, and see if you can get some footage for the few hours before and after Tanner's death on Wednesday night. I know you've already seen the footage from the Wawa camera, with Barry Vaughn and the potato chip truck. That's the timeframe. I just thought the C-View camera might have a wider view of the area and would be worth a look."

"I'll get on it right away then, Chief," Connor said. He hesitated as he started to go out the door. "I guess I screwed that up, didn't I, Chief? I should have thought to go back to them for the Wednesday tapes."

"You didn't screw anything up, Three," Saxby said. "That idea is nowhere on my mind. None of us thinks of everything, and certainly not all at the right time. We just do our best and keep plugging away, and we'll get there, okay?"

"Got it, Chief, thanks," Connor said. "That's a good way to put it. I'll get on it with the C-View and see what I can see."

"Good work, then," Saxby said. "I'll be here for another hour or two. Otherwise, you know where to find me."

Connor gave a thumbs-up and went out, leaving Saxby to gather his own notes and thoughts.

"Thanks, Tate, that was a good update," Detective Dooley said. "I'll admit, when you first told me you were flying out to Minnesota, I thought you might be wasting your time, but now I see that it was the right move. You not only established that Jimmy Dunne isn't our man, but now I think we can say that the whole revenge thing is a bunch of hooey. What did you call it? Oh yes—a smokescreen."

"Yeah, that's the way I'm seeing it now," Saxby said. "We've been peeling away the layers, and I'm hoping there aren't many more left. Could you see what you can find out about Frankie Deutsch, as far as what kind of money we're talking about and who gets it? I remember when we went up to Somers Point, Dikko Wilkes mentioned that Deutsch owned a pair of local motels. It would be interesting to know if there's a partner anywhere in the picture."

"Sure, I can run with that ball," Dooley said. "How about you? Are you going to focus on Paul Tanner?"

"Yes, he's my next focus," Saxby said. "I don't have anything on him yet, other than my gut and those few things I told you about."

"Your gut's pretty good, Tate," Dooley said. "You should listen to it."

"I can't help but listen to it right now, because it's growling at me," Saxby said. "I need to get some lunch. Anyway, I'll check in with you again by tomorrow morning. Aside from the need for a sandwich, another thing my gut is telling me is that this whole thing is heating up quickly."

While Saxby was in the middle of his call with Detective Dooley, Doreen found Sergeant Barstow at her desk.

"Excuse me, Vic," Doreen said, "I have that Mr. Vaughn on the phone, asking for either you or the chief. The chief's been on a long call—I think with that Detective Dooley. Can I patch him through to you?"

"You mean Barry Vaughn?" Barstow said. "The guy who met with us here last week? Sure, send him to me."

Barstow picked up her phone when it rang a minute later. "This is Sergeant Vicky Barstow. Chief Saxby is busy at the moment. Can I help you with something?"

"Hello, Sergeant," Vaughn said. "Barry Vaughn here. You know, the guy who doesn't wear red. I found something that I think might be a piece of evidence that you'll be interested in. I'm only two blocks down from the police station—do you think you could pop over?"

"Mr. Vaughn, we're very busy here," Barstow said, trying not to sound too exasperated. "Is it something you can drop off?"

"I suppose I could, but then I'd have to handle the thing more," Vaughn said. "I've tried to do as little of that as possible. I really think it will be worth your while."

Barstow agreed that she could come right over, and, anyway, she thought to herself, she could use the walk through the crisp spring air to give herself a bit of an afternoon second wind.

Less than ten minutes later, she saw Barry Vaughn sitting on the steps of the late-1800s Victorian which had been carved up into his apartment along with several others.

"Nice to see you again, Mr. Vaughn," Barstow said. "I must say it is a pleasant day for a walk, so thank you for that. Now, if you would please, what was it you wanted to show me?"

Vaughn's answer was to point across to the side of the tiny front yard, to where something was hanging over a fencepost. Barstow walked over to it, picking it up carefully by the edges.

"Maybe that's the red hoodie your detective friend accused me of wearing," Vaughn said. "My neighbor—the one I told you about before—noticed it this morning. She said it was on the steps, about where I'm sitting. She moved it over there to make it easier to see in case someone was looking for it. What do you think, Sergeant? Is somebody still trying to suggest that I'm involved in Jeffrey Tanner's death? I really thought we'd moved on from that."

"I don't think we can rule that out," Barstow said. "Did you or your neighbor notice when this showed up?"

"I was out late last night," Vaughn said, "at a little dinner party with some friends over in Wildwood, and I got home just before midnight. I'm sure it wasn't here then. I bumped into Fanny when she was going out and I was coming in about a half hour ago, and that's when she pointed it out and told me that she'd found it when she took Miss Toodles for a walk early this morning. She's home now if you wanted to get it straight from her. Fanny, I mean. Miss Toodles also, presumably, though it wouldn't be much use trying to get any information from her. Here, I brought a new trash bag in case you wanted to put it in there."

Barstow lowered the sweatshirt into the trash bag as Vaughn held it open. "I'll check in with her, thanks. And thank you for the bag. Would you know your neighbor Fanny's full name?"

"It's Adelman. Fanny Adelman," Vaughn said. "Quite a nice lady, if overly talkative sometimes. She's in apartment two, on the second floor. If you're through with me, then…"

Just then, Barstow noticed that Vaughn appeared to see something behind her, and turned in time to see a white pickup truck pass by as Vaughn gave a wave.

"Sorry, Sergeant, just somebody I know, but I don't think he saw me," Vaughn said.

"That pickup looked very familiar," Barstow said. "May I ask your friend's name? If you think that was him."

"Not really a friend," Vaughn said. "But someone I've known off and on for a year or so. As a matter of fact, I had a job interview with him just yesterday, for a crew boss position. Peter Franks is his name. I've met with him a few times."

"I knew that truck looked familiar," Barstow said. "I met him just the other day. Does he have a construction company of his own?"

"Of his own? No, not yet, but he married into one," Vaughn said. "His wife Annamarie is the niece of Lincoln Barness."

"Lincoln Barness? Of course—the Barness Group," Barstow said. "That's it. Isn't that the company that was trying to get Tanner Construction to take on that big condo project?"

"Yes, that's right," Vaughn said. "But Mr. Tanner the elder was never interested in it, for reasons of his own. I assume they'll be contacting Paul Tanner now, you know, with the recent... how shall I put it... changes in management."

And this guy Peter Franks is Doug Lawson's cousin, Barstow thought to herself. *And Doug Lawson was one of the six, and he's the one who said it was Jimmy Dunne who tried to jump him...*

"Are you okay, Sergeant?" Vaughn said. "You went away there for a minute. Can I get you something to drink?"

"Ah, no, thank you, I was just remembering something, but thanks for the offer," Barstow said. "You've been very helpful today, Mr. Vaughn. Let me go check with your neighbor, Miss Adelman, and then I'd better get back to the station to process this sweatshirt."

As soon as Barstow got back to the station she rushed to Saxby's office, finding it empty. Her next stop was the conference room, where Saxby and Deputy Connor were sitting together at the table, watching something on a laptop screen.

"Hey, Chief, Three," Barstow said, "You aren't going to believe this, I was just—"

"Hang on just a minute, Vic," Saxby said. "You're just in time to see this. We've watched it twice already. This could be a real break."

She set the trash bag on an empty chair and stood behind the two men as Connor pressed a key to start a video playing.

"Three got this from the C-View," Saxby said. "This is

from last Wednesday night, just around the time Jeff Tanner was killed."

"Okay, I see," Barstow said. "So, this is looking from the front of the C-View, away from the intersection and up Texas Avenue, got it."

"Right, we're looking east up Texas Avenue, and we get a wide view of the Wawa and parts of the parking lot up here," Connor said, pointing at the screen as Barstow nodded. "Now look at this." He pointed to a corner of the screen where they could see a car appear and proceed past and towards the Wawa. And there he is. That's Barry Vaughn showing up at 9:23. He pulls in and parks."

"But wait, we're not still looking at Barry Vaughn, right?" Barstow said. "He's got an airtight alibi with the potato chip guy for most of the next half hour."

"You're right, Vic," Saxby said. "We're not still looking at Barry Vaughn, but his arrival defines the scene and the timeframe here. See, look, there's the Herr's truck pulling in right on cue, driven by Vaughn's friend, Chip. Remember when the two of you walked all around the area, thinking that the Wawa would be a good place to park, with traffic in and out, and you could easily walk from there over to the Doyle house to confront Jeff Tanner? All of that works just as well if you were pulled up right in front of the C-View, right? Look at the line of cars along there right in front."

"Okay, that first one looks like an old Chevy Impala," Barstow said, "and then a Honda Accord, or a Camry maybe, and then the Ford Explorer."

They watched as three people appeared from under the camera, piled into the Chevy sedan, and drove away.

"There, now we get a better view of this car," Connor said, pointing to the screen. "And you can see that your second guess was right, it's a Camry. The interesting thing is that there's at least one person sitting in that car for almost forty minutes. We can tell, because every once in a while their foot must hit the brake pedal, and you can see the lights flicker. He's sitting there for a long time, waiting for something."

"I guess he could be waiting for takeout," Barstow said. "Like the wife or friend is inside ordering and paying and all that. Can we zoom in on that license plate?"

Connor hit some keys and the view enlarged to show a clearer picture of the Camry's rear plate.

"Wait a minute, I know that plate," Barstow said, reading aloud. "THX-925. That's Doug Lawson's Camry, isn't it? I've seen it in his driveway every time I drive by."

"Bingo, Vic," Saxby said. "We've already run the plate to verify. Three, fast forward to something more exciting if you would please."

Connor used the controls on the screen to advance the video more quickly. "So, somebody's been sitting in the car waiting for something. It doesn't look like takeout, because we never see anyone come out of the restaurant and go to the car. But look at this."

He pointed to the top corner of the screen for half a minute, until a dark figure appeared from somewhere near the Wawa, apparently waiting for a car to pass before crossing the road to approach the restaurant.

"So, he came from somewhere over there, behind the Wawa or maybe from the Doyle house," Saxby said. "He goes off screen for a few seconds there as he gets right up to the restaurant, and then look—the Camry's overhead light comes on as he gets in the passenger side."

"Oh my God, and there's the red hoodie," Barstow said.

"Exactly. And then the light goes out and they drive away," Saxby said. "And that's about two minutes after Barry Vaughn's car appears from behind the Herr's truck and leaves the Wawa. It sure does look a lot like Doug Lawson sat there waiting while some accomplice went over to the Doyle house, doesn't it? What did you want to show us when you came rushing in, Vic? What's in the trash bag?"

"Something that appears to have been tossed onto Barry Vaughn's front steps sometime in the middle of the night. His neighbor found it this morning. When he found out about it, he called it in and I went over there," Barstow said. She picked up the bag, taking a moment to undo the tie at the top before dumping the contents out onto the conference room table.

Three sets of eyes stared at the thing for a full twenty seconds before anyone spoke.

"The red hoodie."

20

It was Deputy Connor who first broke the silence. "But why would somebody still be trying to point the finger at Vaughn at this point? He's got a good alibi for when we think Jeff Tanner was killed."

"You're right, Three," Saxby said. "But remember, whoever killed Tanner probably doesn't know about Vaughn's friend Chip and the Herr's truck. He may think we've been looking at Vaughn all this time. Hmmm. And now it looks like we might have the real killer on video, with Doug Lawson doing the driving. Lawson is one of the original six boys. I just can't see why he would be involved in killing the others. And why now?"

"Chief, I think I have something on that," Barstow said. "Remember the other day, when you were getting ready to fly out to Minnesota, I went over to check up on Lawson."

"Yeah, I remember that. Wednesday," Saxby said. "You were going to show him a copy of Jimmy Dunne's passport picture to get his reaction, but without mentioning the hit on the BOLO. You mentioned there were two other men there with him."

"Right. So, when I went over there," Barstow said, "there was his friend Bernie Welles, who was staying with him, and the other guy, Peter Franks, who I learned was Lawson's cousin. He said he'd be stopping by on occasion to help keep an eye on Lawson. Anyway, fast forward to this afternoon, when Barry Vaughn calls us and I go over to his place, two blocks down the street. While we're talking on the sidewalk, Vaughn waves at a white pickup as it drives by, which looks familiar to me. I ask him about it and he tells me that was Peter Franks that drove by. Turns out that Vaughn had a job interview with Franks just yesterday, and Franks is with a big property development company. You'll never guess what company."

"Somehow, I think I know what you're going to say," Saxby said. "He's with the Barness Group."

"Bingo. And the Barness Group is the company that was trying to get Tanner Construction to take on that big construction project that Jeff Tanner didn't want to do," Barstow said. "Another thing Vaughn said to me—when we saw Franks drive by—was a comment about Barness. He said he figured now that Jeff Tanner is out of the picture, Barness would probably be after Paul Tanner to reconsider the condo project."

"And that would mean millions of dollars to Tanner and a number of other people," Saxby said. "Oh yes, the pieces of the puzzle are suddenly falling into place. Lawson has a family connection to Barness, but no connection we know of to Tanner Construction. That is, no connection apart from him being one of the six, along with Jeff Tanner, and that's a slim thread."

"Going back to the video from the C-View for a minute," Connor said, "we know it was Doug Lawson's car. If we assume that it was him driving, what do you think about it being Peter Franks crossing the street and getting into the car?"

"Maybe, but I'm pretty sure it was someone else," Barstow said. She had picked up the hoodie sweatshirt and was holding it up to her face, sniffing it in various places as she moved it around in her hands. "This is something I haven't smelled in years. That is, until last week, and now again right now. Cool Water cologne, by Davidoff, I'm pretty sure. I didn't know it was still made. Yeah, that's it— Cool Water. Unmistakable. Paul Tanner was doused in this when he came into the station with that video last week."

"I've never been much of a cologne guy," Saxby said, "but I think I know what that is. Doesn't it come in a rectangular blue bottle?"

"You have a browser open, Three?" Barstow said. "Can you bring up an image of a Cool Water bottle please?"

They waited while Connor worked on his laptop for less than a minute before turning it around so the others could see the screen. "There you go, Cool Water by Davidoff. Thirty-two bucks on Amazon."

"Yeah, that's what I was picturing," Saxby said. "When I saw Paul Tanner at his office on Monday, I saw that he had a full bathroom—like with a shower and everything. He told me how he likes to 'freshen up,' as he put it, late in the day. Have a shave, shower, or whatever. I'm sure I saw that blue bottle on a shelf over the sink."

"My God. He killed his father, didn't he?" Barstow said. "I can't imagine … I mean, how can someone be that cold? He's like Jekyll and Hyde. Half normal man with the other half pure evil."

"It sure is looking that way, Vic," Saxby said. "He wanted his father out of the way so he could take control of the construction company and make the deal with Barness. Somehow, he was able to recruit Doug Lawson to help with his plan."

"And it looks like Lawson was his backdoor connection to Barness," Barstow said. "It must have been about the money for him. I bet Tanner offered him a ton of money. You know, I've met with Lawson a few times now, and I've always gotten the feeling that he was scared, which made sense to me at the time. I figured he was scared because someone—Jimmy Dunne, he thought—tried to attack him. But now I'm thinking that wasn't it at all. He was nervous and scared because things had gotten out of hand and he realized he was an accomplice to murder. What do you think about that, Chief?"

"What I think is that you're right about that, Vic," Saxby said. "We naturally assumed he was all shook up because of the attack. Only thing—the attack never actually happened. I think you hit it on the nail there. He's in over his head and scared half to death. If we're right about all this, he could be our path to Paul Tanner. Because this all makes for a good story, but we need evidence."

"Chief, now that we think Lawson drove Tanner away from the C-View at 9:43," Connor said, "I can go back and try to find other cameras in town that might show them somewhere else. Maybe at either of their homes."

"Good idea, Three, do that please," Saxby said. "But there's one place I'd like you to check first, right after this meeting. I'm making a guess that Lawson drove right over to Tanner's office building and dropped him there. When I pulled into that parking lot the other day, I saw how the entrance faced the hardware store just across the way, and I know they have cameras there. See what the field of view is and if they have footage from that timeframe. Something like five or ten minutes after they drove away from the C-View. I'll be surprised if we don't see Lawson's Camry pulling up and dropping someone off. Ask for Terri Swain and tell her it's urgent. She's a friend of mine and I'm sure she'll help you out if they have anything."

"What do you want me to do, Chief?" Barstow said.

"Doug Lawson is the key to this thing," Saxby said. "And we need to make sure we don't lose sight of him. I'd like you to go home and change into street clothes and get your personal car. Find a good spot a block or two away from Lawson's house, where you can see whoever comes or goes. Take pictures and notes. I need to get with Dooley and bring him in on all of this. Once I do that, I'm sure we can get a couple of county officers to help out, but for the immediate term we're on our own.

"I just thought of something. Isn't there some kind of software that can look at a video image and determine how tall a person is based on their surroundings, like, things they walk by or how long their shadow is?"

"There is, Chief, but I don't know what it's called," Connor said. "I'm sure the state police have it, and I'd be surprised if Detective Dooley didn't have access to it too. I bet it could compare the walking figures in the two videos and tell us if it's the same person. I'll send you clips of both videos as soon as I get back to my desk."

"Great, thanks, Three," Saxby said. "We're gonna need whatever we can get to make Lawson sweat. Okay, guys, we've got work to do and we have a plan for at least the rest of the day. I'm going to get on the horn to Dooley and start working on what comes next. I'll check back with both of you by nine or ten tonight."

As the county seat, the town of Cape May Courthouse, about ten miles north of Cape May, was home to many of the county offices. At 8:30 in the evening, the headquarters of the county detectives was a quiet place. Saxby and Dooley had spent more than an hour going over every angle of the Tanner case they could think of, including a review of the Roseman and Deutsch cases. The chief of detectives had joined them for a condensed review and, after listening carefully, had signed off on their general plan for the next day. One of the department's technical people was working on an analysis and comparison of the video clips that Saxby had forwarded. In addition to the expectation that they would be able to tell the approximate height and weight of the person in the videos, they hoped to determine if in fact the person in the video taken at the Doyle house was the same person seen getting into the car outside the C-View.

Added to that was a brief clip that Deputy Connor had been able to get from the hardware store just that afternoon. That clip, taken by a high-resolution camera mounted on the front of the hardware store, showed the red Camry pull up to the adjacent Tanner Construction building seven minutes after it had driven away from the C-View Tavern at the other end of town. In it, a man could clearly be seen getting out of the passenger side of the car and walking towards the Tanner building before disappearing around the corner as the car drove away. They were told to expect results sometime in the late evening or early morning hours.

"So, how do you want to play it?" Dooley said. "You, me, and a couple from the sheriff's office?"

"I like that, Tom," Saxby said. "Because it's a good show of force. We think this guy's scared and on-edge, and we need to use that against him. Tell him he's under arrest, slap some cuffs on him, and put him in the back seat of a cruiser. That oughta put some fear into him. But what about that friend who's staying with him, Bernie Welles? At the moment, we don't have any basis to think he's involved in any of this, and I'm betting he isn't. But if I'm wrong, we don't want him calling Paul Tanner and putting him on alert."

"You're right," Dooley said. "We're going to need Lawson in custody for at least a few hours before Tanner finds out about it. That's why I say we bring Welles in too —arrest him if we have to. He's got to have access to a lawyer and all that, but I'm hoping we can impress upon him that it would be to his benefit to work with us. If he's just an innocent friend trying to help Lawson—great, we can apologize to him later. If he is involved, well, then I think he'll cave pretty fast when he realizes we're talking about triple murder here."

"Okay, that sounds like a good plan for Welles," Saxby said. "Now the other man, this Peter Franks character. He's got to be in this up to his eyeballs. My people tell me that he's been stopping by every morning. Can we put a loose tail on him tomorrow morning? That might tell us if he's on his way to stop in or what, so we can decide when to grab Lawson."

"I see what you're saying," Dooley said. "We let Franks make his morning visit and then swoop in right after he leaves. Then, if we're having a great day, Lawson decides to work with us early on, spills the beans, and then we grab Franks and Tanner. With a lotta luck and good timing, we'll bag our limit tomorrow."

There was a knock on the door and a uniformed sheriff's deputy stuck his head in. "Excuse me, Detective Dooley, just wanted to let you know that, per your request, we've got two deputies on their way to Cape May to assist with the overnight surveillance. I gave them the contact info that Chief Saxby provided, and I wrote down their own info for you. Here, I made you both a copy."

"Fantastic, thanks, Dave. I appreciate your getting right on that," Dooley said. He took the offered slips of paper and passed one across the desk to Saxby. The deputy nodded at both of them and went out.

"That'll be a big help," Saxby said. "Vic and Three will be able to get a little sleep before all the excitement tomorrow. Come to think of it, I wouldn't mind a little sleep myself. After a stiff drink, that is. How about seven at my place tomorrow?"

"You're on, Tate," Dooley said. "I'll be at your office at seven tomorrow. I think I'll steal your idea about the drink and the sleep too."

21

At seven-thirty the next morning, Saxby was in his office with Detective Dooley going over some information that had come in overnight. The computer analysis of the three video clips was complete, and had determined with a "high degree of accuracy" that the adult man walking across the scene in all three clips was the same person. The memo had also mentioned that the height and weight of that person was consistent with what was known about Paul Tanner. The other significant piece of information had to do with an emergency blood sample comparison test that Sergeant Barstow had ordered late last night. While inspecting the red hoodie, she had found a bloodstain on the left cuff. With Paul Tanner in mind, she had ordered a test of that blood sample against a sample of the blood they had found on Jeffrey Tanner's phone the night of his death. The test had determined that the blood found on the sweatshirt was from the same person as the blood on the phone. Another test found that those samples had a ninety-nine percent similarity to a reference sample from the deceased Jeffrey Tanner.

"So, the blood on the phone and the sweatshirt is not from Jeff Tanner," Saxby said, "but ever so close."

"Right, ever so close," Dooley said. "Because it's from his son. This could be our first bit of real physical evidence that links Junior to the crime scene at the Doyle house. Things are looking up."

Saxby's cell phone rang and he tapped the screen to take the call from Sergeant Barstow, putting the call on speaker. "Hey, Chief, just letting you know that Peter Franks just left Lawson's house," Barstow said. "He showed up with a box of donuts or something, and stayed about fifteen minutes. I saw Lawson come out on the porch for a minute but I haven't seen Welles yet."

"Good morning, Sergeant," Dooley said, chiming in. "How are things on the block? Many people around?"

"It's pretty quiet," Barstow said. "There must be about ten or twelve houses and I'd say only three or four are occupied this week. One lady went out to walk her dog a few minutes ago and I haven't seen her come back yet."

Saxby's questioning look was met with a nod from Dooley. "Okay, Vic. We're on our way."

Ten minutes later, the small convoy of police vehicles pulled up in front of the house openly, but with no sirens or flashing lights. Saxby and Dooley climbed the steps to Lawson's porch together, while the other officers waited on the sidewalk below. Saxby pressed the doorbell button and stepped back. Within a few seconds, the door was opened and Doug Lawson stepped out onto the porch, coffee mug in hand. He looked back and forth at the two men, and then past them to the group of uniformed officers below.

This is good. He's nervous and scared, Saxby thought to himself.

"Why, good morning, Chief Saxby," Lawson said. His voice was shaky. "What's going on? Did you finally catch Jimmy Dunne?"

"No, Mr. Lawson," Saxby said. "But I've seen him and spoken with him the other day after I flew out to Minnesota, where's he's been held in a county jail for the last six months on unrelated charges. He certainly hasn't been in New Jersey in a long time."

"But I don't understand … how can that be?" Lawson said. "He tried to kill me. I know it was him."

"No, it couldn't have been him," Saxby said. "But we can talk about that more later. Right now, I'd like to introduce Cape May County Detective Tom Dooley, who we've been working with on this case. Tom?"

As Saxby stepped aside, Dooley motioned for the two sheriff's deputies to join them on the porch, and moved a step closer to Lawson. "Doug Lawson, regarding the recent death of Jeffrey Tanner of Tanner Construction, you are under arrest for suspicion of conspiracy to commit murder."

Lawson's face went white as he appeared to stumble backwards before reaching out to the wall to steady himself. Dooley recited the Miranda rights as the two deputies closed in on Lawson with a pair of handcuffs.

"But I didn't kill anybody," Lawson said, turning back to Saxby and Dooley as the deputies started him down the steps. "It wasn't me. The whole thing got out of hand, but I never hurt anybody."

"You'll have time to state your case soon enough, Mr. Lawson," Saxby said. "We look forward to hearing whatever you have to say."

Just then another man came out of the house, wearing a t-shirt and with traces of shaving cream on his face. "What's going on out here?" the man said. "What's this about and where are you taking Doug?"

"Mr. Lawson is under arrest, and is being taken up to the county detective's office in Cape May Courthouse," Dooley said. "Are you Bernie Welles?"

"Yeah, that's me," Welles said. "Doug and I go way back. I've been here for a few days to help him keep an eye out since someone tried to attack him about a week ago. Is this about that?"

"We'd like you to come with us also, Mr. Welles," Saxby said. "We've got some questions for you and we'll answer any of your questions that we can."

"I'm not going anywhere until I know what the hell is going on here," Welles said. "Am I under arrest?"

"No, you are not under arrest," Saxby said, "but that can be arranged if that's the way you'd like things to go. It would be a lot easier if you'd come along willingly. We really just want to ask you some questions."

"Whatever Doug and those others were up to," Welles said. "It's got nothing to do with me. I was just trying to help an old friend."

"Fantastic, then," Saxby said. "As long as that's the case, we'll get along just fine. Come on. You can ride with me and Detective Dooley."

After Lawson was booked, searched, and fingerprinted, he was moved into one of the interrogation rooms used by the county detectives. While he waited there, Saxby and Dooley spent most of an hour talking with Bernie Welles in another room.

"It's pretty clear to me that he has no idea about any of this," Dooley said, talking with Saxby in the hallway after leaving Welles alone in the room.

"Yeah, I have to agree," Saxby said. "But at least he's a witness to the fact that both Franks and Tanner had visited Lawson at his house. That could be something, even if he didn't overhear anything. I say we cut him loose but make sure he keeps to himself for a couple of days. What do you think? I have an idea about what to say to him."

"I'm with you," Dooley said. "Let's get him out the door and move on to Lawson."

Saxby sat down across from Bernie Welles after they came back into the room.

"Mr. Welles, as we mentioned earlier," Saxby said, "Detective Dooley and I are investigating a series of several recent murders. I'm sure I don't need to tell you how serious those matters are. At present, we are inclined to agree with your statement that you haven't had anything to do with all that, nor did you know about any of it. It sounds like you were just in the wrong place at the wrong time, with trying to help your friend who you thought had been attacked by some unknown assailant. Are we on the same page so far?"

"Yes. I have no idea about any of this stuff," Welles said. "I was just hanging out with Doug because he said he was worried about someone coming after him. If you're telling me he made it up, well, I don't know what to say about that. I can't believe he'd be involved in murder, but I guess maybe there's a lot I don't know about him."

"Yes, I think that could be the case, Mr. Welles," Saxby said. "So, you are free to go today, and we thank you for your assistance, but I have to ask for your help with something. We think some elements of this investigation are coming together quickly, and we don't want to risk you running into certain people and, you know, accidently mentioning something about what you might have seen or heard today. Is there somewhere you can go other than Cape May, to lay low for, say, two days? We could take you up to Trenton for further processing by the state police, and that can take up to forty-eight hours, but it sure would be easier if we didn't have to do that. Do you have relatives in the area?"

"My sister has a place in Ocean City," Welles said. "She's always inviting me to come visit. I could go right there, if someone could drive me."

"That sounds good, Mr. Welles," Dooley said. "Sure, I can get a plainclothes officer in an unmarked car to run you up there. We appreciate your cooperation with this."

"I think it's time to deal with Mr. Lawson," Dooley said, after they'd left Bernie Welles and taken a short break. "His assigned attorney is in there with him. Decent guy. Name of Rich Baker. I've been across the table from him before. He'll be open to a good deal. I say we start with the videos, then pull out the sweatshirt. I've got it set up to play on the big flat screen on the wall."

"That sounds right," Saxby said. "Unless I'm really

reading it wrong, he isn't going to want it to go much farther than that. Let's get started."

The interview room was silent for a moment when, thirty minutes later, Detective Dooley concluded his narration of the three video clips and closed his laptop. "There's a common term for what it looks like we just saw on the video, Mr. Lawson, and that is 'getaway driver.' Only in this case, we aren't talking about some kind of two-bit robbery. We're talking about cold-blooded murder." A half-hour of discussion followed before Lawson's attorney asked for a few minutes alone with his client.

"We'll be just outside, Mr. Baker," Dooley said. "Take your time."

Saxby and Dooley had enough time to get a coffee in the break room before Lawson's attorney stepped out into the hallway.

"It appears that my client got caught up in something that was bigger than what he initially believed it to be," Baker said. "As long as you are willing to consider various possible lesser and non-violent charges, he is willing to tell you what he knows."

"I've already had a conversation with the prosecutor about this," Dooley said. "And I think we have an understanding in principle. If he cooperates fully, and agrees to testify against Paul Tanner or anyone else involved, I think we should be able to find some appropriate charges that don't necessarily call for jail time. That is, as long as Chief Saxby is in agreement."

"Yes, I will agree to that," Saxby said. "As long as he's willing to tell us everything. And that means right now."

They all three went back into the interview room,

where, after a few minutes of back and forth, Lawson started to tell his story, interrupted frequently with questions from Saxby and Dooley.

"So, you're saying that you really thought Jeff Tanner's death was an accident?" Saxby said. "That's what he told you?"

"Later, yes, but not that night," Lawson said. "See, I knew he was having a hard time with his father—like, they were fighting over how to run the business. He told me he needed to get some blueprints from the house without anyone knowing. He didn't want his own car to be seen, so he asked me for a lift. That's all. Like doing an errand or something."

"It doesn't look like he's carrying blueprints or anything else in the video," Saxby said. "Did he say anything about that?"

"You're right," Lawson said. "I don't think he had blueprints or anything else when he came back, but I just figured he wasn't able to find them. I think he had cut himself on something too, like, he was holding a paper towel or a little rag against his arm, like here, just above the wrist. I didn't ask about it, I just drove. When I found out the next day that his father had fallen off the roof or whatever it was, right around the time that I gave Paul the ride, it scared the crap out of me and I asked him about it. He told me he had seen his father in the house, you know, while I was waiting in the car. He said they had yelled at each other for a while, but when he left, his father was fine. It seemed like he was really upset, and at that time, I believed him, and I didn't push it any further. Now, I don't know. I guess he was lying to me about everything. I swear I never knew anybody was going to be hurt."

"Why do you think Paul Tanner approached you initially?" Saxby asked.

"I've thought about that a lot," Lawson said. "And I'm not exactly sure. There was no love lost between Jeff Tanner and me. Lots of people knew that. After the accident under the boardwalk, you know, with Ryan Dunne, we all ran to that house near the beach that was being fixed up. The Crow's Nest, I think it was called. We were all holed up in there for a little bit, and he tried to blame it all on me. Right in front of the others, he accused me of pushing Ryan against that piling. We all felt terrible already, and then he started in with trying to blame it on me. Truth is, everyone was messing around, but I'm sure it was Jeff who shoved Ryan that last time. I always figured that's why he tried to blame it on me—because he knew it was really his fault. Anyway, that's ancient history. That's why I didn't exactly burst into tears when I heard he was dead, but at the same time, I believed Paul when he told me it was an accident that happened after he left."

"So, you think Paul Tanner might have been trying to exploit the fact that you had an old grudge against his father?" Dooley said.

"I don't know. I guess it could have been that he saw that as something he could hold over me," Lawson said. "The other thing is, somewhere along the way, he must have heard that Peter Franks was a cousin of mine. Second cousin I think—I have a hard time keeping that stuff straight. Anyway, Peter's wife is the daughter of Lincoln Barness."

"It sounds like Paul Tanner saw you as a handy connection in more than one way, then," Saxby said. "You were a foot in the door to Barness, and as a bonus, he figured you wouldn't complain too loudly if something bad happened to his father. The icing on the cake was that you were one of the six boys under the boardwalk, so you could help out with the story about someone killing them one by one for revenge. How does that sound?"

"I think that's probably about it," Lawson said. "His father must have told him about Ryan Dunne and that whole story over the years, so he knew about me. Next thing, he offers me twenty thousand dollars to call the police and say I was attacked by Jimmy Dunne. I'm really sorry about that, by the way."

"Was the deal with Barness ever discussed?" Dooley asked.

"Yes. When he asked me to arrange a meeting with Peter," Lawson said. "He told me about how he hoped when he got control of the company, he could make a deal with Barness for some big condo project. I got twenty thousand for saying I was attacked, but he also promised another thirty thousand if they got that contract."

"Let's talk about the other two murders," Dooley said. "Frankie Deutsch up in Somers Point and Boone Roseman here in Cape May. What do you know about them?"

"Oh man. That is just so terrible," Lawson said, rubbing his temples for a minute. "I really don't know anything about them. I mean, of course I know those two guys, or I did years ago, but not recently. I can only think that must have been Pete. Peter Franks, I mean. He's a distant cousin —barely a blood relation—but we've never been close. I always thought he was kind of a ... what's that word ... oh, a thug. Kind of a thug. It was just a feeling I had, but it kinda looks like I may have been right, right? See, after I introduced him to Paul Tanner, they went off on their own. It's like, once they were connected, they didn't need me anymore. They planned this or that and I wasn't aware of it."

"Didn't they have meetings at your house?" Saxby said.

"Yes, but only once. No, it was twice," Lawson said. "Tanner only ever came over two or three times. The most I can say on that, is, one of those times, I was having my coffee out on the porch while the two of them were inside talking. Bernie had gone out to the Acme or wherever. They were talking in the front room, and they must not have realized that the window was open a few inches, so I heard a little bit here and there of what they were saying."

"We need you to try really hard to remember anything you heard," Saxby said. "Think hard but tell it straight. Try not to fill in the blanks."

"Right. I got you," Lawson said. "I have thought about it, but the thing is I didn't hear much. I remember hearing something about Indonesia. I'm pretty sure it was 'they think someone came from Indonesia.' I also heard the word 'Amtrak,' like the train. A few minutes after that, I know I heard the name 'Jimmy Dunne,' and then I'm pretty sure Pete said, 'I'll need that money for my friend at customs.' I don't know what that meant, but you told me not to try to fill in blanks. I'm afraid that's all I can remember. That was the only time I heard them talking together."

Forty minutes' worth of questions later, Saxby and Dooley ended the interview, with the understanding that

Lawson would spend the night in a private cell at the county facility, followed by one night at a hotel in Atlantic City. Saxby and Dooley went for a late lunch at a nearby restaurant, where they lingered over coffee after finishing their meal.

"We still don't have much in the way of physical evidence," Saxby said. "These guys didn't screw up a whole lot, did they?"

"Unfortunately for us, no, they didn't," Dooley said. "I think we've got enough to pick them up and charge them, but then we're depending on them breaking somehow or turning on each other."

"Doesn't seem there's much reason to wait, then," Saxby said. "Let's grab them tonight."

"Fine. I'll start on the paperwork as soon as I get back to the office," Dooley said, "and we'll plan for eight o'clock tonight."

It was just after seven when Dooley called Saxby to let him know the paperwork needed to arrest Paul Tanner in Cape May was in order.

"I was surprised to hear from the FBI office in Philadelphia a little bit ago," Dooley said. "Seems they've been looking at this Peter Franks guy for some time. Apparently, he's got friends in low places, and has dabbled in some unsavory activities in Pennsylvania, and they'd like to take advantage of this opportunity to deal with him. My boss thought that was just fine as long as he's held accountable for whatever his involvement in our case is. I think they actually moved in on him at his house in North Wildwood a half-hour ago."

"Well, that's a surprise," Saxby said. "But, I guess they

must have something serious on him or they wouldn't be bothering."

"Yeah, that's what I figure too," Dooley said. "In any case, they've taken Franks off our plate, so now we just need to worry about Tanner."

"Tom, can you hold a minute while I take another call?" Saxby said. "It's Vic, and it could be something important."

He tapped the screen to put Dooley on hold and take the call from Barstow. "Hey Vic, I've got Tom Dooley on hold, so I only have a minute, but what's up?"

"Got it, Chief. I knew you'd want to hear this right away," Barstow said. "You know I've been keeping an eye on Paul Tanner. Well, he just came out of his house and took off in his car like he couldn't get away fast enough. Seemed to me like the way he looked around he was worried about being watched. I was on foot at the time, so I wasn't able to follow."

"Okay. Something spooked him, then," Saxby said. "I just found out that the FBI stepped in to deal with Peter Franks, because of something else he's mixed-up in. He must have gotten off a call to Tanner when they moved on him. Was he in that work pickup?"

"No, that's still in the driveway," Barstow said. "He's in a 4-door BMW sedan. Either dark gray or blue. New Jersey tags, but I didn't get the model number."

"Okay, that'll have to do, then," Saxby said. "Cruise by his office, his mother's house, his house again—wherever you can think of, but just look and don't try to intercept. Let me fill Dooley in and I'll get back to you."

"Sorry about that, Tom," Saxby said, switching back to Dooley. "It looks like Tanner may be in the wind. Vic was watching his place and saw him come out, look around like he was worried about being watched, and then take off. She said he's in a dark BMW. Don't know the model but it's a four-door sedan."

"Dammit, he must have found out somehow about Franks getting nabbed," Dooley said. "He's probably panicked."

"That's what I was figuring too," Saxby said. "Where are you right now?"

"I'm on the way into Cape May," Dooley said. "About five miles out."

"I'm headed out now to check out the town," Saxby said. "Let me know when you get here and we can meet somewhere and figure this out."

Saxby was doing a slow cruise along the beachfront when he answered another call from Detective Dooley.

"I'm here in town, over on Harbor," Dooley said. "On a hunch, I swung by that house where Jeff Tanner was killed, and there's a dark BMW 5-Series in the driveway. I'm parked out of sight just in from Texas Avenue."

"Be careful, Tom, he could be like a cornered dog," Saxby said. "I'm just passing Convention Hall right now. I'll turn around and get there in a few minutes."

While executing a quick U-turn near the end of Beach Avenue, Saxby keyed his radio to call Sergeant Barstow, who responded right away.

"Where are you right now, Vic?" Saxby said.

"I'm headed south on Broadway, approaching Sunset Boulevard," Barstow said.

"Okay, keep doing what you're doing," Saxby said. He glanced at his watch. *Damn. Eight o'clock shift change is right now, and we are spread thin.* "Dooley just got in town and he may have spotted Tanner's car near the Doyle house. I'm headed there now to check it out. Keep looking around, but make your way over towards the harbor and stand by to hear from me. Could be something, maybe not."

Another two minutes of fast driving brought Saxby to the turn-in to Harbor Cove, where he had to brake hard to avoid running into Dooley's parked car. After pulling into an adjacent driveway, he approached the other car, finding no sign of the detective. Walking forward another fifty feet, he paused at a bend in the short road to look ahead at the Doyle house, where a dark-colored BMW sedan sat in the driveway. The house was mostly dark, with just a handful of windows spilling out a small amount of light from one or more interior sources. Seeing that the front door stood wide open, Saxby started moving quickly and carefully in that direction, while undoing the safety strap on his holstered pistol. As he came up almost to the front door, he looked up at the façade of the enormous house, seeing that a light was now on at the top of the tower. He was sure the tower had been dark when he'd first started to approach the house.

A voice came from just inside the open door. "That you, Tate? You can come in. I'm pretty sure he ran upstairs."

Saxby moved quickly through the doorway, raising his pistol and a powerful flashlight to sweep the area, seeing that Dooley was on the floor, propped up against the wall to the left of the door, with his legs splayed out in front of him. After taking a moment to satisfy himself that there was nobody else in the immediate vicinity, Saxby came over to kneel beside him.

"What happened, Tom? How are you doing?" Saxby said.

"Well, I've been better," Dooley said. "That bastard shot me with a nail gun. I've got like, six nails in me. I tried to go after him but this one in my knee makes it really hard to move. I'll be okay, but I'm going to have to skip the dance for tonight."

"Yeah, I think you're going to be okay too," Saxby said. He had been probing and counting Dooley's wounds. "They aren't bleeding much. It's Tanner, right? Why in hell didn't you wait for me?"

"I guess because I'm a dumbass," Dooley said. "Yeah, it's Tanner. I thought I saw something in the upstairs window, and I figured I could get a quick look around down here while I waited for you, but he ambushed me and tried to make me into a piece of furniture. He ran upstairs. I think he's having a meltdown. He was crying and raving about how he hadn't killed anyone. Yeah, right. Don't try to tell me that shit as you're shooting me full of giant framing nails."

Saxby keyed his radio to call Barstow. "Vic, close in on the Doyle house immediately, and call for whatever backup you can find. Front door's open, Tom Dooley on the floor just inside, shot five or six times with a nail gun. Not critical but could use an ambulance."

"Take it easy, Tom, help is on the way," Saxby said. "Do you think he took the nail gun upstairs with him?"

"I think so. I'm not sure," Dooley said. "What? Are you telling me that now you aren't going to wait for backup?"

"You're not the only one allowed to be a dumbass, Tom," Saxby said. "I'm going to see what's going on up there.

Maybe I can talk him down before it turns into some kind of big standoff. Send some backup after me when they get here. You're going to be fine."

After pausing at the bottom of the stairs for a moment to listen for anything going on above, Saxby started up. He walked as quietly as possible, with the muzzle of his gun leading the way. He stopped again on the second-floor landing, near the beginning of the spiral stairs, listening. The sound of sirens in the distance grew louder. He started up the stairs into the tower as quietly as possible, stopping midway to listen again. *I knew it. He's out on the widow's walk.*

Reaching the top of the stairs, he paused again to listen before emerging into the small room at the top of the tower. Again, he heard something that seemed to be out on the walkway. A creak, or a footstep, or both. Bracing himself against the center pole of the staircase, he poked his head up into the little room for a look around. He could see the shape of a man at the railing just outside the door, looking outward.

Moving as quietly as possible, Saxby climbed the last few steps into the room and took two steps towards the door out to the walkway. Tanner had not yet moved, and was still looking out into the night sky.

"Don't move, Tanner," Saxby yelled, as he raised his gun. "Let's stop all this right now."

Saxby was surprised at the speed with which Tanner spun around to face him, seeing for the first time that he still held the big red nail gun. The boom of Saxby's automatic drowned out the simultaneous but lesser report of the nail gun, with both bullet and nail hitting their marks.

Tanner stumbled backwards against the railing, shot through the shoulder, but somehow managing to keep his grip on the nail gun. The nail that hit Saxby had driven deeply into his right hand before being stopped by its impact with the gun's hard rubber grip. The shock caused his hand to spasm, dropping the gun to the floor, where it slid towards Tanner and almost to the doorway. The perception of time became compressed and distorted for Saxby as several things seemed to happen all at once. He dove down towards the door, closer to Tanner, reaching to recover his gun with his left hand. Sergeant Barstow burst from the spiral stairs into the room, her own gun sweeping the space before settling on Tanner, who was still out on the widow's walk and was now raising the nail gun to fire it again at Saxby. When he saw Barstow appear, he shifted the weapon and fired a nail that buried itself into her upper thigh. Barstow yelled out and stumbled back a step, but retained her grip on her gun. She dropped to one knee, aiming at Tanner but holding her fire.

"I never meant to hurt anyone," Tanner yelled. The nail gun was aimed at a point midway between the two officers. "This all got out of hand."

"Is that what you told your father before you pushed him over the rail, Tanner?" Saxby said. "It's time for this to end. Drop that damn thing now."

"No, you don't understand," Tanner said. He started to raise the nail gun in Barstow's direction. "I only wanted to talk to him. When I left—"

Saxby and Barstow fired at the same time, Saxby three times and Barstow twice. As Tanner was thrown back to the railing, the temporary fasteners holding it in place yielded and the railing gave way. Tanner's bullet-riddled body was launched into the darkness and down towards the stone patio below.

Saxby holstered his pistol and came towards Barstow, who was now standing and looking down at the nail sticking out of her thigh with a grimace. "How are you doing, Vic? I think you should leave that in for now. Let the doctor take it out."

"Yeah, I think you're right about that, Chief," Barstow said. "Same goes for you and for our friend downstairs. I guess we should be glad he didn't have a .45."

"You can say that again," Saxby said. "By the way, thanks for coming."

He stepped out onto the widow's walk, avoiding the section with the missing rail, and looked down to the patio. Other officers had arrived during the commotion and he could see Sergeant Brody standing over Tanner's broken body. Looking down at the scene, he reflected silently that it wasn't so long ago that Tanner had stood on that patio looking down at the body of his own father.

"Justice done, Chief?" Barstow said, having come up to stand beside him.

"I'd like to think so, Vic," Saxby said. "And I sure hope so. What do you say we head downstairs. You okay to do that?"

"It'll be my first time walking around with a nail in my leg," Barstow said. "But I'll give it a try."

22

Detective Dooley's doctor had just finished checking on him when Saxby knocked on the door of his hospital room the next afternoon.

"Sorry so late, Tom," Saxby said. "As you know, there's a mountain of paperwork whenever there's a shooting, and it goes much slower when you've had a nail shot through your hand."

"Yeah, tell me about it," Dooley said. "How is the hand? Everything going to be okay?"

"That's what they tell me," Saxby said. "Apparently it went through pretty clean and just cracked one bone. It's going to be sore for a while. How about you? You had what, five or six in you?"

"Six. Which is a nice round figure if you've got to be shot with a nail gun," Dooley said. "The x-rays look good, but they want to keep an eye on me for a few days. I can't argue with that. Man, that guy was a good shot with that thing. What a nutjob."

"You can say that again," Saxby said. "Anyway, I guess

we can both be thankful he didn't have a sheetrock gun—then we'd really be screwed."

"Oh, very funny, ha ha ha," Dooley said. "But don't quit your day job just yet."

"Speaking of quitting your day job," Saxby said, "did I hear it right that you…?"

"Yeah, you heard right, Tate," Dooley said. "The wife and I have been talking about it for a while now, and I think it's time. I've been shot a few times, and now this last night with the nails … my luck can't hold out forever, and my pension should be pretty good. We've got friends down in Savannah who can help us look for a place."

"Well, on a selfish level," Saxby said, "I'm sorry to hear that, but otherwise, good for you. You sure have done your bit, and I hear Savannah's really nice."

"Yeah, it is. I guess I'll need to finally learn how to play golf," Dooley said. "By the way, I assume you heard about Peter Franks, right?"

They had both heard, separately, after the evening events at the Doyle house, that Peter Franks had been killed in a shootout with FBI agents, after a short car chase in Atlantic City.

"I heard from the captain that they found a few things connecting him to Deutsch and Roseman," Dooley said. "They've only just started looking, but it's a start. Anyway, it's good news. It's going to be a bad day for law enforcement if crooks ever learn how to clear out their internet searches."

"Yeah, that is really good news, and I sure hope it puts a bow on this whole thing," Saxby said. "Because neither of these guys is going to be answering any more questions. I do like when things get wrapped up neatly, but, well, I don't know … we've just 'caught' two killers and here I am second-guessing everything."

"Try to relax about it, Tate," Dooley said. "We've got a good witness in Lawson, we've got all those videos, we've got Tanner's blood on his father's phone, the sweatshirt. Tanner was trying to get control of the company and willing to kill to do it. Not to mention that the FBI is on it now. Franks was a crook who wanted to make his biggest score ever, and some innocent people got caught up in the mayhem. Call it justice done and give yourself a break. You deserve it."

"Yeah, I know you're right, Tom," Saxby said. "Hey, I'll get out of your hair and let you get some rest. You'll need it for all the paperwork you've got waiting for you when you get back to your desk. And watch out for flying nails."

23

A few days later, Saxby was doing a routine patrol around the town when he decided to go by the Doyle house and see how the work there was going. As he drove up and parked along the side of the road, he could see one of the Tanner Construction pickup trucks in the driveway, along with several of the workers' private vehicles. The weather was calm and pleasant, and the house seemed to be a hive of activity.

As he walked up to the house, he saw a worker at the top of a two-story ladder who appeared to be doing something with the security camera. As he stood watching, another of the workers walked up.

"Chief Saxby, isn't it? I'm the crew chief here, Dave Watson. Can I help you with anything?"

"Oh, no. I was just in the area and thought I'd stop in and see how things are going," Saxby said, holding out his left hand for a shake. "Nice to meet you, Mr. Watson. Good to see all this productivity going on here. Will you be finishing up soon?"

"I think so," Watson said. "Another ten days maybe. Two weeks, tops. I hope that's all. As you know better than anyone, we've had some delays, and I think the Doyles are itching to get back in."

"I'm not surprised," Saxby said. "It's quite a house, and I'm sure they'd like to enjoy it. So, who's running the company now?"

"Mostly Jeff Tanner's daughter," Watson said. "Susan Bingham is her name. Her and her husband. He's got some experience with construction and a business degree, and they seem to know what they're doing. Also, they brought in a guy who used to work with us to be head crew chief. Most of the guys are happy about that. Vaughn's a good man."

"Vaughn? You mean Barry Vaughn?" Saxby said.

"Yeah, that's him," Watson said. "Mr. Tanner—Jeff Tanner, I mean—didn't get along with him, but the others did. Personally, I'm glad he was still in the area and they were able to get him."

"Okay, then. Well, I'd better let you get back to your work," Saxby said, doing his best to conceal his surprise. "Good meeting you, Mr. Watson."

As he started to turn back towards his car, he thought of something, and turned back to Watson, gesturing to the man on the ladder. "I'm just curious. Are you taking the security camera down already?"

"No, the camera's staying, Jerry just went up to fix the time on the thing," Watson said. "Just a silly mistake. When Mr. Tanner asked me to install it the other Tuesday, I had to use the clock in the kitchen for the time, because I had forgotten my watch and I didn't have a phone on me. It was only this morning that I realized the kitchen clock was never moved an hour ahead for daylight savings."

"Ah, of course, 'spring forward' strikes again," Saxby said. "But there's just one thing I don't understand. You said you installed it on a Tuesday. Do I have that right?"

"Yeah, that's right," Watson said. "I installed it myself. Not this past Tuesday, but the one before. I guess that was the 14th."

"And Mr. Tanner asked you to do that himself, right?" Saxby said.

"That's right, Paul Tanner asked me to do it that Tuesday," Watson said. "I'll never forget, because it was the next night that his father was killed. Or he killed his father, I guess, if that's what happened. Crazy stuff."

"Right, I see," Saxby said. "It's just confusing me, because I thought he had wanted the camera in response to the break-in on Wednesday morning, the next day."

"Well, now I'm confused too, Chief," Watson said. "There haven't been any break-ins here."

"But the door from the kitchen to the patio was broken, wasn't it?" Saxby said. "I saw the new door. The trim hadn't been put back yet."

"Oh, that. One of the guys slipped coming in that day and put a two-by-four through the glass," Watson said. "That's all that was. There was no break-in."

"Hmmm. All right, then," Saxby said. "Thanks for explaining that. I'll let you get back to work."

Saxby turned and walked away to his car, pulling off his hat and scratching his head with his good hand. *Leave it to Paul Tanner. Even from the grave he's still playing games with me.*

24

It was a beautiful early-spring day, with a clear blue sky and a gentle breeze coming in from the ocean. It was fifty-five degrees at nine in the morning, on the way to an expected high of seventy-five. Saxby and Angela were finishing up their breakfast at George's Place across from the beach.

"So, are you okay with the plan for today?" Angela said. "Some shopping up the road and then a nice lunch somewhere?"

"Sounds great Ang," Saxby said, "but I thought there was a trip to the winery somewhere in there too."

"Of course, I wouldn't forget about that," Angela said. "We'll have lunch somewhere up near the mall, and then to the winery when we get back down this way after that. Sound okay?"

"Yes, I think that will do nicely," Saxby said. "There's a barbeque place up on the Black Horse Pike near the mall I've been itching to try, if that appeals to you."

"Mmmm, that sounds good," Angela said. "By the way, I

don't think I've asked you yet how your hand is today. So, how is it?"

Saxby stretched his hand out, exploring the feeling. "I think it's better than yesterday. Stiff, but not much pain. This is the first day I haven't taken anything. I mean, it's early yet, but so far, so good, five days later."

After settling the check, they walked outside and lingered on the sidewalk, gratefully inhaling the fresh sea air. Though the ocean was several hundred feet across the street and beyond the sea wall, they could still hear waves crashing on the sand and the insistent squawk of gulls calling to one another as they soared over the surf, tirelessly searching for their next meal.

"You know what Ang," Saxby said, "I know you want to get to the mall, but do you mind if we take a few minutes to sit on one of the benches up there and watch the ocean for a while? We have time, right?"

By way of answer, she took his hand and, after checking for approaching cars, led him across the street to where the few steps led up to the promenade, where they parked on the nearest bench.

"Honey," she said, "I promise you that we will always have time to sit and look at the ocean, for as long as we need to."

At about the same time, Sergeant Barstow was a half-hour into a routine patrol around Cape May, when she turned onto Madison Avenue and noticed a group of vehicles gathered in front of one of the big Victorian houses on an otherwise quiet stretch of road. Approaching slowly, she saw that the Ford pickup truck in the driveway of the house bore the logo of Tanner Construction, and one of the two cars on the street in front of the house was the Acura TL sedan that she recognized as belonging to Barry Vaughn. She parked the cruiser in front of the other cars and walked towards the three people standing at the bottom of the steps leading up to the porch.

"Why Sergeant Barstow," Barry Vaughn said, as she approached the small group. "How nice to see you. Is this a social call?"

"As a matter of fact, Mr. Vaughn, yes, it is," Barstow said. "I just saw you here and stopped to say hello on a beautiful spring day. But also, Mrs. Bingham, you might recall that we met briefly when I came over to your mother's house after your father's passing. Please accept my condolences again, on your brother Paul's passing. Your family has had a tough time of it this month. I'm very sorry."

"Thank you, Sergeant, that's very nice of you," Mrs. Bingham said. "I do remember when you came to speak with my mother that day. I remember that you were kind to her, and I appreciate it. Sergeant, this is my husband, Burt Bingham. Burt is going to be taking over the daily operations of the company now. With help from me of course, and Barry."

"Oh, so, you're back with Tanner then," Barstow said, looking at Vaughn with thinly veiled surprise on her face. "I must say I didn't see that coming, but I hope you do well."

"Actually, Barry and I go way back," Burt Bingham said.

"And we work well together. Susan's father had, shall we say, his own way of doing things, but that's all water under the bridge at this point. We're going to be making changes and looking for growth opportunities, and Barry's going to be a big part of that."

"That all sounds great then," Barstow said. "Do you have a background in construction, Mr. Bingham?"

"I do, yes. I had my own company," Bingham said, "back fifteen or so years ago, but not as big as Tanner. Now's my chance to shine and I'm not going to let Susan and her mother down."

"Burt was always anxious to take on more responsibility with the company," Mrs. Bingham said, "but my father and Paul were stubborn men. With loving respect to them, things are going to be different now."

"Well, I wish you the best, and again, my condolences," Barstow said. She looked up at the house they were standing in front of. A colorful new sign hung from a pole just off the sidewalk near the stairs to the porch. She pointed to the sign. "The Crow's Nest Inn—that sounds familiar. Isn't this the house... after that tragic accident..."

"That's right, yes, it is," Mrs. Bingham said. "This is the house the boys ran to after Ryan Dunne's accident under the boardwalk. I'm sure they were all terrified. As I understand it, they spent some time here arguing about what to do and who to call, before one of them finally left and told his parents. It was a moment my father always regretted, and I think it haunted him at least a little bit through his life. Anyway, the family of one of the other boys owned it for a long time until my father bought it from them, also a long time ago. We're going to spruce it up and re-open it as a Bed and Breakfast. Hopefully close to its former glory."

"Well, I hope there are happier days in its future then," Barstow said. "Good seeing you again, and meeting you Mr. Bingham. Have a good day now."

Mrs. Bingham turned away to take a phone call as Barstow started back towards her cruiser, passing Barry Vaughn on the sidewalk.

"Thing's certainly have fallen into place nicely for you then, haven't they?" Barstow said.

"Yes, they have, Sergeant," Vaughn said. "But I'm mildly disappointed that you don't seem happy for me. I was at least a little bit of a help with your case, after all."

"That's right, you did give us a little help," Barstow said. She held his gaze for a moment. "And yes, I'm always happy to see people doing well. It's just that it can be strange how neatly things come together sometimes. But hey, that's my problem, not yours. I hope you do well with your new position, Mr. Vaughn. Good day."

As Barstow got into her car and drove away, Burt Bingham climbed the stairs to the house as Mrs. Bingham came back over to Vaughn.

"Oh, I have those files you wanted me to look over," Vaughn said. "I've made some notes and added some cost estimates that we can go over in the office next week. I'll get the box out of my trunk and put it in your car for you. It's a little heavy."

As they walked to his car, he hit the button on his key fob to pop the trunk. He reached in to pick up a box from among a half-dozen other boxes that filled the space.

"Look at all those boxes," Mrs. Bingham said. "Are you in the middle of moving to a new apartment?"

"Oh no, it's just old stuff I need to drop off at the thrift store," Vaughn said. "I was up early this morning going through drawers and closets. You know how it is. Stuff I don't need anymore. I'm heading over there right after I leave here."

Ninety minutes later, after dropping the boxes off at the Liberty Thrift store in the nearby town of Rio Grande, Barry Vaughn leaned against his car in the parking lot, allowing himself a few minutes to smoke his first cigarette in hours. When he was done, and had ground out the butt on the blacktop, he popped a Listerine Breath Strip into his mouth and checked his watch. Just past eleven. Plenty of time for him to get back into Cape May for his lunch appointment with the men from Barness.

It was after dinner that evening when sixteen-year-old Heather Ryder was starting to lose hope that she was ever going to find what she was looking for. She began a careful search through the last few racks of donated clothes while her mother stood by the counter, chatting with the lady working the register. It was fifteen minutes to closing time, and they were the last customers in the store.

"It's for the school play," Mrs. Ryder said. "Beats me how it fits in, but there's some big musical number where they want all the kids to be wearing oversize pull-overs in different colors. Heather's assignment is red, and we've been looking all over for a big red sweatshirt, and can't find one anywhere. It was her idea to try the thrift stores, so this is kind of our last hope."

"I can imagine what that's like," the saleslady said. "I remember when my daughters used to go all over town looking for exactly this or that. I learned to just get out of the way. You know, I just remembered something. See those boxes over there against the wall? Someone dropped those off earlier today and we were planning to sort through them in the morning. It's mostly men's clothes, but you can look through them if you like."

Mrs. Ryder thanked her for the offer and walked over to tell her daughter about the boxes. Heather's rummage through the last racks had been fruitless, but her face brightened slightly as she learned that there was another place to look. She knelt next to the first box and started to look through it.

It was a minute after opening the third box that she pulled the sweatshirt out from the bottom with a squeal of delight. "Oh Mom—look! It's like new, and it's a beautiful red. It's huge, but it's perfect!"

Thanks to his long-time love of trivia and history, Tate Saxby knew that the famously hot 'dog days of summer' were named for that sultry, sweaty, stretch from mid-July to mid-August, when Sirius, the Dog Star, appears to rise along with the sun. Most people just knew that the dog days of summer were *really hot.*

That summer was no exception. While many visitors and residents alike packed the beaches and took dips in the ocean to get some relief from the heat, others donned shorts and linen shirts, or airy sundresses, to shop, stroll, or dine their way along the shady streets of the historic town center. Many of those people found their way to the sprawling grounds of the historic Physick Estate, where a local arts group had transformed the lawns and paths into a compact version of a county fair. There were games, pony rides, and face-painting for the kids, along with a sno-cone booth to cool them down and satisfy their sweet tooth. People lined up at a variety of food trucks, and a roped-off patio area had been made into a beer garden, complete with fake palm trees and music from a steel drum trio.

As Saxby strolled leisurely through the area, enjoying a double espresso and a cookie from the refreshment cart that Starla's Café had set up, he spotted Mark Allen seated at the WCFA Radio table. Allen was handing out key chains and water bottles to anyone who stopped to talk, along with flyers for the historic WWII Lookout Tower near Sunset Beach, where he served as a volunteer tour guide.

"Well, hello there, Chief Saxby," Allen said, as Saxby approached. "If I said 'is it hot enough for you', would I be the first person to say that, or the tenth?"

"Oddly enough, Mark," Saxby said. "You would be the first person to say that to me today. And by the way, the answer is yes. I like it hot in the summer, but ninety-two in the shade is hot enough. How are things going here? You getting a lot of people to visit the tower?"

"I think so," Allen said. "I tell them it's breezy and cool at the top, and anyway, there's a beach, a restaurant, and a gift shop nearby. You know—exit through the gift shop. I've been meaning to ask you, Tate, don't you think it's about time you came on my show again to talk about your crime-fighting exploits? Listeners always love it when you're on. I'm sure they're itching to hear more about that Tanner case back in March. That was a hell of a thing. These cases you've been having over the past few years have really been something. I mean, geez. Somebody should start writing books about your exploits."

"Oh, I don't know about all that," Saxby said, after

laughing out loud. "I don't know if my exploits would keep people awake long enough to finish a whole book."

Saxby was distracted by something that caught his eye across the lawn, and missed most of whatever Allen said next. "I'm sorry Mark, I just saw someone over there who I need to grab before he gets away. Hold that thought and I'll be back in a minute."

He left Allen to greet the next visitors to the booth, and made his way through the crowd to where a cart was set up to put on an old-fashioned Italian Marionette show. An ornate and loudly-colored frame surrounded a miniature stage of about three feet across, where a pair of marionette puppets were engaged in an animated dispute that involved hitting each other repeatedly with sticks, delighting the children who sat on the grass watching. As Saxby came up to the edge of the small crowd, the man who had caught his eye, Barry Vaughn, was handing a few bills to a little girl of about twelve, who held hands with a woman who Saxby guessed to be her mother. The ladies started away in the direction of the sno-cone booth, leaving Vaughn by himself.

"Chief Saxby," Vaughn said, as he turned to see the other man. "You surprised me. You just missed my sister and her daughter. They don't care much for sand, so I'm doing my best to show them around town. Are you on the job, or just enjoying the fair?"

"Oh, I'm always on the job," Saxby said. "But I'm enjoying the fair too. It's nice to get out and see people having a good time. You know, keep in touch with what people are up to."

"Sure. In your position that sounds especially important," Vaughn said. "Did you get to see much of the marionette show? I'm not sure what it's about, but it looks like fun. My niece liked it."

"They are fun, aren't they?" Saxby said. "I remember the first time I saw one of these shows. It was an event something like this. I must have been about seven or eight. Younger than your niece."

"Do you remember what the story was?" Vaughn said.

"No. Not that I recall," Saxby said. "The main thing I remember is that the characters were arguing about something or other, and, just like this one today, apparently hitting each other with sticks is a normal part of it. I was mesmerized for a while, as they jumped around the little stage, yelling at each other and knocking each other down. And then, after it ended, and they were taking it all apart, I was astounded to see that these characters going about their business in the little play were really just puppets. They were just puppets on strings, and it turned out that someone behind the curtain had been controlling them all along. It was confusing to me, you know, I was just a little kid. I thought those puppets were doing what they wanted to do, but actually it was all someone else, pulling their strings. You know what I mean, Mr. Vaughn?"

"Yes, I think I do, Chief Saxby," Vaughn said. "But tell me, that was a long time ago. Did you ever figure out the rest of the story?"

"No, I never did figure it all out," Saxby said. "Not completely. Or I should say...not yet. But there's still time, and I'll keep thinking about it, in between everything else.

Anyway, I see your sister and niece are on their way back with sno-cones. I'll let you get back to your family."

"Well, until next time then, Chief Saxby," Vaughn said.

"Right, until next time," Saxby said. "Maybe I'll catch you later."

ALSO BY MILES NELSON

The Privilege of The Dead (2018)

To Die No More (2019)

Murder At Exit 0 - *A Cape May Mystery* (2020)

Murder Is A Shore Thing - A Cape May Mystery (2022)

Made in the USA
Middletown, DE
16 September 2023

38511093R00179